PRAISE FOR MILES ROZAK

"*Starship Found, Child Missing* is escapism full of guts and glory. A perfect balance of military realism and science fiction." - Rachel Aukes, bestselling author of multiple novels in USA Today's Recommended Reads.

"Rozak's latest novel, *Starship Found, Child Missing*, opens right out of the gate by grabbing the reader with engaging characters who you'll immediately want to know more about. Then he plunges them into a grand adventure and puzzling mystery, hooking the reader into a brand new universe full of danger and wonder." - Rick Partlow, former U.S. Army infantry platoon leader and bestselling science fiction author of the *Space Hunter War* and *Drop Trooper* series.

"Grab this book and hold on tight. Miles Rozak has written a story that will launch you from your living room chair into a galaxy packed with technological, futuristic wonders. This novel is a blast!" - Scott Bartlett, bestselling author of space opera and military science fiction novels.

"Engaging right from the jump. I loved the action and suspense. Tyson Gage is my kind of hero." - Toby Neighbors, bestselling author of the *SSG Vanhorn Series* and *Armor Brigade*.

"A great book. It started off giving me Alan Dean Foster's *Glory Lane* kind of vibes and took off from there. A former Marine turned guitar maker in space—just don't get between him and his son or dog." - William S. Frisbee, bestselling military sci-fi author of *The Last Marines*, and U.S. Marine Corps veteran.

"Total enjoyment from start to finish. No matter the technology change—you are always a Marine who honors his or her code of honor. This book will definitely be a winner." - Dennis Whalen, Master Gunnery Sergeant, US Marine Corps.

"Few authors are able to grab and hold my attention the way that Miles Rozak did... I couldn't wait to keep reading. Just plain excellent! A page turner to the end." - USA Today bestselling author Jasper T. Scott of the *Cade Korbin Chronicles*.

STAR CENTURION

ALIEN SHIP FOR SALE
BOOK 2

MILES ROZAK

Star Centurion:
Alien Ship for Sale - Book 2
Text copyright © 2023 by Miles Rozak
All rights reserved.

Published by Megaulcite Press. Cover art and design copyright © 2023 by Megaulcite Press, including one image from G.G. Tsukahara/shutterstock.com.

Edition: 07/13/23

CONNECT WITH MILES ROZAK

Hey, my friend!

Amazon doesn't always let people know when the next book comes out.

So for author updates and release alerts, you can join my spam-free newsletter at milesrozak.com. I'd love to connect with you there personally.

Plus, just for joining, I'll send you my the prequel book to my *Mercenary Galaxy* series, *Oracle of the Galaxy,* for FREE.

JOIN THE CONVERSATION

Come say "hi" in my rocking Facebook group, the SciFi Readers Club!

I built this group to be a fun getaway from all the division on FB—where you're always welcome among friends. So come join us for some fun conversations around novels, movies, and everything science fiction! You can find us here:

www.facebook.com/groups/scifireadersclub

Edition: 07/25/23

CHAPTER ONE

ENGULFED in a seemingly endless array of stars now within reach, we shot through the expanse—but not in our ship.

The utter silence seemed to amplify our labored breaths within our helmets. Rebreathers attached to our jetpacks piped in air that felt unnatural since it was one-third of Earth's atmospheric pressure, one hundred percent oxygen.

But that was intentional. Our training as bounty hunters had taught us to wear battle suits for two hours before extravehicular activity to let them pressurize with pure oxygen.

That rids the body of nitrogen to keep gas bubbles from building up in your joints, so painful that you can lock up in space.

As you can imagine, that would be bad.

Things you learn out in the Big Dark.

It had been twelve weeks since I'd purchased the *Gambit* from Steinbreaker's dealership and hired the proprietor, who'd already been its science officer/engineer, and the helmsman, who looked like a translucent stingray to round out my crew. There was a lot I still didn't know.

Like piloting, tactics, or even the art of delegation as the corvette's captain.

But here we were.

Tess, Celin-Ohmi the mollusk, Bond, whose full name we'd learned was Bondranamir and who'd fought with us in the Battle Mech Tournament, Steinbreaker, whom I called Fuzzy McCuddles because of how much he hated it.

And Maggie. Let's not forget my crazy dog who, at fourteen years old, was experiencing some kind of canine renaissance after her nanite treatment. I think she might live for another three decades.

Now, into the expanse of stars, Tess fired thrusters on the jetpack I'd bought, and I flew right behind her. The rest of our crew was back on the ship.

Our jetpacks hadn't been standard issue since we'd been promoted to Zenith in the fugitive recovery agent ranks of the Commonwealth.

That just meant we could now hunt Blue Bounties. They fetched higher payouts than the Greens we'd started with. Still, my team was gearing up for an undercover operation in the League of Desai—with or without the government's help—and that had led me to a weapons outfitter who'd kitted us in this tarnished armor we'd purchased from the Wildcard vendor.

Unmarked armor like this made it clear that we weren't fighting for any flag. At least not in any official capacity. It had the "rough-riders, take-no-prisoners" vibe in the gaze of mercs and security types disembarking from ships at the spaceport or standing sentry with loaded guns.

The kind of vibe that made spacers avoid you.

Well, except for Fuzzy McCuddles. On his two-foot-tall stature, the armor looked more like a metal onesie or maybe a Halloween costume you'd put on a toddler.

"Embrace the cuteness, doctor," I told him. "It's just who you are."

He hated that and me because of it.

But the helmet could do nothing for his giant ears. Wildcard had to special order one with slots to accommodate them. It wasn't my fault that he looked so funny trying to walk down the spaceport terminal with his mini-blaster and little battle suit.

Like he was practically shouting, "Hey, everyone, shoot my exposed earlobes because even if you can't hit my torso, any drunk Imperial Storm Trooper could hit these mud flappers from five klicks away!"

I mean, what the void?

You might as well get a full suit of armor and leave the back open, then run into battle with exposed butt cheeks. That's just asking for trouble if you ask me.

I wondered how many nerve endings he had in those ears. When the light hit them from behind, you could see all the blood vessels in those giant things—so, no—I wasn't planning on taking Steinbreaker into combat any time soon.

His talents and intellect, which were considerable, were better suited back on the ship where he could put his wealth of knowledge about everything from xenomarine biology to Randall-Sundrum drives to use as our resident scientist and ship engineer.

Despite the alien's furry appearance, he'd make a terrible child's toy because he was always smoking cigars and had such a negative disposition.

We'd vowed not to use our real names anymore from here on out, except with each other, and stick to the call signs each one on my team had stenciled on the corner of their armored chestplates.

They called me Stryker, and Tess was Rubicon. Rubi for short.

The two of us shot through space toward the maw of the shuttle, keenly aware of the species I'd catalogued from the spacewalk I'd taken with Hidalgo into a derelict ship like this one—the hostile species we'd never identified but which had been thirsty for blood.

I wasn't looking for more unsolved mysteries. I had enough of those with my son.

"But I doubt this is like that," Tess reassured me in the Gambit when we'd been acclimating, waiting for our suits to pressurize.

And she was right. The destination for today's EVA was a shuttle, not large by space fleet standards, and not military. It was for civilians who needed transport.

That made it all the more strange.

Because we were now staring at its dead hulk, still listing with smoke.

The forward section of the craft in question was crumpled and breached by what must've been a round from a kinetic weapon that had cored through its ablative armor and interweave layers, leaving the inside exposed to cold space.

Unless something was still alive.

Something to explain that distress signal that had pinged off our ship, the *Gambit*, in a loop. We wouldn't have heard it if we hadn't moved in close enough to investigate.

Tess and I jetted toward it with nothing between our flesh and the void except the airtight seals of our helmets and suits that shielded us from the radiation and conditions of the Big Dark.

"What are we doing here?" she asked on our internal comm through the cybernetics implanted when we had joined Magnum. "No one could've survived this, Stryker. The ship's a dead wreck."

"Hey, if Emin Braddock told me to meet his guy on this ship to talk through terms, I want to be able to tell him I exhausted every possibility," I said. "He's my only link to the League of Desai."

"But his contact is gone. Look at this shot they took through the bow. No flight crew could've survived that."

"Then how do you explain that looping distress signal? The sections behind here still look intact."

Braddock had told us to meet his man at Terminal Nine on Hendarii Station because it was public and wouldn't raise suspicions with all the passengers boarding, disembarking, and milling around.

But that ship had never arrived. So, we'd been forced to hack its flight plan, and that led us here to where it had been hit.

Hidalgo's words returned to me from the day we'd explored a shipwreck like this one. Sure, that was military and dwarfed this craft, but the ominous silence and looping distress call, and uneasy feelings were all the same.

"Are you ready?" I could still hear his voice. "It's just like we practiced. Give the mental command to your thrusters, nice and easy."

I swallowed hard through the lump in my throat. We were all still shocked by his passing, even though it had been almost three months.

Floating ahead of me, Tess touched the epicenter of the breach that had splintered with cracks from the kinetic round. The resulting hole in the shuttle was large enough for her to slip into the forward compartment, which she did, avoiding the edges of sheared-off metal and pulling herself into its opening with a kick like a mermaid through water.

"That's what I mean," she replied, now inside. "The signal we intercepted was looping, so the flight crew could've activated it in the final throes of asphyxiation."

"Thanks for that rosy mental picture there, doc, but the signal didn't come from the cockpit, remember? It was farther back, which—like I said—proves that someone else could be in here. I've got the tools right here in my belt to override the emergency hatches, so if you'll just give me a minute..." I grunted and fired a burst from my jets. "Would you please wait up?"

"Scrat, it's a mess in here," Tess said.

"Well, that's what happens when you get shot up with a ship-mounted rail gun," I mumbled, pulling myself into the breach that had caused uncontrolled decompression in the forward end of the ship.

Drawing my blaster, I recommended Tess do the same.

I'd kept Bond back on the *Gambit* because he'd now received training in fugitive recovery like us, but we were so constantly hunted by Yakuza that I wanted someone working the guns in case they showed up in this system.

Our helmet-mounted searchlights scattered stark beams of white across skittering shadows on the deck plating, causing the shadows to flee away like monsters retreating for unexposed corners.

"I don't like this," I said out loud, then initiated a gentle burst from my thrusters to the first emergency hatch and tried to muscle it open.

No luck.

My hands went to work on the internal mechanisms of its control panel to trigger the manual safeties override. "That should do it. Okay, stand clear," I said. "If the next section does have atmosphere, this hatch will blow out when we break the seal."

I paused, concerned for her safety until she flattened herself against the collar that encircled the entry. My pulse pounded with unanswered questions.

Why would someone attack this shuttle?

Finally, I managed to crack open the hatch. Nothing happened.

So by grabbing handholds, we pulled ourselves through, as if swimming through the lack of gravity in the mysterious ship. The absence of passengers is what disturbed me.

Shreds of clothing, a few odd shoes, and globules of blood floated, suspended in the airless space of the compartment.

"Gage, where's the passengers?" she asked, her voice now tight with alarm. Tess looked like she might become sick. Her eyes widened behind her faceplate.

"You good?" I asked with a hand on her shoulder.

She nodded quickly but didn't speak.

I led us through the subsequent hatch. No one was here. Not even bodies.

And by the time we reached the third one, my heart was thudding inside my chest. "Where's Sigourney Weaver when you need her?"

"Hey, what am I—chopped liver?" Tess asked.

"I actually like chopped liver," I said.

"You would," she said with a disgusted scowl.

Tess had been giving me the cold shoulder since yesterday, ever since I spent 200K from our bounty hunter earnings on this pair of jetpacks and some other equipment after she'd insisted we not spend anything. The pricey plasma grenades hadn't helped.

According to her, we should've used those precious

credits to pay down debt with Polariti and Magnum. It was a fair point, but come on! Jetpacks.

The crew had outvoted her, three votes to two.

Tess and Steinbreaker wanted us to cut losses and put as much space as possible between us and the Yakuza ships that had been on our tail.

The rest of us felt the key to survival, even if we couldn't win, was to at least to do them some damage to make them think twice about pursuing us, to wear them down until they decided that hunting our craft just wasn't worth it.

That was putting a strain on our resources, and the question was who would break first—the Yakuza leadership or our bottom line.

"This hatch is stuck, and my Jedi mind tricks aren't working on it," I said, holding up my simple tools. "And looks like I am fresh out of duct tape."

No response from the Ice Queen. Not a grin.

"That was a dad joke," I said. "Okay, fine. Looks like I'll be using the jacker. Good thing I bought it on that shopping trip, right?"

She rolled her eyes and looked annoyed.

I attached the small, octagonal device to the control panel and waited. "It's decrypting," I said. "The guy at Wildcard said it takes a minute—that is if he didn't sell me a dud."

I was no expert on the female mind. Let me just get that out of the way. My late wife once talked me into reading a book called *The 5 Love Languages* because she'd heard from her friend that it could work wonders for communication.

So, being young and earnest, I said, "Sure!"

The basic gist of this book was that we all had ways of

receiving love that might not be self-evident. We expect other people to get it, but they don't if their love language is different.

For Amber and me, that meant I had to stop buying her trinkets just because gifts were my preference. To her, acts of service were more meaningful, like taking out the trash or unloading the dishes, and that did help our marriage a lot.

So, is that what's happening here?

The author of that book outlined five love languages, which to me meant one glaring omission.

You guessed it. Not one chapter on jetpacks.

Tess released a groan over our comm link. "How long does this take to work?" she said.

"You got a better idea?" I replied. "Be my guest."

I squinted at the jacker. True, the device looked like a Transformers accessory from 1990, but everything else we'd bought from Wildcard had been legit. "That guy had better not have ripped me off," I grumbled under my breath.

"What was the total you blew at that place?" Tess replied with an arching eyebrow. "All good investments, right, Savvy Shopper?"

I was getting used to this since she'd been standoffish since we left Vorak-3. The two of us had shared one delicious kiss on Taggermore before the Battle Mech Tournament, but since then, tensions had begun to rise. Whenever I tried to figure out why, it only seemed to push her away.

I mean, she was here.

Tess was here with me, but I just kept getting the sense there was something that she was hiding, something distracting her that she wouldn't say, not any one thing that I could point to. It just seemed like something was... off.

The jacker beeped twice on the control panel. Finally, this hatch was ready to open.

"See," I said. "All good investments from Wildcard. Okay, let's stand back and keep weapons hot."

Tess braced herself against the bulkhead, aiming her blaster. "Roger that," she breathed, her upper lip now moistened with sweat.

With a last exhale, I activated it. The hatch exploded toward us with the force of escaping air.

Inside the compartment, the lack of all sound sent chills down my spine.

Section by section, the interior lights blinked off until we froze there, immersed in the darkness, with only the lamps of our helmets to pierce the shadows with shaky white beams.

Her sharp scream turned the blood to ice in my veins.

Movement off to the starboard—a boot, a smudge, and then it was gone.

"Rubicon!" I called, frantically searching the space for my partner. "Rubi, where are you? Rubi, respond!"

CHAPTER TWO

GRUNTS AND PANTING came through on my comm.

I triggered my HUD and found the blinking icon representing Tess on the ship's schematic, which I'd downloaded. Keeping the HUD overlay active but reduced to fifty percent opacity, I swiveled, pushed off the collar, and dove for her.

A dark assailant slammed into my flank like a linebacker, pushing me off course, driving me into the bulkhead. My head bounced off the inside of my helmet, but it was cushioned by memory foam.

I drove my left elbow into the attacker. That left him stunned for a millisecond.

Crouching against the interior, I pushed off and struck him across his visor. Superhuman strength from my nanotech enhancements turned what would have been a solid strike into one that left spider cracks in his faceplate.

Gripping a railing in one hand, I grabbed his head with my other and slammed it into the bulkhead. His visor fractured with a hiss of air.

The attacker convulsed and then fell slack.

"Help me!" Tess pleaded. "This thing is too strong!"

A humanoid figure had her wrists pinned and looked to be reaching for her helmet.

So, I fired the tow line from my right vambrace. The cable shot out, deploying its grappling hook. It snagged the armored plating over his shoulder blade. I jerked it back, retracting the cable with mental commands.

The two of them—Tess and her attacker—flew toward me. From its sheath in my chestplate, I drew my combat knife and sunk it into the combatant's ribs.

That elicited an inhuman shriek. I stabbed him twice more until he let go.

In the clinical glare of my helmet, I caught a glimpse of what lived inside for the first time. An elongated skull twitched, its skin drawn and pale, gnashing gums and spiked teeth too big for its mouth.

It was the same alien horror I'd encountered on the hunt with Hidalgo. I switched my helmet to thermal imaging, but before I could wheel around, Tess shouted, "Watch out!"

Another one sprang from the shadows and drifted across the compartment, firing at me from a carbine like mine, strafing my armor with its streaks of plasma.

The heat signature from its weapon burned out my vision, causing my HUD to dim the display, even while making my reticle glow. We traded fire, and Tess intervened with subsonic plasma rounds from her blaster.

Arcing fire shot out from somewhere. I tracked the target and returned the favor until it died off. Two of the aliens were creeping toward us along the bulkheads.

No, there were four.

The sight was eerie, the cores of their weapons flared

bright in my thermal imaging, but their bodies were remarkably dim inside their pressure suits, which meant they must've been cold-blooded or maintained a chilling core body temp.

Four of them opened up with their blasters, which was a problem with limited cover.

I grimaced, pressed up against the bulkhead, trying to avoid their assault. Diving behind a passenger seat, I could scarcely emerge to return fire.

Hunkered now behind the barrier, I licked the sweat from my lips and caught a glimpse of why the aliens were unloading ammo at such a high rate. My body was already laced with adrenaline, but when I saw what they were up to, my stomach dropped.

"They're providing covering fire for the other ones climbing into an escape pod," I yelled to Tess, who had ducked behind the passenger seat across the aisle.

"Stryker, that isn't the mission," she said. "We can't afford to lose any grenades. We have to conserve what's left of our stockpile, so we can save up to finally go dark."

I set my jaw. "The only thing worse than them killing us would be these terrible things getting loose. I have to do something."

Celin-Ohmi, from back on our ship, the superintelligent mollusk, cut in. "Stryker, this is Aerial," she said. "I don't know what you two are doing in there—but it will have to wait."

"We're a little tied up right now, Aerial!" I snapped back. "I can assure you; we're not wasting time!"

"Be that as it may, sir, one of my drones has picked up an Ekibyo-class destroyer. We need to leave now before it closes to within range of sensor scans."

"Scrat!" I seethed. For twelve weeks now, we'd been

taking bounty hunter jobs until I could finally convince Braddock to set up this meet, but we'd been constantly harassed by Yakuza's ships bent on blowing us out of the sky after our victory in the arena that had cost them untold millions in wagers they'd placed on the other team—based on Hidalgo's assurances to Shintox that he'd make sure we didn't survive.

Not to mention costly losses to their fleet and personnel.

They didn't believe in the saying, "Forgive and forget." Suffice it to say we weren't exactly their favorite crew in the universe.

"Rubi, we've got company!" I called. "Gotta go! Now that we know the contact's not in here, maybe Braddock will meet us in person."

"After he just tried to kill us?!" she said. The space crackled with energy as she snapped off rounds at the ravenous aliens.

"You mean this bullscrat? We don't know that Braddock's behind this. There'd be easier ways if all he wanted to do was to get rid of us. No, I think we've stumbled into something else. What, I don't know, but we're out of time to investigate."

"True. But what'll we do about all our charming new friends?"

"Forget them," I said. "Yakuza's out there! Lead the way —I'm right behind you. I'm gonna drop an Officer Friendly."

"An Officer—Gage, are you nuts?!" Tess shouted. "Give me a minute!" Grabbing a handhold, she rocketed into the next compartment with a hard burn of exhaust from her thrusters.

I closed the gap right behind her. Blaster fire pinged off our armor.

Pausing at the hatch, I holstered my weapon, then grabbed a grenade from my utility belt and pulled the firing pin. "So long, you sons of bjoreks!" I screamed, pitching the bomb into their compartment.

Closing the blast doors, I shut the aliens in with the bomb I'd nicknamed an Officer Friendly. It was a far cry from the military issue of the twenty-first century.

Booms like thunderclaps heralded heat waves of positively and negatively charged particles exploding from the plasma grenade in a flash that I knew would vaporize all organic life in the blast radius.

"Go!" I urged Tess. We shot out of there with our jets on full burn.

The concussive force of my Officer Friendly shook the ship with a roiling heat that sublimated metal. On our way out, I pitched a second one into the shuttle's thruster assembly because I had to make sure that escape pod didn't get clear with any of those living nightmares inside.

Shockwaves rocked the hulk of the vessel as it went critical.

A ball of plasma blossomed behind us at a range that wouldn't be lethal but still gave us an extra push. "Wahoo!" I yelled. "You feel that behind us? Oh man, I'm riding the wave!"

"You're lucky these suits block out radiation," Tess shot back in a withering tone. "You can't afford to lose any more brain cells."

"Jetpacks, though, right? All good investments! These T-600s really came through."

She snickered but added, "Don't think I'm not mad."

"I heard you laugh," I said.

"I didn't laugh. I coughed."

"Sure you did," I said quietly. "Whatever you need to tell yourself."

Tess and I joined our station-keeping starship at a hard burn from the thrusters on our jetpacks. She radioed Steinbreaker to let us in, and the outermost access hatch cycled open.

"I told you these things would be worth the credits," I said as the first airlock sealed shut behind us.

She looked away, and the lights in the airlock pulsated red.

"You did great out there," I said, making a point to raise my voice over the sound of overhead nozzles dousing us with decontamination sprays.

I couldn't make out her silent expression through the swirling mist illuminated by the lights that alternately flashed in ultraviolet and infrared spectrums.

I'd actually gotten used to this spectacle designed to sterilize whatever contaminants the decon sprays hadn't. It reminded me of the car wash near my childhood home with the garishly colored light show that mixed with suds as you drove through it.

It's amazing the things that you can get used to. There were so many things that felt foreign to me in the twenty-ninth century, but there were little sights and sounds like the airlock cycle I was getting used to from repetition of use.

Tess removed her helmet and tousled her shoulder-length hair. Her crystal blue eyes had taken on an even more icy quality than usual, so I turned right back around and keyed open the second hatch.

Gesturing to the open airlock, I added a winning smile. "Please, after you, my lordship," I said.

"Keep it up," she said. "And the only one sitting across from you tonight will be that precious jetpack... because you'll be eating alone."

"Hey!" I replied with furrowed eyebrows. "You don't think you're overreacting just a wee bit about all the new gear we purchased?"

She brushed past me into the ship.

We both headed to our separate quarters to change out our armor for crisp and clean flight suits. Then, she followed me into the cockpit.

My workstation was forward to hers as the captain because, according to the *Gambit's* design, her chair in the gunner's position had an elevated line of sight through the canopy, which was elongated, ample vertical clearance for both of us to maintain a clear view, even if we did have to ride in the front almost stacked on top of each other.

Bond had been training her for the gunner position since he'd been through flight school and was an accomplished pilot—more than anyone could say for Tess or me at this point.

Thankfully, we had Celin-Ohmi to do the actual flying. She was back in her dedicated compartment, encircled by flight control and navigational systems, which she interfaced with and helmed via the neural motherboards hardwired into her nervous system in the water tank she swam in twenty-four seven—since her alien race was aquatic.

Just like the ocean-dwelling creatures on Earth, the Quonella never stopped swimming. I'd always found it fascinating how sea life swam when they slept.

When Tess came in, Bond sensed her bluster and

must've wanted no part in it because, in deference to her, he climbed down and walked the short corridor to the comms station aft of us, where he took a seat.

Next to him, Steinbreaker was grouchily manning his console and muttering his discontent about something.

"Did you think I wouldn't see you up there?" I asked Tess.

We'd might as well dive right in.

"What do you mean?" she said. "This is my seat."

"Not when we're in an active engagement," I reminded her.

She just balked.

"Bond, would you please take the gunner's chair?" I asked.

"Gage, I can do it!" Tess protested. "Why don't you think I'm capable?"

I groaned. "Nobody here is questioning your level of talent or ability," I said. "It's only a matter of experience, remember? You don't see me taking the weapons with enemies in system. That's because I haven't been to flight school or taken their educational track on space combat. Neither have you. Bond has."

"Fine," she said, climbing down to switch places with the Oshwellian.

"Navigation, what's the likelihood of that Yakuza ship picking us up on its sensors?" I asked over the ship-wide comm channel that was often active and the five of us shared.

"It's currently on a vector that should keep us out of its range," Celin-Ohmi responded. "If they remain on their current trajectory."

"Which we won't take for granted," I added, stress digging into my gut. "Listen up, people. I don't want anyone to panic, but if it's not already obvious, meeting Braddock's guy was a total bust, so that means, unfortunately, we're going to need to make our budget stretch a little longer because it looks like we're still on the run."

"How bad is it?" Bond interjected.

I looked down. As captain, I carried the economic—and literal—survival of this crew in my hands, a fact I'd accepted as a high honor when I bought this starship and took over as captain, but which had recently only seemed to make me lose sleep until I could bring them some piece of good news.

One thing a competent leader knows—in the absence of good news, don't fudge on the truth.

I cleared my throat. "You all know I believe in total transparency. We'll review our profits and losses in the morning. But for now, let's just say that we don't want to burn any more fuel than we have to, so we're going to wait this out until that Yakuza vessel is gone before we make any maneuvers that could draw unwanted attention. Celin-Ohmi, cut our thrusters and reduce power to the point that our energy signature is as discrete as you can make it while keeping us ready for maximum thrust in case things go south. And let's hope that destroyer completes its patrol and keeps right on going. Hopefully, we'll be on our merry way."

A somber silence fell over the ship because we all knew that wasn't likely. Our ship was no match for Yakuza.

Maybe today, our luck had run out.

I barely breathed as the seconds ticked by, and my heartbeat thrummed in my ears in time. We waited amidst the ambient beeping of telemetry and rolling hum of the engines.

"This would be easier if we went dark," Tess pointed out.

"Nobody likes a backseat driver," I replied with a clench of my jaw. It wasn't my finest moment, but I was stretched to the brink.

With irritation, she unbuckled, stood up, and added on her way out, "I'll be in the rec room if anyone needs me."

"What's her deal?" asked the Oshwellian.

"It's complicated," I said to Bond, not wanting to start another argument. Someone had to keep this crew together.

But Tess and I were at an impasse. We had a fundamental disagreement about how to handle the money, and it seemed to be getting worse. The two of us liked to joke around, but it seemed like our divide had only deepened.

She had been outvoted, three against two.

The crew had agreed to split up our haul from bounty hunter work equally among the five of us since each of them helped with every job.

Bond had even gotten licensed with Magnum and had earned his promotion to Zenith last week after turning in enough bounties to be rewarded with that designation.

But collective purchases or investments could only be made by majority rule and equal contributions from each crew member.

Ultimately, I had veto power since I held the majority stake. I'd put up most of the credits for this ship, so that had to count for something. That seemed fair to everyone else.

My purpose was to keep the crew motivated by not only uniting around common missions but also giving each a piece of the pie.

To me, that was the best way to do business. Every

member of the team shares the risks, and each one gets a cut of the rewards.

That would sound great if we were winning.

If we weren't primary targets of the second biggest criminal syndicate in the galaxy... and getting ready to join the first.

CHAPTER THREE

"SHE'S RIGHT, YOU KNOW," Steinbreaker said, breaking the silence, "about picking a fight we can't win."

"I can't believe you're not backing me up on this, Steinbreaker," said Celin-Ohmi, her tone laced with hurt and betrayal. The translator matrix at the base of her tank adeptly translated electrical signals from her brain's left hemisphere into speech we could all understand, including her emotions and inflections, a technology Steinbreaker had worked on himself.

"I *am* backing you up—by saving you from this vendetta that will get us all killed!" he growled before softening. "This is why I didn't want to sell this ship to an outlander— or anyone else. I knew you might try to conscript them for this lost cause of yours, and I didn't want to see you go through that again."

"Oh, so you think the Quonella—you think the plight of my people—is a lost cause?" Her voice trembled with anger.

"No! That's my point," said the engineer. "Haven't your

people been through enough? When is it going to end, Celin-Ohmi?"

"It's going to *end* when Quonella are free from their slavery to Yakuza!" she said. "You talk like I'm the only one who's been hurt by them, but you're forgetting about the others onboard! Each of us here has a reason to fight. Look at what they did to Bond—trying to force him to pilot their ships into those Antrydium freighters in the shipping lanes, just like they've been doing to my people for months. The only difference is he's a land-dweller, so they couldn't threaten to drain his water tank if he didn't comply! And Gage—look at him. He lost his child, but he's actually trying to help us, Steinbreaker—no thanks to you! See, these people have causes, too. It's not like I'm on some crusade of vengeance all by myself. There are real people's lives at stake here, many more than our little crew!"

"I know," said Steinbreaker. "I know, and I'm sorry. I didn't mean to infer that—"

"I'm with her," Bond interjected. "I'm with Celin-Ohmi. Once we showed them up in the Battle Mech Tournament and cost them millions in sports bets, you think they're going to just let that go? No, at this point, it's become an interstellar stain on their reputation. They have to resolve it."

Steinbreaker blew out a breath which became a hacking cough, probably from the cigar. "I don't think you people appreciate the gap in our capabilities. Take Ekibyo."

"You had to bring that up?" Bond said with a groan.

"Yes, I had to bring that up! You know why? Because I'm *Gambit's* engineer. That means my job is to keep this ship running and inform the captain of her capabilities. Look at the specs of Ekibyo destroyers next to ours. That should make it clear. We have no chance—and that's only *one* class of destroyers. Imagine fleets with three different types. You people are entertaining a fantasy!"

"Didn't say we could do it alone!" Bond retorted. "Obviously, we need some allies. But now that I've got my license, there are three of us who can take jobs, so that's three times the income. Not right away, but maybe in time, we can use that money to keep upgrading our weapon systems."

"To do what?" the engineer balked. "To destroy all of Yakuza? Phaw!"

"To hurt them enough that they'll leave us alone," I interjected. "We can't keep running forever. We have some alliances in the works, remember? Mercedes offered to pay us if we can establish a relationship with Emin Braddock in the League of Desai, which I need to do anyway if I'm ever going to get into the Free People's Protectorate, where they're holding my son."

The furry scientist barked out a laugh. "And how's that working out for you, Captain?"

I almost wanted to throttle his neck. "What are you— some kind of therapist now? Everything's not lost with our League contact. Today, we just ran into a snag."

"Be careful of the company you keep," said Steinbreaker.

"Not saying I *like* the prospect of working with the League of Desai," I retorted. "But we're pretty low on options here, Steinbreaker. And you know what they say— the enemy of my enemy is my friend. It is one place to start."

"Until you're not watching your back," he warned me. "Fighting Yakuza is a losing venture, and if you continue down this road, Captain, you may manage to blow up a few ships. But long term, you're not going to succeed at anything except for draining all of our bank accounts—and we'll still end up dead when it's over. Look, I'm sorry, but Tess is right. Going dark is the only way."

A somber silence fell over the *Gambit*.

The first one to break it was Celin-Ohmi. "You don't know what it's like to be controlled by someone more powerful than you, forced to watch yourself execute orders that haunt you for the rest of your life."

No one said anything after that.

How could Steinbreaker argue with her?

The bottom line was that he and Tess thought we should put away as much as possible to save up for what they called "going dark." In this case, that meant taking our ship's transponder offline.

Their plan had some clear advantages. The light years we'd logged had taught us our ship was common enough that Yakuza couldn't track us by appearance alone without a transponder.

That would be like tracking a Honda if you had the license plate number and VIN versus looking for one if you didn't have anything on it.

Going dark was the one way to travel without any record of where you'd been.

Without a transponder, we wouldn't show up on sensor arrays of Yakuza ships like the one in this system.

Free to come and go as we please—as long as we steered clear of the authorities and didn't mind docking in dangerous places.

It was tempting.

Technically, the *Gambit* was a corvette, but the privatization of war and enforcement—combined with its widespread commercialization—had made this bad boy a common sight in the unwashed masses.

A consumer version of it was trendy among spoiled young spacers, sort of like how the Hummer in the 2000s, a vehicle inspired by military use, was suddenly being driven in Hollywood by everyone from Britney Spears to Arnold Schwarzenegger.

This was like that on steroids. Some say that goes without saying with Arnold, but you get the idea. In a galactic federation where corporate conglomerates built weapons for a living *and* owned entire planets—war had a glitz of its own.

Many private military companies used our model on security escorts for mercantile ships and patrolling worlds. At only twenty-three meters long, it was a favorite of federal law enforcement working undercover.

At least, that's what I'd heard.

So, we'd have no problem with blending in.

The latter two uses—PMCs and Law—usually formed a *deterrent* for Yakuza from attacking a random ship like ours if one of their soldiers would cross its path, sort of like how a typical gangster would steer clear of squad cars in the heyday of the American mafia.

They had no reason to pick that fight.

Yakuza thrived by staying in the shadows, out of the limelight. The less the government meddled in their affairs, the better that was for their business at large.

After all, the popularity of our corvette is why their leaders had chosen it for the convoys that were making surprise attacks on the Antrydium freighters. Their after-market upgrades to drives and engines were hidden "under the hood," so to speak. Even the most deadly weapon system was tucked back into the big ventral shaft to keep it concealed from prying eyes.

So, at least, the *Gambit* was fast and deadly.

At least, we had that going for us.

But we were outnumbered, outgunned, and outclassed by Yakuza's fleet, and the stress of being hunted constantly was starting to wear on my crew. Who could blame them?

Somehow, I needed to keep us together.

But there were two strikes against going dark.

It was illegal. That meant we'd lose our licenses as fugitive recovery agents for the Commonwealth. And that meant no more income. We didn't have time to learn a new trade. That's why Tess wanted to pinch every penny—to build up a nest egg to cover our bills so we could go dark without needing jobs.

Problem was, in the meantime, to make that money and build up a buffer, we needed these positions for our fuel and gear.

Neither was cheap.

Not with the light years we needed to log to stay one step ahead of those bjoreks working for the Japanese mafia.

Maybe she was right. Maybe it would be easier to run if they couldn't track us. I'm sure it would be. But the fact was, we couldn't run forever. We'd just be in a holding pattern. That might keep us alive a little longer, but it was just delaying the inevitable.

Someday, we'd step out of a bar on a remote world and be gunned down before we made it to the spaceport. I didn't know how it would happen for sure, but I knew it would.

We all did.

Maybe that's why we'd been growing more edgy, fighting about things that didn't matter.

Just like a car's VIN where I had come from—the transponder on each ship was registered with the government, so removing or trying to change it out as the owner was against the law.

Sure, you could try, but you wouldn't make it far with traffic control the next time you wanted to land. And we'd definitely lose the government contracts we depended on for survival.

Plus, going dark, being harder to track, wouldn't help us find Oliver.

After months of scouring the gal-net and fugitive recovery agent database, my only lead was what Mercedes from Task Force Cyberblade had suggested may offer some benefit—see if I could build a connection with the snitch that she'd worked with before in the League of Desai, Emin Braddock, then wait for further instructions. At least, that's what Mercedes had insinuated without coming out and saying it.

He was a powerful Caudanum Mathum in the organization who ran their operations on a world called Vedana. She'd hinted at as much as she could without getting in trouble. If the underworld where the League trafficked was as deadly as whatever clues I'd been able to scrape together from my interrogations and dives into the gal-net, I wouldn't go in there unarmed.

No, despite how much Tess hated it, we couldn't put enough away to go dark. Not while we were pursued by Yakuza.

Not while we were planning to infiltrate a syndicate even more deadly than they were.

It would only take one guided missile to turn this ship to debris forever. I worried about the risks to our crew as long as the bad guys had bigger load outs and better equipment—not to mention entire fleets.

All the savings in the world wouldn't mean anything

until we could hold our own against both of those organizations. Why couldn't Tess and Steinbreaker see that?

As much as I respected and admired them both, they had decided I was being reckless when my only motivation for buying jetpacks or grenades or upgraded cannons was the safety of the *Gambit* and her crew.

But that meant we wouldn't be able to go dark for a very long time, and we'd have to find a way to evade Yakuza until then. I'm not one to back down from a fight.

Our ship's engineer didn't see it that way. And neither did Tess.

Sometimes I wondered if that was the only thing wrong as the weeks rolled by. Her withdrawn behavior had started to make me wonder if I could trust her in general.

After all, if the woman didn't trust me enough to tell me what was really going on inside her, what else could she be hiding?

To be honest, I had some questions.

Like why, on Galiano Island, had Tess been the first one in Pell's ship when I got there, descending its ramp right next to the man?

Standing there.

Right next to Ollie's abductor.

For weeks, I'd been trying to ignore that question because I didn't want to believe it—but could they somehow actually be connected? Could they have come back through time together? Her and Pell?

No, that was crazy.

But when I thought about it, I mean, why not?

She could've shown up at the restaurant the day before when I met her for lunch ahead of Pell's crew. I had no way to rule that out but no way to verify it.

The only inconsistency in her backstory was between

her claims of how long she'd known Devon and what he'd seemed to insinuate. Tess claimed she'd first met him the day before me at the Hummingbird Pub, while he'd seemed to think they had some kind of history.

Maybe it was nothing.

Maybe I was expecting too much, too fast. After all, we'd been complete strangers less than six months ago. It was only the trauma of our journey through time and Oliver's disappearance that had twisted our story together. Now that we both had time for a breather, who could blame her for needing space?

But that wasn't all that I didn't know.

I didn't know why such a well-connected mob boss in the most powerful criminal syndicate would risk his neck and those of his crew to test the limits of time and space in subversive ways that shouldn't be tampered with and brave the treacherous journey through a wormhole to a remote island outside of Vancouver in January 2024.

Had he come to our site for the meteor? Because the Centurions had never explained that.

Or was he actually there for my son?

As completely preposterous as that may seem—after all, what's one little kid have to do with it, four years old and kind of a screw-up—who can't even keep his own sneakers tied? I don't see what Sarmonicus Pell would need with him.

Did he know something about our future? Was there something unique about Ollie?

I'd turned it over and over in my mind until I was ready to pull my hair out, until I was so mad I could punch through a wall. Actually, I had done that a couple times, now that I was all souped-up on nanites. It was kind of cathartic.

But it didn't change anything. It didn't change the darkness I was stumbling around in ever since my son disappeared.

It didn't change the fact that I dreaded his birthday when he should be in kindergarten, but instead, it would be the first one without an Oreo cake and a tiger-themed present.

And the first one without his dad.

There were a lot of things I didn't know.

I didn't know how I would keep this crew safe with Yakuza constantly gunning for us and, even if I did, how I'd make it another day without my child. I didn't know what had become of my Ollie or how he was getting along.

Most of all, I didn't know if or when our paths would cross again this side of heaven. Or whether the four years we'd spent together would be all that I'd know.

I kept pushing those thoughts down so I could function. So I could be the man that my son needed.

I kept telling myself that it would be worth it. And for his sake, I hoped I was right.

"Captain," Celin-Ohmi spoke up. "The Ekibyo ship has turned around and is headed our way."

CHAPTER FOUR

"THE YAKUZA CRAFT is on an intercept course with us," said Celin-Ohmi. "Their long-range sensors have detected us. It's Ekibyo-class destroyer *Hantakira*."

"Great," I said, shaking my head. "I was starting to miss Marekk-Thuul. I haven't seen that captain for days."

Ekibyo was Japanese for "pestilence." They couldn't have chosen a better term. Of all the ships the syndicate had sent after us, the *Hantakira* seemed to be most determined, although the verdict was out on whether they'd come to kill us or turn us into hostages—since we always jumped out of the system at the first sign of their patrols. The few times we'd traded fire out of sheer necessity while making a hasty retreat from the system hadn't gone well.

Our repairs to the *Gambit* were extensive and costly.

Heavily armored, armed, and fast, their vessel was outfitted with laser batteries and missile turrets, one of two destroyer classes capable of multidirectional firing arcs, but it was the twin mass driver cannons its superstructure was built around that put fear in the hearts of their enemies.

Destroyers like these could deal serious damage in

groups against cruisers and battlecruisers—so one clean hit from their MDC would annihilate a little ship like ours. How many sleepless nights had I spent trying to work out a solution, when every encounter, we were tempting fate?

I feared the day they'd catch us off guard and deal a critical hit with that cannon. It was only a matter of time.

"Incoming missiles!" Bond alerted me. "Deploying countermeasures."

So, it begins.

"Celin-Ohmi, bring us around!" I said. Even if we did minimal damage, we had to make at least *some* kind of effort on our vector out of the system to show them that the fight hadn't left us, that there was venom still in our fangs.

"Aye, aye, Captain!" the helmsman replied.

The roar of our engines spinning up almost drowned her out as spillover g-forces pushed us into our acceleration chairs, memory gel absorbing the inertia not already diminished by our ship's dampeners.

Celin-Ohmi brought the *Gambit* around. Attacking missiles could be seen briefly streaking across our view in a flash. The *Gambit's* point defense cannons rattled, launching our guided rockets with warheads that burst, expelling a hail of spheres.

Our bombardment pelted their incoming missiles with not only kinetic but cybernetic force, scrambling guidance systems as strips of foil flitted into range of their targeting systems, crippling their ability to find a good lock. Gouts of flame punctuated the darkness.

Hitting our wall of countermeasures, their missiles exploded, most at relatively safe distances, but it was hard to tell with the naked eye if we'd scraped by without any secondary damage. Others strayed off course and vanished into the eternal dark of the void.

But from that void flashed *Hantakira's* lasers before we had time to react. His energy beams slammed into our shields, sending a tremor down the spine of the *Gambit*. The console rumbled in my white-knuckled grip.

The defensive barrier enveloping our hull shook with duress under the impact of their heavy lasers, rocking me forward into my restraints.

"Energy shields down to sixty percent!" Bond reported from his workstation. "We can't take many more hits like that, Captain!"

"Celin-Ohmi, evasive maneuvers," I said, buying time.

My mind raced through our available options, which didn't take long because there was only one destination that made any sense in this situation—an asset this destroyer wouldn't dare to face off with—the one we'd been headed to next, anyway. Now, we'd just have to step on it. "Celin-Ohmi, get us out of here!"

Before she could respond, another blast from *Hantakira's* laser batteries raked our hull with tremors, testing the boundaries of our defenses. Something astern of me— maybe in the engineering section—pitched and groaned. Not knowing what those noises represented, my stomach lurched at the ominous sounds.

"Evasive maneuvers!" I said with more heat. "Helm, get us the void out of here!"

"I'm trying, Captain," said Celin-Ohmi. "But something's wrong with our acceleration."

"Something's wrong with our acceleration?!" I said with a grimace. "Guys, I don't like the sound of that!"

"I see the problem," Steinbreaker put in. "We've sprung a minor leak in the moderator array from where one of his missiles detonated too close to our ship. We're leeching antimatter from that thruster bell."

"Can you fix it?" I asked. "What about the damage control bots?" But I knew that was a last-ditch effort, not something we had time to address in the middle of a space battle.

Our engineer blew out a breath. "Sure, we can fix it— but not here—in a repair bay with the ship powered down."

"What does that mean in the meantime?" I asked.

"That means until I can make the repair, our top velocity is going to be about twenty-three percent lower than normal," he said. "And that will drop with time until we can dock and patch up that leak."

"I can't execute evasive maneuvers at this diminished velocity," said Helm. "The destroyer already has the advantage of speed, even when we're in top condition. But the bigger concern is that we need to reach a certain threshold of output for an FTL jump. With this leak, we're falling short of that."

"Which means, we're sitting ducks," said Tess.

In all the chaos, I hadn't noticed that she'd returned to her comms and sensor station, but there she was. I breathed with relief, then groaning, ran a hand over my face. "That's not what I wanted to hear, Celin-Ohmi. There's got to be another solution. Come on, people, think!"

"Stryker, *Hantakira's* hailing us," said Tess. "How do you want to respond?"

I grimaced. "Can you send it to voicemail?"

"Captain, we need to get clear of his guns and punch in the jump coordinates," Bond urged me. "Until then, I don't think we should fire weapons. Our shields can't take another hit like that last one and now, we're too slow to evade him."

I ran a hand over my crewcut. Scanning the tactical display on my station, my eyes fell on the neighboring moon. "Hmm, what do you do with a car when it's out of gas?" I mused quietly. "I think I have an idea. Patch their captain through on the holo screen."

"Aye, aye," Tess said with a tinge of sarcasm, as if any of this was my choice.

The holo image flickered to life. The two-dimensional square display screen of the *Hantakira's* captain floated midair in front of our canopy. Marekk-Thuul was a male Thrawlenian, a pseudoarthropod species.

His body was plated with a carapace, the back half of it segmented, extending behind him, supported by six legs that made clicking noises on the deck plating whenever he spoke. The front half of his body arched upward, allowing him to face bipedal races like humans head-on, towering over us at a height of eight feet.

He had sinewy arms with fore-claws covered in the same natural exoskeleton as the rest of his body, the profile like that of a Minotaur—but two parts scorpion and one part man.

His metasoma, or tail, held bloated segments ending in a barb called the telson, a vesicle-like organ with poisonous glands. From there, his venom would travel through the stinger when he injected it into a victim.

Not that I'd ever witnessed the ritual but was told about it dozens of times in the dirty dive bars where unsavory characters hung out after hours and told their tales of distant journeys to whoever was there to listen.

Beneath Marekk-Thuul's hollow, black eyes, was an orifice encircled by muscular tentacles that writhed like serpents whenever he spoke. For humans, the sight of him alone could be difficult, even before he'd commanded destroyers.

The survivors of navy ships he'd attacked, in interviews before being whisked off to asylums, often spoke of their lives in two distinct stages, the years before they'd seen Marekk-Thuul.

And the descent that occurred after.

He was a powerful *wakagashira,* a regional boss presiding over ten gangs, each of whom had thirty members, in this case, the sailors who traveled with him. He was our nemesis, dispatched by Yakuza, hunting the cosmos for our little ship and commander of the destroyer *Hantakira.*

He always came onscreen with a bounty hunter standing at his either side, anonymous guards clad in armor like ours, each with custom markings on their chestplates—one had a bird of prey, and the other had some kind of family crest—the only signs of self-expression beyond their blank faceplates and burnished armor, hunters turned guards who'd sold their souls to the other side long ago.

I'd spoken to Marekk-Thuul before. Each time, I left sick to my stomach for reasons that were hard to articulate. Interactions with the Yakuza captain triggered a creeping sense of dread like a stain on a garment that wouldn't wash out no matter how much it was scrubbed or bleached.

"Surrender your ship and crew, Captain Gage," Marekk-Thuul intoned from the audio transmission accompanied by his horrid image. "Or you will be destroyed."

"Looks like we don't have a choice," I responded, averting my eyes. "Would you consider a cease-fire until then?"

"A wise decision," said Marekk-Thuul. "All this running around, taking fire from superior weapons. Come now,

Gage. Why? What's the objective for wasting your fuel and valuable resources when we can all see how it ends?"

I drew in a deep breath. "Let me make the necessary arrangements. We need to rearrange some cargo, because as you can see, we don't have much room for storage in here. But I'll hail you when we're ready to receive your boarding party."

"You are allowed," the captain intoned.

After I cut transmission, Celin-Ohmi said nervously, "Captain, I hope you know what you're doing."

"There was a mission, Apollo 13," I said, "that I'm sure Tess is going to remember. The NASA crew was supposed to be the third manned mission to walk on the moon. But instead, their oxygen tank exploded when they were in orbit, so Mission Control and the astronauts had to figure out how to get them back home."

"The slingshot maneuver," Tess said, a glimmer of hope creeping into her voice. "If we had a gravity assist from that moon, it could increase our velocity enough to make the jump to recondite space. Is that what you're thinking?"

"That's what I'm wondering," I said. "Celin-Ohmi, only you can do the math. What do you think? Would that be possible?"

She fell silent in her dedicated compartment aft of the blast doors astern of the rec room. I could picture the room where she operated because we'd held briefings there many times. One continuous wall of data encircled her as swam inside her tank that sat on a pedestal full of tech that was the AI system.

Our FTL core was immediately behind this room, jettisonable in case of serious malfunction. It had to be very close to Celin-Ohmi, our OI (Organic Intelligence), due to the insane sophistication of the calculations needed for jumps into wormholes.

Waiting for signals to be sent or received down cables, even at the speed of advanced fiber-optics, introduced unsustainable delays and false positives in the calculations, a hard-learned lesson for space travelers in earlier times. That's why all ships generally followed this layout with their AI and FTL core, well, except for the superintelligent mollusk. Once you located a starship's drive core, the AI would be adjacent to it.

"My calculations indicate that its dense gravity *would* give us the necessary boost in energy to reach the minimum expenditure required for the jump into recondite space," she said. "But there are two problems. First of all, the sudden reversal in g's would turn us to goo, even with our inertial dampeners. Secondly, it's going to be clear right away that we're defying *Hantakira's* orders. He could shoot us, no?"

"What if we push our inertial dampeners to their max?" I asked her. "Would that bring the effects into acceptable limits?"

"That would take too much power," she stated.

"Without diverting power from the thrust it would take to execute that maneuver or from our shields," Stein-breaker added. "You've got max inertial dampener capacity, maximum thrust, and max-level shields. No. In this situation, we can only have two of the three—or else, we risk a reactor meltdown."

"Is *Hantakira* in range for his tractor beam?" I asked.

"I assume he's waiting on you," said Tess, who also monitored sensors at her console in addition to the comms duties. "Looks like he's keeping his word and giving us time to make arrangements."

"That smug son of a bjorek," I said, shaking my head, almost angrier that he was giving us such a wide berth than if he'd been moving in for the kill shot because it was so disrespectful.

He didn't even see me as a serious threat.

That part of the dynamic needed to change, but today, maybe it actually was to our advantage. "Maintain the thrust we need for the slingshot," I said. "But lower our deflector shields to zero and energy shields to half power."

"What?!" balked Tess. "Do you know who we're dealing with?"

"That's going to leave us defenseless," Bond said.

CHAPTER FIVE

"GUYS, EITHER WAY, IT'S A RISK," I said to my crew, tension so thick inside the Gambit that it felt like the climate control system had malfunctioned and the air had thickened to a stifling soup of humidity, several degrees higher in temperature. "The way I see it is this. Would you rather be captured, interrogated, and tortured... or take a risk on a narrow escape? I'll admit that second choice includes a distinct possibility of getting blown up, but... those are the options we have."

"Great speech," Tess said with a golf clap. "I don't mean to say, 'I told you so,' but if we'd disabled our transponder, like I'd said—"

"That's easy to say in hindsight," said Bond. "But it doesn't help us right now. I'm with Gage. If we cooperate with Marekk-Thuul, then we're all dead for sure."

I was impressed at how the young Oshwellian's self-confidence had grown over the time we'd been working together, about four months, counting our weeks of preparation for the Battle Mech Tournament. Our work together was so intensive, that by this point, the three of us had become pretty comfortable speaking our minds and telling each other exactly what we thought in no uncertain terms.

That was the only way we would've lasted. Sure, we gave each other a hard time. Didn't want things to get too boring. But no team can work together long term without wanting the best for each other and also feeling the freedom to express their ideas without censure. To me, we had both in spades.

"If we do the slingshot, worst comes to worst, we go out swinging—and it might actually work," Bond said. "Anything else on offense, Captain?"

I nodded and said, "Countermeasures on my mark."

"Countermeasures?" he asked with some skepticism. "They haven't shot any missiles."

"I know, but we're not going to do critical damage with any of our current load outs. That'll temporarily keep him from firing missiles, plus the smoke and strips of reflective foil will make it hard for him to get a lock on us with lasers. Our explosive charges won't cripple *Hantakira* but they'll be a distraction, a nuisance, long enough to give us a head start," I said.

"I'm with Gage—Steinbreaker is, too," Celin-Ohmi volunteered for both of them.

"That true, Steinbreaker?" I said, eyebrows raised.

"Yeah," he said, drawing out the syllable with a ripe sense of disdain.

I drew in a breath. "Helm, you're go for the slingshot maneuver. If it works, rendezvous us with the *Excalibur*. If it doesn't work, all of you should know that it's been an honor."

"Eh, don't get all sappy on us," Steinbreaker groused. "If we're going to do this, let's go all in, ronk! Enough back-and-forth, lukewarm commitments!"

I shook my head with a sober chuckle. Any place would be better than here, as long as we could make the jump before our shields took any more damage from that laser fire, or worse, they unleashed their MDC.

But if we could make it to the dreadnaught *Excalibur*, the pride of the fleet and base of operations for the CMC Joint Special Operations Command, I knew we'd be safe. No destroyer—or any one capital ship, for that matter— would dare take on that behemoth.

Plus, Mercedes was stationed there at the moment, and they held my other ship which had belonged to Shintox, so we had two reasons to go.

Three—if you counted not dying.

"Fire," I said. "Celin-Ohmi, take us in."

Anti-missile rockets whistled out from our launch tubes and exploded across the enemy's bow, littering their targeting systems with foil that would divert energy-based attacks amidst the confusion of smoke and shrapnel that I hoped would at least leave a few scratches.

Celin-Ohmi barreled us into the orbit of the barren moon. Hot strands of plasma streaked across our canopy, building into a frightening blaze of heat radiation and friction caused by our penetration into its atmosphere.

The seat restraints cut into my shoulders and seemed to strangle my circulation as the moon's intense gravity whipped us around the heavenly body like a runaway coaster and spit us out on the other side. I swore we were going too fast.

It was all I could do to brace myself, and I worried about the rest of the crew. We careened around the side of the moon, and the *Gambit* rattled in protest. Things were shaking so hard that I pictured bolts along the welded seams coming loose and the whole ship shaking apart. We shot past the Yakuza destroyer.

The only reference point I could compare it to was when, as nine-year-olds, me and my friends built a ramp in the snow over a rusty car at the bottom of Whitaker's mountain and shot down that hill on our flexible flyers in a sledding excursion that ended in three concussions and a broken nose.

Through my viewport, stars coalesced in a vortex distending the fabric of time. Recondite space. It was the catch-all term people used in the future to describe the higher dimensions of reality that weren't that well understood. Using our Randall-Sundrum Transfer Drives, or RST, we intersected them—or maybe they intersected us?—via exotic wormholes enabling a transfer between almost any two points in the universe. If it was charted, it was possible. All of it blew my mind.

I'd made a mental note long ago to ask somebody more knowledgeable for more details about the mysterious precepts of FTL, how it all worked, but until now, that had never seemed as critical as staying alive or taking on the next feat in my ongoing mission to rescue my son.

The science officer, Nilza, had taught me a few tenets of the science when Oxhorn had brought me aboard the Centurion corvette. I hadn't wanted to believe any of it, because of what it meant that I'd lost.

But then again, I'd been in shock about waking up in the distant future.

Steinbreaker had once tried to explain something about how I was thinking about it all wrong, trying to conceptualize it in three dimensions—well, four, if you count time—when interdimensional travel through wormholes really worked nothing like that.

I still couldn't get my head around it but figured maybe I'd ask him more later about Recondite space. It wasn't the jumps that boggled my mind so much as them being instantaneous. I shrugged. Sometimes, it seemed better to not over-analyze. Instead, I accepted my smallness in the grander universe and that there were wonders I may not understand.

I blinked, and the ride was over. A new canopy of stars now engulfed us, pristine, each point of light like a diamond against the velvety black of night, immersing us in the cosmic birth and death of phenomena I couldn't fathom.

My neck and shoulders were sore from the wild slingshot maneuver, but nothing I couldn't recover from.

"Phew!" said Bond. "What in the void? That was awesome."

"It worked!" Tess said with clear elation.

"Celin-Ohmi, I could kiss you right now!" I said, my fingers laced behind my head.

"I don't have lips, Captain," the helmsman responded. "But anyway, thanks for the sentiment."

I leaned back in my chair and laughed. "Yee-haa."

"What does that term mean—'yee-ha?'" asked the helmsman.

"It means when the bad guys were about to get us, you ramped the General Lee!" I said.

"Tell me, Captain, is that a good thing?" she asked.

"It's a very good thing, Celin-Ohmi—though I don't expect you to pull that off as often as Bo and Luke Duke did," I said. "The writers of that show were one-trick ponies."

"Gage, what is a one-trick—"

"Ugh, never mind!" I said. "Some people just don't get my references. It just isn't fun when I have to explain it."

"What about all the things we explain to *you*, you voiding kerlanzi?!" Steinbreaker griped.

"Hey Dr. Furball, there's no reason to get testy with me!" I snapped, thankful he didn't understand my comparison, because if he had, Steinbreaker would be lecturing me right now about how unscientific it was. That show wasn't even logically consistent with itself. After all, cars in the seventies and eighties didn't just jump other cars without a ramp!

But that didn't stop me from getting a laugh about the comparison anyway.

"Besides," I reminded Steinbreaker, "I'm the captain. Which means you do what I say, or else I put you up for adoption at the nearest kennel—because as far as furry companions, you're a lot more testy than Maggie. And you smoke."

"At this rate, I'm going to void *myself* before this mission is over," he grumbled.

I rolled my eyes. Voiding yourself meant spacing yourself—stepping outside of the airlock without a proper supply of oxygen—so he was joking.

"Now boys, do we need to separate you two?" Celin-Ohmi said in a motherly tone.

That shut him down because those two shared a funny dynamic.

Whenever the mollusk raised her voice in the slightest, he grudgingly complied, maybe because he felt responsible for the subjugation of her race by Yakuza, since he was the one who first introduced them to the technology that eventually got them into that situation.

If that were the case, Steinbreaker was just being too

hard on himself, but what did I know? Feeling responsible to her seemed to sort of keep his surly nature in check. Otherwise, he'd probably be nearly impossible to bear.

This way, he got on your nerves but stopped just short of that. Seemed like a win to be riddled with guilt. Well, for some people.

The really *special* personalities.

"Hey, on a brighter note, check out that view," Tess interrupted.

"See, Steinbreaker," I said. "Why can't you be more of a ray of sunshine like our friend, Tess?"

"Oh, for Ancients' sake," he mumbled. "The scrat I put up with around here."

I grinned. "Celin-Ohmi, prepare us to dock with the *Excalibur*."

With a chuckle at our fuming engineer, the helmsman agreed.

The *Excalibur* was awe-inspiring in our forward view-ports. It had been nicknamed "The Federation Dreadnought." That wasn't an official class in the CMC, since their largest capital ships were carriers and battlecruisers, which were typically about seven hundred to eight hundred meters from bow to stern.

"Dreadnought" was a casual term people seemed to use in either admiration or scorn in reference to the *Excalibur*, depending on whom you were talking to, since the sheer scale and armaments of the behemoth stole your breath when you approached it in space, 1.5 kilometers from bow to stern, turrets, and torpedoes so massive and devastating, they were beyond the capacity of any ship's armor and shields to defend against.

Those who appreciated the government's protection

saw this as a show of strength—while those who didn't considered it hubris.

Love it or hate it, the *Excalibur* was unyielding. Appointed with the most powerful weaponry of any capital ship in the Commonwealth, the fleet's crowning achievement and a symbol of military might.

Each time I'd boarded it, everyone I'd met among the twenty thousand people onboard at any given time, from bridge officers to maintenance techs, all seemed to take pride in their responsibilities. They exuded a culture of excellence, optimism, and mutual honor.

Since Task Force Cyberblade, home of the Centurions, was a SpecOps unit under the leadership of the Joint Special Operations Command, Mercedes Jain worked on *Excalibur*, too, when she wasn't deployed on missions.

Since the meeting with Braddock's contact had gone so terribly wrong, I needed to ask her what our next steps should be.

But I had a second reason for coming aboard the *Excalibur*. My guess was that a face-to-face with Braddock would be coming, and in that case, I wanted to have my second ship on hand to make him an offer he couldn't refuse.

Once Braddock saw what we'd found inside it, I believed he'd be very eager to work with us. It was time to go big or go home.

It was a solid move by Mercedes to use her connections to get permission for us to deposit the corvette we'd stolen from Shintox in the hangar bay of the *Excalibur* after we'd defeated him in the Battle Mech Tournament—because I'd needed to stow the craft somewhere, somewhere out of the way where Yakuza wouldn't be able to get their hands on it. We had enough trouble from them already with only one vulnerable craft to defend, and we didn't need a second one.

Well, until we did.

But I wasn't planning on using the *Lizard King* (okay, I'd had fun with that name as a classic rock fan) as another set of guns in our battle against the Yamaguchi-Gumi or Yakuza in general.

No, this prized craft was my bargaining chip with the League of Desai.

And even though the Centurions had a vested interest in keeping it from falling into the wrong hands in their role as the most elite private military unit that was contracted by the federal government, I still had full rights of ownership.

After all, Shintox was my bounty, fair and square. I'd tried to bring him in, and he had resisted, then tried to kill me. Multiple times.

As a Magnum hunter, I'd been authorized for lethal force, and I'd done what was necessary. In those situations, whether the defendant is turned in or killed in self-defense, any property they've signed over as bail is confiscated personally by the fugitive recovery agent responsible.

Still, I truly appreciated how the Centurions had been willing to keep the *Lizard King* for me until I had returned.

I was eager to report back to Mercedes on our progress and get her recommendations on where we should turn next with Braddock. The fact that his contact's shuttle had been sabotaged by a mysterious species was a wrinkle I hadn't expected and only complicated a situation that already felt like it was slipping away. *Braddock is my only lead*, I reminded myself.

We needed to get this locked down.

But it wasn't clear what my next steps should be—or whether there was more going on than I'd originally been told.

CHAPTER SIX

"ENGAGING AUTOPILOT," Celin-Ohmi announced as we came within range.

Security was tight. Due to the *Excalibur's* strategic importance in the CMC, there was always a risk of terrorists hijacking a craft that would otherwise have good reason to dock there, then plowing it into the dreadnought upon approach of its hangar bay in a kamikaze attack.

That's why the ship had its own dedicated traffic control for incoming vessels and was uncompromising about its demand that all incoming comply. If their sensors couldn't confirm that the *Gambit's* autopilot function was active our entire approach, I knew our ship would be turned away and two of *Excalibur's* turrets would rotate in our direction.

That much was clear from the electronic manual Mercedes had sent me ahead of time to prepare for our first docking here.

Armored blast doors installed for extra protection parted vertically. Blue light poured from the opening, as their computerized traffic control system guided us through the force field at the entrance that was there to prevent decompression, even cycling down our landing gear as we entered the hangar.

We scooted inside, most of *Gambit's* weight kept off the landing gear by our engaged gravimetric drive. As they taxied us into our designated berth, I finally exhaled. It was uncomfortable letting someone control our ship, computer or not, who wasn't part of my crew, even for a short time.

In this case, there was no getting around it.

Control returned to Celin-Ohmi, and she completed her routines of shutting down drives and putting the different ship systems in standby or turning them off as needed. The rest of us unhooked our harnesses and filed into the rec room. I untwisted the hatch in the deck at our feet and led my crew down the ladder to the lower deck, where we made our way out through the stern on our cargo bay's ramp.

I yawned with a stretch. Disembarking after a long flight reminded me of climbing out of the car at the rest stop to pick up Red Bull and Doritos on one of our family vacations or an away game with my baseball team.

A blonde representative with her hair drawn up into a tight bun and dressed in a uniform was right there to greet us. That we did *not* have on family vacations or away games with guys from the dugout.

"Welcome to *Excalibur*, everyone," she said with an attentive smile. "Captain Gage, it's so nice to meet you."

"Thank you for having us," I said with a nod, returning her firm handshake.

Bond, Tess, and Steinbreaker nodded their approval, each of them mumbling a warm reply.

"I'm Clara," said the representative. "Operator Jain's looking forward to seeing you. Right this way, please."

We followed her, and I noticed the guards with blaster rifles posted in the hangar for security. Other small craft were lined up in this, the public bay for general access by delivery drones dropping off supplies, shuttles escorting delegations, envoys, commanding officers of other ships, and other visitors with the appropriate government clearances.

Our tour guide, Clara, keyed open a hatch and escorted us into a busy corridor running down the length of the ship, filled with uniformed people who passed us headed in the other direction and the occasional robot mopping the deck.

The Excalibur was so big you could get all the cardio you ever wanted just walking around inside its passages which were painted dull shades of gray in horizontal lines punctuated by tract lighting and the occasional black and yellow stripes to demarcate dangerous areas or access hatches.

Sometimes exposed cylindrical shafts ran along bulkheads over our heads, carrying the ventilation system or water, and sometimes not. Tess elbowed me and gave me a look.

Apparently, she'd caught me ogling the bulkheads like a dumb idiot.

I couldn't help it that I was still amazed by the inside of a spaceship. There wasn't much to see in this part of it, but even the way the robots took care of things was pretty cool. The corridors were immaculate.

I shrugged. "Can't help it that I'm easily entertained," I whispered.

She rolled her eyes, but before she could speak, we were interrupted by the sound of panting on the internal comm link the Commonwealth had so graciously implanted inside of my head.

"Do you hear that?" I asked with a squint.

She nodded, keyed into the same team channel.

"Crap, where's Steinbreaker?" I asked.

Hearing me in his comm link, Bond spun around. "I thought he was with you guys."

I craned my neck down the corridor behind us. It took me a minute because of the people that were walking past us, but then I spotted him doubled over with his hands on his knees, one hundred yards or so behind us, coughing and wheezing with some kind of asthma attack.

"Ah, come on," I said at the sight.

Bond asked the tour guide to wait up, while Tess and I charged back down the corridor. Moments like that made me feel like a bad captain because I'd forgotten that the little guy's legs were all but five inches tall.

Most of his height was head and midsection. This was like power-walking a mini-Schnauzer. Pick up the pace, and his heart was likely to burst. "You look like a walking public service announcement for the American Lung Association," I said as we reached him.

"Seriously, though," Tess said, biting back a smirk, "are you okay, Steinbreaker?"

"What's... the... American... lung...." he wheezed out between gasps.

"If he's really that curious about it, I think he's probably fine," I said.

"Stop," Tess said, chiding me and crouching down for the engineer. "Tell me where it hurts."

"It feels kind of tight right in here," he said with a trembling knife hand on his sternum that was covered in green fur peeking out over his gray coveralls.

"Don't coddle him," I said. "That is pure evil. He's just trying to manipulate you, now."

Tess flashed a glare my direction and patted Steinbreaker's back. "I think he was having an asthma attack. I don't know why you're so mean to him," she said.

She picked him up like a wounded child and held him, patting his back. "Don't worry. I can carry you, so you won't have to walk anymore. How's that? Is that better?"

Steinbreaker leered at me from over her shoulder with a self-satisfied grin.

I knew it. He'd planned this. I scowled, not sure what he was trying to prove, but pretty sure it was at my expense. *Ah, who cares?*

His gloating laughter came out silently so that Tess wouldn't hear it.

"Laugh it up, fuzzball," I said under my breath. The Han Solo reference was over his head, but so were most things. *So what else is new?*

At least, he wasn't complaining.

"Come on," I said. "What a recovery, Steinbreaker. Good for you, buddy."

"It was hard," he wheezed.

Shaking my head, we rejoined the others and continued toward the elevator. After boarding, the doors chimed a few minutes later and opened, so we followed Clara to Mercedes' compartment where the tour guide announced our arrival.

When the hatch slid open, the chocolate-skinned woman was there to greet us, smiling warmly in her navy and gray uniform with gold trim on the sleeves.

As a private military company contracted by the CMC but serving at the behest of their version of JSOC, her unit, Task Force Cyberblade, didn't follow the traditional military ranks and protocol that I knew from Earth.

But I'd served alongside plenty of private security contractors, too.

Many Americans had no idea what a huge role they'd played in the wars of Iraq and Afghanistan. In fact, private contractors often outnumbered our troops in both of those conflicts. By the summer of 2020, our country had over twenty-two thousand contractors stationed in Afghanistan, about twice the number of American troops.

Now, the majority served in non-combat roles, but the ones who did fight by our sides, over half of which weren't even American, changed the landscape of war the world over.

Like any other potent combination, combining war and profit led to some volatile results, some of them positive when it came to protecting innocents who didn't want to or *couldn't* serve in large enough numbers to defend their ideals.

But the implications could be very dangerous. Sometimes, they did things without oversight, except from their CEOs.

I didn't think all private security contractors I'd met in Iraq and Afghanistan were terrible. They were doing a job. Many were retired Army and Marines, so kudos to them for coming back to defend their country at a time in their lives when many would be content to rest on their laurels, mow the lawn, and coach Little League.

The government didn't even honor their deaths the way they did with official members of the Armed Services, and that was a real shame. Because the statistics don't lie. More of them died in action than us.

You see, the privatization of war is complicated.

It's not something you can tie up with a bow like a gift for the next generation. It requires leaders with a strong moral fiber to keep it from becoming the worst connotations of the word "mercenary."

So, that's what I hoped this was. I was still getting to know the Centurions, but I'd talked to her enough times to see that Mercedes was one of the good ones.

"Gage, I'd like you to meet my daughter," she said, welcoming us into the bright compartment with clean lines and the aesthetic of a briefing room mixed with a modern lounge.

"You bring her along on missions?" I asked, trying not to sound too intrusive with her personal affairs.

The operator grinned. "No, not usually. Obviously not when there's a clear and immediate danger, but some of this job is waiting around, you know, filing reports? I learned a long time ago that if I don't take advantage of the down days to have her here, we're not going to see much of each other, are we, pumpkin?"

She said that last sentence with a tug on the collar of the little girl's uniform and followed that with a quick brush of her sleeves to make sure the girl was neat and tidy. "This is Sierra," Mercedes said. "Sierra, this is Mr. Gage."

"Hi," the little child said with a wave. She shared the same striking chocolate-toned features as her mother but had her hair teased in a shorter style that contrasted with her dainty frame.

Sierra was just a bit taller than Oliver. That brought a pang to my gut because I knew they were the same age.

How much had Ollie grown since I'd seen him? He was with someone else now—a stranger—who didn't give a rip about him or what he needed to grow up strong.

Someone else was watching him grow and deciding who

he'd become, without a second thought for his father. Teaching him what?

How to be a criminal?

How to deceive and manipulate people?

Or maybe Ollie was locked in a cell like some kind of trophy. Maybe their scientists were using him for experiments. Maybe, he wasn't even alive. Clenching my jaw, I swallowed hard and willed myself back to the present, just like I'd done countless moments before now. I wasn't going to let all those thoughts consume me and drag me down to the abyss.

Mercedes and her daughter Sierra were here in the *now*, and that's where I was, too, if I could regulate my emotions.

I cleared my throat. "And what do you want to be when you grow up?" I asked the girl.

"A mathematician... or a singer," Sierra said.

You gotta love kids. "Well, there's plenty of time to decide which path to choose," I said, then added, "Or, you could do both! Mathematical Opera might become the next big thing in the music scene."

"It actually is," Mercedes replied. "But only with one race that I know of, the Entorlyn. They're so much more intellectually advanced than humans that they get bored with either discipline in isolation. But when one of them combined opera music and calculus, he became a major pop star on their concert circuit."

I chuckled, shaking my head. That's what happened half the time that I tried to make a comment about culture or tech in the twenty-ninth century. There was still so much I didn't know that I'd only gotten a little better about not sticking my foot in my mouth. "There I go, blundering my way into the hearts of space people everywhere," I remarked.

"I think you've definitely done that," said Mercedes with a wink and genuine smile.

Sometimes I wondered if she had a crush on me, or whether she was just that empathetic. Either way, no use complaining. "I wouldn't go that far, but thanks for the compliment," I said, then got down on one knee so that I'd be on her daughter's level. "Sierra, it was an honor to meet you."

The little girl giggled, then trotted off.

"Mercedes, you know Tess."

"Good to see you again," said Tess with a bright smile, and Mercedes actually hugged her.

"And these are two other members of my crew, Bondranamir—we call him Bond—and our engineer and science officer, Steinbreaker."

"How do you do?" asked Steinbreaker.

"Nice to meet you," said Bond with the traditional two-pointed gesture the Oshwellians made when meeting someone. The first time I watched him do that salute, I thought he was picking lint from his shoulders, although I'd never tell *Bond* that.

Who was I to judge the way another man said, "Hello?"

Mercedes invited us to sit around a circular table of frosted glass that was lit from below. "How did it go with Emin Braddock's contact?" she asked.

"We waited at Hendarii Station, just like Braddock told me over my quantum pad, but the shuttle he indicated never showed up. I had Steinbreaker here hack into its flight plan—hope you don't mind."

"Next time, let me do that part," she replied. "Because I'm authorized to pull up that sort of information, but... "

she grimaced, weighing her options, "it's not that serious of an infraction, so this time, I'll let it slide."

"Right, thanks," I said, shooting a glance toward Steinbreaker, who looked stunned and a little uneasy. "Okay, moving on. We followed that shuttle's route, and we found it."

"Okay," said Mercedes.

"I know this was the right one because the shuttle number was emblazoned right there on the flanks and tail, the way that they usually have it," I began.

"It was attacked," Tess interjected. "Shot clean through with a kinetic weapon."

"The shuttle?" Mercedes clarified.

"Yeah," I confirmed. "And get this—there were a few pieces of clothing, like shredded remains and a bit of gore, but other than that, there weren't any passengers or flight crew."

"None?!" Mercedes was incredulous. "Did you find any indication of where they might've gone? You said it took a kinetic round. Was the hull breached so badly that they might've all drifted into space afterward?"

"No," Tess said. "You should've seen this. That wouldn't have made sense, even for the flight crew, because there was a breach from where they took that slug, and I could fit through it, but I had to wiggle my way through it. The hole wasn't big enough or in the right position that it would've just sucked everyone outside."

"Well, and plus, in a forward section that small, venting atmosphere wouldn't have enough force to drag everyone outside a hole like that, at least until perhaps they ran out of oxygen, but that flight crew would've been wearing a type of EVA suit that's regulation for their job. They prepare for contingencies like this. Now, if they'd been forced to survive in that situation for enough hours, well, maybe... "

"I don't think it had even been that long since the attack had happened," I said. "The shuttle was listing and drifting smoke when we got there, and the passenger sections still had power. That brings us to the other freaky thing about this whole situation." I paused and drew in a breath. "When I was hired at one of the admission centers for Magnum Corp on Kepler-442B, the first op I went on with my sales trainer was a derelict ship, and our bounty was missing in that case, too. Just like this time, there was no one onboard, and just like this time, we were attacked by the same unidentified species. I mean, I haven't lived here that long, so it's not that surprising, right? But my trainer, Hidalgo Ross, had been doing this for decades. I don't even know how old he was, but you can look him up. I just know he'd been bounty hunting for many years, and he'd never heard of or seen this alien race before. So, that was the really weird thing about it. Couldn't find them in the database either."

"You said you were attacked," said Mercedes. She brought up a holo screen from the center of our conference table and began tapping notes into a touchscreen keyboard native to its glass surface. "What did they want? Were you able to engage them in communication?"

"No, not these monsters," Tess said, her eyes glazed over, staring into an unfixed point in the middle distance. "It was a nightmare. One of them almost ripped off my helmet before Gage intervened, and then they just started shooting."

"Okay, so they were armed," she said.

"Some of them," Tess continued. "They all had EVA armor and helmets, and the armed ones had us pinned down at one point with their blaster fire. We would've died if—"

"I had to use a TR80," I said. "Well, two of them, actually."

"Scrat," said Mercedes, rearing back with wide eyes and a frown. "You guys are using plasma grenades on those ops? You guys aren't messing around."

"We had to," I said with a shrug. "Like Tess told you, they were firing on us, and we were badly outnumbered. I'm telling you; this species is crazy. Honestly, I don't know if they're even capable of rational thought. It's that bad. They're just like crazed, out of their minds. Bloodthirsty killers and nothing more."

"He's not exaggerating," Tess confirmed. "It was awful. I mean, Gage was cracking jokes the whole time, but you know him. That's like his M.O."

"Dark humor's just a cheap way to cope," I said. "But when we use deadly force, it's only as a last resort and according to the regs governing our actions as law enforcement agents of the CMC government."

"Understood," said Mercedes. "We don't like it when it has to come to that, but that's why you carry a firearm. I'm sorry you two had to go through that. Did you catch any video on your implants from these two encounters that you could upload here to my pad? I can follow up to see who this was and try to figure out what they were after."

"I have footage recorded from both ops that I'll share with you, absolutely," I said, exhaling with relief that someone would be looking into it.

CHAPTER SEVEN

"I HAVE A QUESTION," Tess said, cocking her head. "Why us? Why did you pick Gage and our crew to set up communication with this gangster? None of us have ties to the League of Desai, so it's not like we have any inside experience, and we're bounty hunters, fresh off the boat. Sure, Gage and I have military experience—him more than me—but that was a completely different era. We're still getting used to life in this time. We're obviously not members of your government task force. Why not send in one of your people?"

Mercedes lifted her hands off the table, palms facing downward, and glanced at each of us. "Let me assure you, Ms. Rodriguez, each of you will be paid the sum we agreed on, assuming you achieve the mission objective."

"I get all that," said Tess, nodding her head. "I'm not questioning you or the CMC's ability to pay us as independent contractors, but I've put my life on the line for this job already. So has Gage. I understand our contact with Braddock is part of a larger covert operation, and there are limits on the details you can share. But I think we deserve a little more background. If we're going to risk our lives, we need to know why and what our actions will achieve toward Oliver's rescue."

I shifted in my chair, wanting to interject, because Tess' question made me uncomfortable.

Of course, I understood why she asked it. She had every reason to ask, but I didn't want Mercedes to let off the gas for even a second and wonder if we were the best fit for the job.

This was my child's life we were dealing with. I needed each team member to be all in.

Because my only goal was to get on that restricted continent.

The Free People's Protectorate had so far been shrouded in secrecy on Samudra, the planet where the Centurions had said Pell was holding my son. Unless they'd moved him or sold him or who-knows-what-else. In that case, I'd make sure those scumbags in the League would spill his location and tell me where to look next.

Trouble was, I didn't have the security clearances to find out what I needed to know for a successful raid, much less the assets to make that happen.

That's where I hoped Mercedes came in.

Because I hadn't been completely forthcoming with my crew. Yakuza had already pushed them to the brink, so it had never seemed like the right time to tell them, but I was planning my own mission to rescue Oliver and I needed them to contribute some hard-earned credits to hiring a team of mercenaries for it. I didn't know how they'd receive that.

Going rogue wasn't ideal. But what other options did I have left?

After months of delays, I had serious questions about

whether the Centurions would follow through on my son's extraction.

And how much longer I could stand by.

My attempts at gathering intel to do it ourselves were falling short, as were my attempts to earn the windfall it would take to hire operators.

That's why it was too soon to tell them. Hopefully, that wouldn't make things worse.

Like many worlds vested with the Ambani faction, Samudra's name was of Gujarati origin, out of respect for their founding family. In this case, that translated to "the sea." The M-Class planet had only one continent surrounded by water. Anyone could see that, but on the galnet, this entire land mass was blacked out—redacted for "privacy mandates." That was my first roadblock to getting an operational picture.

The entire continent, Khadakala, was taken up by this Protectorate with zero images available to outsiders. That didn't help me scope out the location. I couldn't even see its topography or infrastructure.

Before Marine Commanders begin a mission, one thing they do is evaluate it for potential risks on multiple levels. What are the enemy's capabilities? What are the terrain and weather? The enemy can use those to their advantage, especially if we don't know what to expect.

Leaders take stock of the capabilities of friendly troops —their level of training, manning levels, the condition and maintenance of vehicles and equipment, morale, availability of supplies, and the physical and emotional health of their people.

This process wasn't just for commanders. All Marines had to be aware of hazards before going in.

And all I had to prepare for this one was a blacked-out

land mass on a map and vague assurances from Mercedes that her task force had gotten approval to, "if possible, extract your son when it's viable to put boots on the ground."

Sounded like a line of scrat from the bureaucrats.

In other words, "Gage, go void yourself." No word yet on whether I'd be able to come along with them in a support capacity if their brilliant raid or extraction ever came to fruition—or whether I'd have to form my own team.

Because mark my words, I was going.

It was just a matter of time. I wouldn't rush it as much as that killed me. The waiting. All these forsaken delays. But, I had to wait until I had intel, assets, the complete operational picture, and a plan for mission success.

I had to assume that my kid was still in the custody of Sarmonicus Pell. A shaky assumption with no guarantees— but that was my only lead.

If the mob boss had given or sold off my son to someone else, then I would grill him for where to search next, and—

"Gage... hey!" Tess shook my shoulder. "Snap out of it. Mercedes asked you a question. You listening?"

I blinked, clenching my jaw. "Sorry—what?"

"I was just asking what you know about the Free People's Protectorate," said Mercedes.

"An M-Class planet with favorable conditions to human life, it has one continent surrounded by water, which on the SkyCam, is redacted," I said with a sarcastic level of cheer.

I was sick of this conversation already, and we were just getting started—because how long would they give me the runaround? How long would Braddock give me the runaround?

For three months, I'd called him repeatedly and did everything short of begging for a meeting. He'd been the only name Mercedes gave me. But that ronk was whacked —more paranoid than a meth addict with a heart attack on his first night in prison.

My heart began to drum faster. My ears were getting hot. My throat constricted, making me want to get out of my chair and start breaking things, tearing the perfect art off the bulkhead.

I slowed my breathing and asked instead, "Who do we need to talk to on this ship to actually get something done?"

There was no need to raise my voice. If Mercedes couldn't see the murder in my eyes that waited in the shadows for Sarmonicus Pell, she didn't know me, and we'd wasted our time.

"Hey, let's give her a chance to explain," Tess said with a soft hand on my arm.

"There's some really bad things going on in the Protectorate, and Sarmonicus Pell's at the center of it all. It's more than just Oliver. This goes way beyond your son," said Mercedes.

"You work for the Commonwealth government," said Tess. "Why can't you just go in there? It's been a long time for Gage to wait for some kind of progress report."

Mercedes drew in a deep breath and looked down to gather herself, the white glow emanating from her conference table highlighting her angular features. "When Zenith Corporation arrived on the unvested world of Samudra to colonize it and bring it up to our standards of industrial progress, there were people already there, indigenous ranchers who'd been raising morshgur in the mountains for generations, family clans who'd already rejected being vested with the Ambani faction when they'd tried to take over."

"Every people has the right to determine their own form of governance," Steinbreaker commented.

Mercedes nodded. "Exactly." Turning to us, she added for our benefit, "He's quoting the CMC constitution. Now, many would see these ranchers' refusal as a missed opportunity to improve their quality of life with the influx of jobs, modern infrastructure, automation, and economic gains that come with a takeover that they'd experience with either Ambani or Zenith Corp. But not everyone sees a privileged position in the CMC as good. The rancher clans didn't want the sweeping changes that Zenith or the Ambani faction would usher. They felt it would threaten their way of life which had been passed down from generation to generation for thousands of years. And they were right. It would. Since the CMC is a democratic federation, not a tyranny, the native population in that situation has the right to work out a contract with the vesting company on terms they would be comfortable with. If they can't come to an agreement, it gets appealed to the Senate, or the conglomerate leaves and goes somewhere else."

"So what happened?" I said, still ticked off over where we sat on the progress of things.

"Well, these native ranchers had been unvested, used to doing things their own way. Sure, they were centuries behind other planets but had been self-reliant. They demanded that they'd have to retain complete control of their continent, Khadakala—and that meant no outside interference from CMC law enforcement, military, or federal government. Complete autonomy to manage their affairs. No outside interference. All Zenith wanted was to come in there and do deep-sea mining. They were just interested in the mineral deposits in the planet's vast ocean, so they didn't mind. They took that deal. Forty years later, after they'd stripped the seabeds of terrestrial metals, the mega-corporation packed up and left, leaving the planet to once again serve as host for these humble livestock herders according to ancient traditions. Zenith still maintains control of the planet, as they typically do in those scenarios, but haven't had any active projects there for over a hundred years."

I rubbed my temples, already sensing where this was going.

I liked to think of myself as capable, but even the most squared-away operator couldn't change the laws of galactic federations, and that looked like what we were up against.

"Did you have a question, Gage?" Mercedes asked.

"No, carry on," I said, crossing my arms.

"No one really visited Samudra for years, because there was nothing to see, no spaceports or tourist destinations or anything to really draw outsiders. Even their ocean had become toxic from the years of deep-sea mining. Now, it was just herds of morshgur grazing in the mountains and the clans who took care of them. Everyone had pretty much forgotten about it."

"Until Sarmonicus Pell showed up," I guessed.

Mercedes nodded in confirmation. "He moved in quietly. Disguised his shipments, forged manifests, covered his tracks. The CMC didn't even find out about the colony he was building there until it was already erected in the valley, hidden on every side by the mountains and primitive ranches. He saw something in the Free People's Protectorate that the rest of the federation had forgotten. The contract they'd signed with Zenith Corporation, now binding law guaranteeing that our government would never interfere in their affairs. Not federal law enforcement, the Navy, or the Marines. Not even the Centurions. Unless the Senate would actually bring this to a vote and overturn that long-standing contract, Pell can do whatever he wants as long as he's standing on Samudra soil because the Protectorate is nearly sovereign. There's nothing any of us can do about it."

"Why doesn't the Senate just overturn it?" Bond spoke up.

The young Oshwellian had been quiet. It was nice to see he was still engaged.

"You kidding?" balked Steinbreaker. "That den of serpents is riddled with corruption from what I've heard."

Bond's eyebrows furrowed.

I forgot that he was too young and idealistic to realize how, if this was anything like Earth, politics was a game of one-upmanship where candidates would strike up a deal with anyone to get their own little piece of the glory—and even more to maintain it.

Mercedes winced a little and responded, "Since we can't change the laws, my superiors have tried to reason with the Capital. But at the end of the day, too many Senators on the verge of reelection are beholden to the ones footing the bill for their campaigns. The League of Desai has such a big stake in their political futures and their families that I don't think it will come to a vote any time in the foreseeable future."

"But if the League is committing some kind of atrocities in the Protectorate, wouldn't there be a public outcry?" Tess interjected. "Because then, we could capitalize on that to apply pressure on the Senators, to convince them to take action."

"What kind of atrocities are we talking about?" asked

Bond, shooting a glance at me with his reptilian eyes that stood out against his cerulean skin.

"That's just it," said Mercedes. "There's no public outcry because nobody knows what they're doing there. Unfortunately, this situation is so sensitive, that again, I'm very sorry, because I understand how difficult this is, especially for you, Gage, but due to its highly classified nature, I can't go into the details. But suffice it to say that no one knows outside of upper levels of the CMC what's really going on in the Protectorate because if they did, there would definitely be an outcry. In fact, that's exactly why we must keep everything secret. Because if the citizens of our Commonwealth knew what Pell was doing, law and order would collapse under the pressure of the widespread panic that news would induce."

I drew in a breath to steady myself, clenching, unclenching my fists, watching my blood vessels bulge with each flexion under my tightly-drawn skin. "Let's talk about the raid," I said. "Is it heavily guarded?"

Mercedes pursed her lips in reply. "Very. That's where you all come in. Pell's instituted a no-fly zone over the entire continent. It's heavily fortified with point defenses and two Orbital Defense Platforms. Again, because of the contract, by law, we can't even get close to do proper reconnaissance. Their planet's forces have already demonstrated their willingness to shoot down any vessels that even come within sensor range, and officially, we can't retaliate. That's why we need someone on the inside. Top wants to get one of our Centurions into that compound to get us more intel about the location, so we know how to plan an insertion. But we've got to be careful. If Pell and his forces sniff out our involvement, it's over—and we could lose all the hostages."

Swallowing the lump in my throat, I thought that I might be sick and diverted my gaze.

But Mercedes held me in a hard stare, her palms flat against the table. "Braddock is my informant," she said. "He's never been to that planet, but he's got connections and he's our best chance. The problem is that in the past five months, he's gotten paranoid about spies in the League of Desai. Spies from his biggest rival who he thinks is plotting to usurp his position. Since then, he's refused to talk to anyone associated with the government, even me. I've lost contact with him."

Mercedes looked directly at me. "We need someone to broker a deal with Braddock in order to get one of our people inside. That's why I first approached you, Gage. I think you're the ideal candidate."

"You mean to infiltrate the Protectorate, right?" I tried to correct her. Maybe, she was finally coming around.

"No," she said, her hands moving quickly, palms face down over the glass table—like she was taming a dog. "Think about it. The moment that Pell catches you on his property, he'd use your son as leverage against you, and the mission would be compromised. But there's a security risk that's even more serious. Let me be clear. *Only* our Centurions can go into the Protectorate for reasons I'm not at liberty to discuss. You know this, though, right? We've been over that many times."

I'd heard it.

That didn't mean I understood or accepted it. It didn't mean that it made any sense, but I didn't think we'd ever see eye to eye on those perspectives. That's why I needed plans of my own.

Just in case theirs didn't work out.

CHAPTER EIGHT

"YOU STILL HAVEN'T ANSWERED why you chose Gage," Tess pointed out. "What makes him and us your number one options?"

I was pretty sure I knew how Mercedes would answer that, but it took seeing Tess' confusion to realize that perhaps I'd never clearly communicated those reasons to her and the rest of the crew.

That was disturbing. I'd been so engulfed in my own grief and determination to see things through, that I'd neglected to cast the vision like I should have for the rest of my team.

"There are four reasons that I chose Gage—and the rest of you by extension," Mercedes said. "First of all, like I mentioned, Braddock shut off communication with me and any other member of this task force—or anyone else associated with the government—for that matter, five months ago. I needed to find a civilian whom I could trust to reestablish contact. That leads me to the second reason. Sending a civilian in undercover for an operation like this is fraught with risk because we have to create an artificial background for that person, but it's really hard to scrub all evidence of their actual identity from every security cam and record on the gal-net. Because you can bet, the League of Desai will check. If I send in someone to talk to Braddock, and he looks them up on the gal-net and finds anything that contradicts the cover story I give them—they're dead. Instantly. And then I have to carry that around, that knowledge that my actions led to the murder of an innocent person who was just trying to help. If that happens, Braddock's going to suspect it was me behind it and I've blown any chance of ever getting intel from him again, then word gets around the League to be on the lookout for undercover agents, and our jobs become harder to do. Meanwhile, I have to explain to the children of that undercover agent what happened to their mother or father —or let them grow up with no explanation. Starting to get the picture?"

She waited for each of us to acknowledge, and we all nodded.

"Tess, you and Gage, on the other hand, are already ghosts. You had no previous identities on record that I needed to try to conceal from the League because you literally did not exist in the Commonwealth of Member Civilizations until we rescued you from Pell's ship."

"I'm sorry—that doesn't make sense," said Tess. "You just defeated your own argument, because obviously Pell knows who we are, and you said he's one of the League's five main bosses. He knows we're on the loose, so you're telling me he wouldn't put our faces on some kind of mafia watchlist to warn all his gangster buddies?"

"No, Pell would," Mercedes said with a laugh. "I didn't say he wouldn't recognize your *faces*. We have ways of changing your appearance to fool a lower-level ronk like

Braddock. Remember, I'm only talking about working with him for as long as it takes you to cut a deal. Hopefully, one meeting."

"What about biometrics?" Bond asked. "What if Pell did biometric scans on them when he took them hostage? Especially because they said they were sedated on his ship, so he would've had plenty of time to do that."

Mercedes shrugged. "That's possible. Basic biometric scans do facial, retinal, and vocal scans. The higher-end ones take DNA imprints. But in either case, they only check data points to determine a person's identity against the database of those who've already been registered with the government at birth. Like social security numbers and birth certificates from your time, Gage and Tess. Our federal database doesn't include anyone born on an unvested world. A *lot* of criminals come from unvested worlds and unfortunate circumstances so that only rein-forces your cover. If Pell scanned you, the results would've just read, *UNLISTED*. Going forward, we can equip you to deceive the more basic scans, and you'll be good to go."

"What about his personal motivation?" asked Stein-breaker. "Gage is a very stubborn man."

"Yes, he is," Mercedes agreed with a chuckle. "My third reason for choosing you was that you can see how difficult Braddock can be to nail down. I knew that anyone trying to make contact with him would have to be relentless—and your son's predicament has made sure of that. I didn't mean for that to sound cold. As a parent, I can't imagine what you're going through. But if it was me, the worst thing would be sitting on my hands if I didn't have some active way to help. So, I knew you'd need some way to contribute."

"You think?" I grunted.

"What's the fourth reason?" asked Steinbreaker. "You said there were four. We might as well check off the list."

"This is where it got interesting," said Mercedes. "After what happened in the Battle Mech Tournament, now Gage has what the League of Desai wants more than anything—physical evidence showing how Yakuza has been so successful in their attacks on the supply chain of Antrydium—Shintox's ship, the *Lizard King*, what you discovered inside it."

"Ah, the Quonella," Steinbreaker said. "It's a shame we didn't get to that one before she was gone. We might've saved her."

"We can still save the rest of them," I said. "If we can get Braddock to help us."

"Let's not get ahead of ourselves," Mercedes warned me. "We're not asking you to do that. I'm just asking you to offer that evidence and Shintox's ship to Braddock in exchange for entry into the Protectorate for one of our own to do recon, whom we'll pass off to him as a fixer with a convincing backstory."

"Speaking of Yakuza," I pointed out. "I avoided bringing this up before. I didn't want you to think we couldn't handle business and think it disqualified us from your job, but I'm just going to say it. We have a problem. Yakuza must know we're still looking for contracts and licensed by Zenith because they seem to be deploying drones to the planets where Blue Bounties are active. At times, we've only been in system for half a day and we're like, 'Look, here comes a Yakuza destroyer, ordering our surrender. Firing at will.'"

"Yakuza won't touch you on Vedana, because it's a stronghold for the League of Desai," Mercedes stated. "Plus, you're going to be flying in the *Lizard King* with the new transponder our techs are installing, forged identities and disguises. Yakuza's the least of your concerns."

"Until we turn over Shintox's ship to Braddock and have to get back in our own," Tess muttered.

"Let's focus on one thing at a time," I said, chewing my lip. "You said we'd be wearing disguises?"

"Yes," said Mercedes. "Most of the biometric scans you'll run into at local businesses or in the dens of low-level bad guys are the more garden variety—facial, retinal, and vocal checks. Those we can help you overcome with biomasks, retinal implants and vocal modulators based on audio logs from your cybernetics."

"Wait, *most* of the biometric scans?" I said.

"Well, the higher-end ones take DNA imprints, and our disguises can't bypass those, since they take an accurate snapshot of your genetic code. But don't worry, you'd only run into those at public spaceports or hospitals or law enforcement offices."

"So, don't get arrested," Tess volunteered.

"Exactly," Mercedes said.

Just then, a control panel chimed next to the hatch, and Oxhorn walked in. Filling a uniform like that of Mercedes, his gaze swept over us, an appraising glare, steely-eyed, weathered, and uncompromising. The man stood there with his hands on his hips.

My chest tightened in a visceral reaction at the sight of him.

Thaddeus Oxhorn.

I hadn't expected to see him anytime soon. The air still felt stifled between us. He probably sensed it. How could he blame me for feeling burned about his handling of the standoff with Pell on the day my son was abducted?

That was a lot to absorb. What was I supposed to do now—just sit here and forget about that?

He was the man in command of the ship tasked with Pell's capture before the mob boss had made an effective escape as I looked on. Oh, that helpless feeling. I could feel my blood pressure starting to rise, my fists tightening under the table with nothing I could do about it.

Trust me, I'd tried to convince myself that Pell had caught us flat-footed that day when he'd disabled critical ship systems with a blast from his EMP weapon. After all, trustworthy sources—the crew on our bridge—had said those things were incredibly rare and expensive to boot.

Still, it nagged me.

I couldn't help but wonder, if Thaddeus Oxhorn had done something differently, would my son be here today?

"What kind of biometric scans do they use in the Protectorate?" I challenged him. "I'm asking for a friend."

Mercedes lips pursed and she crossed her arms, because they didn't need to answer that question and was probably wondering whether it was a good idea. I could see her wheels turning.

"I don't think that's any of your concern," said Oxhorn with a critical squint, "since you'll never be going there, Gage. That's not the role we need you to play. I'm sure Mercedes explained that."

"Oh, I have—at length," said Mercedes, her eyebrows raised as she cocked her head with annoyance at my continued broach of the subject.

"If you're going to provide any value to our Task Force on this operation, we need your assurance that you will not —under any circumstances—try to enter the Free People's Protectorate on Samudra," Oxhorn stated. "Can you make that commitment or not?"

I furrowed my brows. "Well, I'll be honest. At first, it was my knee jerk reaction—any parent would feel the same way. But from what you've described so far, I'd have to be a lunatic to think some jarhead from the twenty-first century could cobble together enough people and resources to infiltrate a place that well-guarded."

Technically, that wasn't a lie, because going in there *had been* my initial knee jerk reaction...

And I was that kind of lunatic.

"Look," I continued. "You guys have a lot of red tape and scrat like that to work through to get this extraction op going. That I can buy. But let's be honest, Thaddeus. It *has* been three months."

I raised my hands in a dismissive shrug to telegraph my innocence. Then I stood and cleared my throat, as if we were getting ready to leave.

Frowning, I scratched the back of my neck, then shot him a look of disdain. "I'm just wondering if the Centurions still have what it takes. Sure, maybe you did at one time, but the League of Desai's become very powerful. I get it. You've been in the game for a long time, Oxhorn, but Father Time's a real bjorek, isn't it? No shame in admitting when you've lost your edge—when it's your time to hang it up. Right, guys?" I glanced around at my team, as if my question deserved an answer.

Tess seemed lost in a sort of bewilderment. Bond looked confused about where I was going, and Steinbreaker had stiffened on his booster seat, stricken as if he'd seen a ghost. Crossing my arms, I glanced around the bulkheads as if I wasn't in any hurry to hear the Centurion's reply.

Like *he* was the one on trial.

A long series of seconds transpired so thick with tension that I don't know whether anyone breathed.

"You're talking about the most elite Special Operations unit in the CMC," Oxhorn finally ground out, his tenor near a deep growl. "If you want to stand here and question my competence, you go right ahead. But *not* Task Force Cyberblade, not on my watch. There are too many good people working here who put their lives on the line every day."

Good, I thought. He was taking the bait.

Maybe he was a little bit testy about his impending retirement. I'd thrown a low blow to question his fitness for service, one that I'd never do. But I enjoyed making him squirm, and maybe I'd finally pinpointed a soft spot.

If I could get Oxhorn to accidentally spill even one detail about the Protectorate, my machinations would all pay off... or, I'd get kicked off of this ship.

Well, you know me.

I continued pressing my luck. "And yet, you're planning to deploy a team of operators into the Protectorate armed with biomasks and retinal implants—measures that are only effective on *entry-level* biometric scanners."

I chuckled and shook my head. "Nothing like defeating a mission before it begins with a poor commander strategy. We both know those biomasks won't cut it in the Protectorate, because they use top-of-the-line equipment to check DNA imprints of everyone crossing into their border."

All of that was a wild guess, but based on what Mercedes had described, my hypothesis was worth a shot.

Her eyes narrowed at me in reply. "I didn't say we were sending Centurions into the Protectorate with those measures—I said we'd be sending *you* into the meeting with Braddock that way!" she said, her cheeks flushed with indignation.

These people really didn't like when I insulted their task force. Their unit cohesion was solid. Good for them.

"Have a seat, Gage," Oxhorn growled. "We have technologies for Protectorate scanners that you are not privy to."

"Oh, I'm sorry," I said with a grin. "Maybe I misunderstood something you said."

"Maybe we should let someone else talk," said Tess, embarrassed by all my missteps. "You'll have to forgive our captain."

But Oxhorn had already let a valuable piece of information slip, something he thought I'd known already. I actually hadn't.

The methods of disguise they'd give us on this ship wouldn't get me into the Protectorate without discovery, but their task force had some *other* form of technology that could do the trick.

I just had to figure out what it was and how to get my hands on it.

"I'll broker your deal with Emin Braddock," I said, walking up to within inches of Oxhorn's face, "if you can promise that your superiors will send in a team for my son."

"We'll do what we can—I can't promise more than that," he said without flinching.

A chime from the panel announced a visitor.

"Come," said Mercedes.

Our tour guide, Clara, froze in the entrance when the doors slid open. Sensing the tension that hung in the air, she seemed unsure about how to proceed.

"If you'll all excuse me," Mercedes said, likely relieved for the interruption. "I need to take my daughter to her learning program. Bond, Steinbreaker, it was nice to meet you. Thank you both for your valuable assistance. If you'd like to follow Clara, she can lead you to our mess hall, and you might enjoy some down time there while Tess and Gage complete their orientation on some new gear with Oxhorn."

Flashing me a stern look, Bond picked up our furry engineer and carried him out behind the assistant.

I think *everyone* was mad at me.

CHAPTER NINE

OXHORN LED TESS and I into the corridor, the question ringing out in my mind—if he had done something differently in the standoff with Pell, would Oliver be here? It was the type of question that could drive a man to the bottle until he disappeared inside it and seldom returned to the land of the living.

God knows I'd seen that story play out in too many brothers from the battlefield.

And whenever I indulged that line of thinking, it never ended anywhere good. No one was going to crawl back for me. I could fade and wither like so many in my situation, but that wasn't my way. I had to find some means to rise above this, or I'd never work well with these people, and I couldn't do this on my own.

If I could, I'd already be in the Protectorate. No, we'd already be home.

I willed myself back to the lessons learned after years of grappling with Amber's death on the highway when Ollie had been only one. I'd never been able to reconcile myself to the reckless disregard of some kid who'd leave a party with a blood alcohol level way above normal and get behind the wheel of his car to plow into my wife at the red light.

No matter how much I tried, that wouldn't make sense. How could it? How can some things that some people do to other humans make sense?

They can't. That's the only answer.

They can't.

We think we're punishing the perpetrators of crimes against us with the grudges we hold, but we're not, because most times, they'll never even know or care how we feel about what they did.

Bitterness only hurts ourselves.

At the bottom of the bottle that almost killed me, that's the hard truth I came to back then, and that fact had been what jolted me awake.

I was about to throw my life away by the very mechanism that had ended the days of my soulmate. That's how much it ate me up inside, perseverating on one man's depravity, when there was nothing I could do about it.

How had I forgotten this?

Forgiving the man who'd killed my wife was one of the most freeing things I'd ever done. It actually helped more than I'd expected. It didn't make everything suddenly okay, but it did clear away cobwebs enough that I could see my way to starting again.

If I could do that—forgive the man who killed my wife—maybe I could work on giving Oxhorn another chance. Maybe there was more than one way to look at it. Mine couldn't be the only perspective.

He'd been outgunned by the leader of the most powerful crime syndicate in the Commonwealth on a day he was just trying to do his job. His superiors hadn't equipped him with the proper defenses for an EMP weapon.

So, really, that was on them.

I knew Sarmonicus Pell was my enemy. But was the captain who'd faced off against him?

He led us down the corridor of the *Excalibur* to a lower level by way of the lift and into an octagonal compartment where an orb hovered at my eye level. It was about the size of a basketball, but the silver metallic sphere emitted a dull hum and floated midair.

"This is the G-2600," Oxhorn explained, dipping his chin.

"No way," I said, "that looks like the spherical UFO's the Pentagon testified about before the U.S. Senate in 2023."

"Remember that?" Tess said, shaking her head. "Can you believe that report went under most people's radar at the time? That was before a respected member of US Intelligence sued the feds that same year."

"Well, it was covered by major news outlets, but if you weren't watching TV that night, the news got buried in most people's feeds with all the political stuff going on."

"Hmm, if I remember my history," said Oxhorn, "that must've been after your first contact but before that contact was really made public."

"Exactly," I said. "Just another day in the comedy of errors we call the public rollout of human contact with non-human species."

"How much did your government know at that point?" Oxhorn asked, growing more curious.

"More than they were letting on in the news," Tess said. "Much more."

"Yeah, but when you think about it," I replied, "even

what they *did* make public back then should've raised some major red flags. In their testimony to the United States Senate, the All-domain Anomaly Resolution Office (or AARO) said the spherical orbs were the most common of the 650 UFO cases they were investigating. Of course, back then, AARO still claimed they had no evidence of alien activity, which was laughable considering how they also admitted the orbs were one to four meters in size with no visible means of propulsion—yet had been seen traveling at velocities of Mach 2 and coming to a complete stop midair. A spherical craft traveling at supersonic speeds without any sign of a heat signature? Come on. That was way beyond anything we'd engineered in 2023. The writing was already on the wall."

"Just one of many more dominoes that kept falling in the decades after we left Earth the year after," Tess said. "Kind of a shame we weren't there to see it."

"And miss all *this?*" I said, spreading my arms. "Are you kidding me?"

Laughing into her hand, she pushed my shoulder.

"Your authorities didn't understand how this spherical drone's propulsion worked, then?" said Oxhorn. "Well, let me show you its capabilities. They'll come in handy where you're going. This drone's superconductors create its own artificial magnetosphere. That enables it to use the magnetic field of whatever planet you're on to fly and maneuver. I'll give you a quick demonstration. Computer, begin G-2600 targeting simulation forty-six-alpha."

Suddenly, the bulkheads around us seemed to vanish, and we found ourselves standing in a river valley with vast sloping hills on our either side. On one grassy summit, an antelope-looking creature paused from her grazing to glance our way. Her ear twitched in the wind as a flock of

African birds took flight behind her, filling the expansive blue sky.

My breath caught in my throat at the sense of realism that made me come up short. A thundering sound in the distance was approaching. We felt it under our feet.

Mentally, I knew this was all holographic, but my heart started pounding nonetheless as a juggernaut of an animal crested the hilltop from what looked to be a couple hundred meters ahead, then began charging into the ravine, headed straight for us like some mutated hybrid monster, half rhinoceros, half Triceratops.

"The G-2600 syncs to one of your neural implants," said Oxhorn. "You two get to decide which one."

The charging beast kept barreling toward us, snorting displeasure in a hard gallop, making me a little uneasy, though I knew the thing wasn't real.

"For this demonstration, I'll work it manually," Oxhorn said. "G-2600, evaluate the battlespace for hostile targets."

The rounded sides of the spherical drone folded out, revealing omnidirectional turrets. Instantly, two targeting reticles flashed red on the snout of the gigantic beast that was thundering toward us.

"Engage," said Oxhorn.

The orb's turrets fired a blistering hail of laser pulses into the advancing monster, causing it to bellow with pain. The galloping beast tried to reverse course under the barrage of lasers but was so huge and cumbersome that it got tripped up in its own legs, each of which was like a tree trunk, and stumbled into an awkward slide, hitting the dirt in a mighty crash.

"End simulation," said Oxhorn. "Now, which one of you wants to sync with it?"

"Oo, I'll go!" Tess said, one hand shooting into the air

like a kid on the first day of second grade. "If it's okay with you, Gage."

I shrugged. "Actually, I think that would be great with my plan," I said.

She smiled, rubbing her hands together. I loved that side of her personality. It's one reason we got along.

Oxhorn deactivated the sphere of metal and zipped it up in a black canvas backpack which he handed to Tess. She slung the pack over our shoulders, and ironically, I realized we were being siloed by the government.

Just like ours in the USA had siloed those working on UFO's.

When the twin towers fell on September 11th, the event that led me to join the Marines, Joint Special Operations Command was being led by Army Major General Dell Dailey, who reported to Air Force General Charlie Holland, head of U.S. Special Operations Command at MacDill Air Force Base, Tampa, Florida.

Since that was my only reference point for a Joint Special Operations Command (JSOC), here in the CMC my guess was that Oxhorn's Task Force reported to the equivalents from their own Navy or Marines, since the CMC didn't have an Army.

So, it was no surprise to me that my little crew, being nothing more than outside contractors, would most likely never get to meet their top brass—but would rather be relegated to contacts who'd worked with us in the past, who knew us—in this case, Mercedes and Oxhorn.

It was always best to keep your outside contractors siloed in Special Ops. Everything on a need-to-know basis.

Kind of like how the U.S. government handled contractors they brought in to reverse-engineer UFO's in my lifetime. When the truth came out about UAP's (Unidentified

Anomalous Phenomena—or Aerial Phenomena in common terms), testimony I could now access in the twenty-ninth century from historical archives recounted stories of engineers isolated with one or two others in classified labs.

They'd been given the task of studying how a certain part of technology from recovered alien spacecraft worked —without talking to other teams working on the same project—even though they could've all benefited from collaboration. But dominos had already started to fall in revelations of that government cover-up before we'd left Earth in 2024.

In April of 2020, the Department of Defense authorized the release of three unclassified Navy videos where pilots were stunned by impossible craft.

The next year, our director of National Intelligence released a report that examined 144 reports of UAP's. They could only provide an explanation for *one* of them and admitted the rest could not be explained.

Mounting pressure led to the first public hearing on UFO's in half a century in 2022 when our House Intelligence subcommittee met, demanding more information.

Some ascribed the sightings to glitches in imaging systems of aircraft, but that didn't explain the instances cited in the same government report of pilots recording near misses with them. Sources like Navy pilot Ryan Graves described how the UAP's flew by some exotic technology that seemed to defy laws of physics. Their absence of propellers, rotors, wings, or visible means of propulsion reinforced that assessment.

The next year saw another hearing, this time with the Senate Armed Services Subcommittee on Emerging Threats and Capabilities. There, Dr. Sean Kirkpatrick showed video caught in the clear light of day, not over infrared sensors, of a metal sphere soaring over the Middle East above an active military zone. No means of propulsion or lift that could be explained by our current levels of technology but traveling at an extreme velocity.

In the clear light of day.

Trying to dismiss any evidence of extraterrestrial activity, he admitted the sighting was one of 650 that his office still couldn't identify.

But few people outside of government were prepared for the whistleblower who, in June 2023, filed a legal complaint with the Intelligence Community Inspector General.

His claim?

The United States Intelligence Community had multiple alien spacecraft and bodies of non-human pilots in their possession—but had been hiding these facts for years from the U.S. Congress and American public. It sounded like the rants of a conspiracy theorist.

This whistleblower was anything but.

David Charles Grusch had worked for an agency of the Department of Defense (DoD) tasked with the collection and analysis of geospatial intelligence and the agency in charge of collecting U.S. satellite intelligence. He was vetted, called "above reproach."

That prompted a hearing by the Oversight Committee in the House of Representatives. And the rest is history. The real story took more decades to unravel. It's remarkable how long we can deny things that we don't understand.

I'd been one of the most skeptical people, right up until the night a UAP landed not far from our cabin where we'd been staying in British Columbia with my son and my dog.

And now, Tess had one slung over her shoulder in *a backpack*, of all things. I shook my head.

Life would never be the same.

Oxhorn produced a pair of shock cuffs that we typically used to apprehend fugitives in our line of work. "Gage, put out your wrists," he said.

I gave him a sidelong glance. "You know, I was working up to trusting you," I said.

"Shut up, and give me your wrists," he repeated.

"Maybe just a wee bit of explanation would—"

"Oh, for Ancients' sake, I'll do it," said Tess, sticking out her arms.

Shooting me a dirty look, Oxhorn cuffed her and said, "Now, break them."

"Uh, you want me to—" Tess ventured, eyes wide at the risk of electric shock that we'd both seen the restraints deliver many times to an errant criminal dumb enough to test their limits and try to escape.

"Yes!" bellowed Oxhorn. "Try to escape. Just try it."

I winced as she squeezed her eyes shut and yanked her wrists apart. The inner ring of the shock cuffs snapped off with her abrupt motion, and they disengaged, enabling her to shrug out of them.

"Hey, that's cool!" said Tess.

"Gage, on this job, you're going to be playing the part of a fugitive on the run from her. You're going to need these to keep up your ruse. This is how you establish credibility with Braddock without needing to actually commit a crime."

"You could've just explained that ahead of time," I said with a shake of my head.

"What if Braddock sees us together after that point?" Tess asked. "Isn't that going to blow our cover?"

"He won't, because you're going to change your identity again after Gage escapes. That's when you swap out your disguise for the second fake profile we give you—a member of Stryker's criminal gang."

"Whatever smoke and mirrors you've got in mind had better be pretty good," I said, "because we're putting our lives on the line, here."

But Oxhorn had already turned his back.

He walked through the open hatch, and we followed him through the corridor to a new compartment that was pitch black except for a circular ring of lights visible on the distant deck after we'd stepped inside.

"Time to get acclimated with our Chief of Disguise—meet Dimitri," Oxhorn said. "Good luck, and you all have fun."

I heard the hatch swoosh closed behind us as he left us, engulfing us in even deeper darkness until a spotlight switched on overhead. Its beam lit up a thin, hunched-over figure in a Task Force Cyberblade uniform. Dimitri regarded us with weary eyes. He spoke with a light Russian accent from the center of the light circle that put a gleam in his slicked black hair. "Tess, Gage, come over here and let me take a look at you," he said.

As I stepped forward, lighting strips embedded in the deck at my feet lit up, revealing a gangway with railings, and I took the opportunity to grip them carefully to avoid the steep drop-off on either side.

Turning back to Tess, I could make out her expression in the dim glow. She looked just about as lost as I was.

"They like to keep us guessing, these Centurions," she said.

At the end of the gangway, we reached the circular platform. I tried to give Dimitri, the agency's Chief of Disguise, a handshake, but he ignored the gesture, plunging right into my face with pencil-like fingers.

"Let's see, here," he said.

I almost instinctively defended myself before I realized what he was doing, probing, checking my facial bone structure, pinching my skin as if it were a lump of dough in his hands.

When he was finally satisfied, Dimitri turned to Tess, intent on giving her the same facial work-up.

"Is that really necessary?" she asked.

So began a strange but informative ninety minutes of briefing on some really amazing techniques of disguise that I expected would come in handy when we'd need to conceal our identities planetside on Vedana.

When we were done, Oxhorn escorted us from that creepy compartment through *Excalibur* to meet up with Bond and Steinbreaker in Hangar Bay B—not the general one that received supply deliveries, delegations of fancy diplomats, alien ambassadors and the like.

The *secret* hangar for sensitive and classified equipment like the craft I'd confiscated from Shintox and had stowed in this very bay, since where we were going, I'd have to become somebody else. It was time to retrieve my bargaining chip.

And see if our bet would pay off with the League.

CHAPTER TEN

TESS and I joined the rest of our crew. Our boots clicked across the vast metal deck with a determination of purpose. We'd received our orders and everything we needed from Task Force Cyberblade, and the sounds of maintenance, repairs and refits greeted our ears from the end of the cavernous bay, a distant, albeit industrious racket of clanging, banter, and power tools.

This hangar was where Centurion operators returned from their missions in corvettes or attack craft, where crews were scheduled to repair and refit any damages done to their ships and whisk their casualties away to Med-bay. And while we'd been in our meetings, one of those teams had transferred Celin-Ohmi from our ship into the water tank of Shintox's ship that had been vacated of its Quonella when we'd discovered her body in that compartment after Yakuza had drained it on the day of the Battle Mech Tournament.

Once they'd realized we'd stolen his ship, they'd been able to do so remotely, and the Quonella swimming inside had been helpless to stop them.

"There she is," I said, running my hand along the silver hull of the *Lizard King* that *Excalibur* techs had buffed out with wax to make the corvette as alluring as possible to our mafia kingpin.

"Yeah, but why waste a brand new Transponder on something we're going to get rid of?" Steinbreaker complained, shifting his bearing in Tess' arms.

"You do know you're a real buzz-kill," I said.

"I'm just saying, they could've swapped out *our* Transponder first."

"No," I said, "we're trading this ship with what amounts to a mafia capo whose biggest rival was its former owner. Braddock's not going to want it if the voiding thing works like a tracking device for Yakuza whenever he powers it on. Come on, you used to sell vehicles!"

"It does make sense, Steinbreaker," said Bond. "A government agency can get away with illegal mods to a ship like this one if they're planning to make a trade with a mobster. They don't want it to get tagged by a member of the local law enforcement as belonging to Yakuza. Plus, it's registered to Tyson Gage, so that would blow our whole cover."

"That's why we've got to leave the *Gambit* here with the Centurions. There's no other way to hide our identities. So, we'll be on the *Lizard King* from now on, until we trade it to Braddock," I said.

"Then we get right back in the *Gambit*, and Yakuza's right back on our tail!" shouted Steinbreaker.

"I'm sure we'll think of something," I said, fidgeting, realizing my heart was racing. I stood there chewing my lip, eager to know what we'd be facing on the planet owned by the man who might be my link to the Protectorate.

There were only two levels of authority above Emin Braddock in the League of Desai, the underbosses and the Sansthana Vada, which included Pell.

So, when we stepped foot on Caldera Island, we'd be in Braddock's domain. Sure, Vedana was vested with the Ambani faction, but under the pomp and circumstance of their political ties and that shiny veneer was the cold, hard reality of the way things worked.

That whole planet was his.

Various makes and models clogged the shipping lanes over Vedana. We'd already begun our descent in the *Lizard King*. Civilian ships dotted the space around us like an invasive plague of locusts.

"Look at this traffic," I said. "This place must really be popular."

"The prudent thing to do would've been to learn everything we could about this planet before we entered its atmosphere," said Tess.

"Yeah, yeah," I said but fell silent. Maybe I was sick of the runaround from Braddock or the runaround from the Centurions, but before I reviewed the intel Mercedes had given us on this world, I'd just wanted to get a visual.

Now, I couldn't even do that.

Because after penetrating the clouds, we'd drawn close enough to the surface that an ocean and land mass were visible in our viewports, but an ominous shroud of soot-colored smoke was expanding into the sky over the port, obscuring the place where we needed to land.

"Traffic control on Caldera Island's warning me not to approach until their visibility improves," said our helmsman and navigator.

"Thanks, Celin-Ohmi," I said. "We'll comply. Where do you guys think that smoke's coming from? All I read so far was the top page of the holo which said that Braddock lives in the city of Oathel Beach on Caldera Island. Figured I'd read the rest of our intel once we could get a visual."

"Typical man," Tess commented. "But to answer your question, heat and seismic activity indicate the presence of a large volcano."

"Which means that isn't smoke," said Steinbreaker. "It's a mix of water vapor, carbon dioxide, gases, and ash."

"Who asked you to be part of this conversation?" I teased him.

"As long as we're both on the same comm channel, I feel morally responsible to correct your stupidity," he dead-panned from his station.

I squinted at the billowing obstruction below. "If those people live that close to a volcano, wouldn't that wreak havoc with their air traffic?"

"Not necessarily," Bond chimed in. "But they would have to control everything coming and going due to variances in visibility and keep an eye out for major eruptions."

"Well, while we're up here killing time, let's finish going through the intel packet on this planet so we know what we're up against," I said, then activated Frederick from my neural link.

Mercedes had sent the locale documents to my

quantum pad. Since he was my pad's interactive AI, they were accessible to him as well. I could either read through the information myself or go through it with Frederick, which could be helpful, because when I thought of additional questions, he could answer those, too.

I didn't consult him on everything, but sometimes would summon his avatar which took the form of a rotund, overly formal chap from nineteenth century England. He was useful and entertaining enough that I'd had Celin-Ohmi merge his programming with our ship's systems before we left, which did two things.

It made Frederick quite a bit smarter and enabled him to walk around, now a life-sized, iridescent hologram that I sometimes caught roaming the ship, choking down a holographic crumpet with a gulp of imaginary tea.

He kept insisting he was on a diet, but I told him to not worry about it since he wasn't gaining any actual weight.

That just elicited a scrunched-up nose and blank stare from behind his wire-rim spectacles, making me wonder whether the avatar actually knew he wasn't alive.

Apparently, the non-sentient limited programming of his personality matrix was convincing enough to make him act in ways that seemed pretty lifelike to me, albeit on the ridiculous side in keeping with his assigned persona.

"Frederick, I'm sure that by now the people on Caldera Island have figured out how far from that volcano they've got to live to avoid getting steamrolled by molten lava, but they're still close enough that all this steam and ash seems to be messing with their air traffic control and incoming ships. What's their upside to living close to it?"

"Well, my dear boy," Frederick said with a puff on his briar-root pipe before taking it out and pointing its tip in my direction. "As a matter of fact, living near active volcanos poses both risks and benefits. Layers of ash can smother crops and cause respiratory problems in livestock. As you pointed out, ash from eruptions can damage infrastructure, contaminate water, and delay space travel— but it also has some benefits."

"Really?" I asked, drumming my fingers in irritation as we waited for the airspace to clear. "Benefits like what?"

"Captain," our navigator interrupted. "The island's traffic controllers require I give up control of our ship, their standard procedure for landing. This must be a heavy tourist spot. As you can see from the ships around us, the landing queue's quite extensive, and with the occasional eruptions, they're saying this is the only safe way to do things. But it will require me to switch to autopilot and let them guide us in."

I crossed my arms. Normally, if I was familiar with the planet, if we'd been here before, that wouldn't be such a big ask. But I didn't like unknown variables, and we hadn't even completed our assessment of this location.

We knew it was controlled by the League of Desai. Would it be smart to give their traffic controllers total control of my ship before I knew who they had on their payroll? No.

"Celin-Ohmi, tell them we'd like to remain in their airspace for the time being but will coordinate with them when we're ready to land."

A pause.

Then she responded, "They're warning me that if we don't land now, we'll lose our place in the queue."

I blew out a breath. "I was hoping to finish our briefing packet. How much time do we lose if we give up our place in line?" I asked, getting annoyed with these people already.

A tense moment passed. She returned to our channel. "Well, they say we've caught the front end of the dinner and gambling rush, so if we don't take this spot now, it could be another nine or ten hours before they can accommodate us."

"Nine or ten hours?" I said with a scowl. "Fine, take us in. I guess we'll have to learn more about the planet when we're on the ground."

She turned control of our corvette over to unseen forces below, and we entered the approach lane designated. Because of the traffic and reduced visibility, they had us circling the spaceport at such a glacial pace that I told everyone they could unbuckle and move around.

The volcano had come into view. This wasn't the cone-shaped variety that we'd built as kids with vinegar and baking soda. This thing boiled up from a massive crater in Vedana's crust. Erupting splatters of glowing orange spewed from vents in the deep depression. Giant plumes of steam and gas dispersed into the air from its summit. From the sky, the planet's famous volcano looked like a gurgling cauldron of lava that could boil over if it weren't for its recessed rock walls.

"The size of that voiding crater!" I marveled.

"It's actually not a crater," said Steinbreaker. "It's a caldera, hence the name of the island."

"Whatever," I said. "Is there a difference?"

"Calderas and craters can both be formed by volcanic activity," said Frederick. "But they're not the same. A crater is a bowl-shaped depression formed by an explosive eruption, lava flow, or meteorite. But a caldera is a much larger depression. Its creation requires an eruption so massive that the magma chamber beneath the volcano drains out, causing it to collapse in on itself, sometimes creating lakes or bodies of water underneath."

"Wow," I said. We finished going over our information about every aspect of the planet and its inner workings, and then I called a mission briefing around Celin-Ohmi's tank.

"You wanna get out of here, take a look around town?" I asked Tess with a nudge of my elbow.

"You buying?" she asked.

"As long as you can control yourself," I huffed in return.

"Stop!" she said with a smile in her voice and pushed me away.

Sometimes, she still seemed mysterious to me. One day, she'd feel distant, detached, while other times it seemed like we really connected.

I shrugged and drew in a deep breath, just grateful for the opportunity to be around her.

"In all seriousness, guys," I said, "Tess and I will be assuming new identities when we step off this ship. Bond, you're a little harder to disguise because of your Oshwellian heritage, so just to be safe, keep your helmet on when you're not on the ship. You and Steinbreaker will each need to sleep here in the private quarters."

"That's fine," said Bond. "That's where I usually sleep anyway."

"Do you mind feeding my dog?" I asked him.

"Oh no, you don't!" roared Steinbreaker. "You're not leaving that rabid monster on board unattended with me! Not a chance."

"Maggie's not going to be unattended," I said gently, fighting a smirk. "I just asked him. You'll watch her, right, Bond?"

The young Oshwellian shrugged. "Yeah, no big deal. Why are you so afraid of her, Steinbreaker?"

The furry engineer's eyes bugged out, his wide ears pressed hard against his head for second, before relaxing. "I —I'm not afraid," he protested. "It's just that she's filthy and undomesticated—"

"Okay, that's settled," I interrupted, not letting him ramp up any further into one of his anti-dog rants. We were all well aware of his terror of Maggie and being tossed around as her personal chew toy.

It was completely unfounded.

Dogs often love to gobble up treats or doggie biscuits as rewards for good behavior, but not Maggie. She'd only take a genuine cow's bone. That had been particularly hard to come by out here in the Big Dark, a project I was still working on.

But our engineer? Come on. She wouldn't chew him.

His bones were way too small.

"Listen up, guys, here's the plan," I said, after retrieving the rigged shock cuffs Oxhorn had given me from the weapons locker. "Braddock has made it clear he doesn't want to work with anyone tied to the feds anymore, so I'm going to be posing as a thief, Henry Stryker. The new transponder on this ship has been registered to that name. Our cover story is me and my ship have been captured by this bounty hunter." At that point, I gestured to Tess. "And she's landed on Vedana to round up more bad guys, when I break free from her custody. Braddock will see me—if we play our cards right—as a criminal on the run who's trying to unload this stolen ship to cover my tracks and evade authorities. That's why I'm in such a hurry to trade."

"We'll be posing as part of his crew, so Bond and I will case the streets, work the drone, and move in if the situation demands it," Tess said.

I nodded. "As much as possible, keep your helmets on at

all times if you're not on the ship, unless you are in disguise. We're on Braddock's turf, now. His spies are everywhere, so watch your six. We'll be coming in for a landing here, so grab your gear. Okay, you're dismissed."

CHAPTER ELEVEN

TESS and I returned to our private quarters to activate our biomasks. I activated the database with a mental command and a sea of faces populated in the augmented reality holo display of my HUD generated by my neural implant. Dimitri had given me access to the disguise database as part of the software upgrade when he trained us on their techniques.

"Only show me identities compatible with my bone structure," I said.

The list of faces shuffled and only displayed the best choices that I could pull off with zero detection, dummy profiles with matching biometrics that had never existed.

Perfect.

I tapped the one in the holo display under which the ship's transponder had been registered on *Excalibur*.

Henry Stryker.

A status bar told me it was scanning then prompted me to apply the mask. I unzipped the canvas pouch from inside my chestplate and dumped the contents onto my hands which resembled a patty of rubbery material but actually contained billions of nanites programmed to form themselves into my profile. I smooshed the patty onto my face and waited while a tickling sensation spread across my skin.

Two minutes later, I glanced at the mirror and had to do a double take, because the look was so convincing.

Just like that, I was someone else.

Our helmsman/navigator instructed us to brace ourselves, so I grabbed the stability bar on the bulkhead to steady myself. Our corvette touched down on a private landing pad amongst thousands of other ships.

It was clear that we'd entered a tourist trap. Any lingering doubts of that fact were quickly dispelled as Celin-Ohmi completed her post-flight checklist and gave us clearance to step outside.

We both cracked up at the sight of each other. Tess had a wider nose with a spatter of freckles, plumper cheeks, and thinner lips. I had angular cheekbones, a pointier chin and my nose was different. She kept wanting to touch my new skin, but I batted her hands away.

After we'd finished teasing each other, Tess slipped the backpack with our spherical attack orb over her shoulders, her enhanced strength from the nanite treatment making the added heft easy to carry.

"Any final words for your funeral arrangements?" Stein-breaker said as we suited up.

"That's cute," I said. "Let's confirm call signs. No real names from now on. I'm Stryker, Tess is Rubi or Rubicon, Bond is Bodega for his culinary skills, Celin-Ohmi's Aerial for obvious reasons and Steinbreaker is..."

"Edmund!" he called out. "My call sign's—"

"Hedgehog," I said. "Okay, loud and clear. Bond, you hang back and let's have Tess escort me through the spaceport. Then once she's changed her disguise, you come find her."

"Roger that, Captain," said Bond.

"Yep," Tess said, not sounding too excited about it. She holstered a blaster carbine, one of the N-50's we'd trained on and had become comfortable handling in our everyday line of work.

I hesitated at my weapons locker, reaching for the plasma blade called the Reckoning until I thought better of it. No doubt, Braddock would be confiscating my weapons at some point before this was over, and our standard issue carbine would be less tempting for his gangsters to lift then a premium weapon like this one.

I'd have to keep it stowed here for later.

Plus, there was the minor matter of playing the part of an unarmed criminal until I got the upper hand. Ugh. Details. Come what may, I didn't want to lose it. By now, the sword had sentimental value since it had been a gift from Hidalgo.

Tess grabbed the metal collar of my armor and gave me a jerk backwards. "Come on, you unvested space trash, you're under arrest."

I rolled my eyes, then stretched my hands behind my back for her to slap on the shock cuffs. She did, then pushed me. Roughly.

"Easy!" I said.

"Gotta play the part, you voiding kerlanzi."

"Doesn't mean you have to *enjoy* it," I said, narrowing my eyes. "You've been waiting for this moment, haven't you?"

She chuckled wickedly and slapped the control panel of the ramp to open our cargo bay.

Tess shoved me down the ramp and plunged us into the

crowds of people, both human and alien, that were streaming through the long terminal. Among them I spotted adults with the haggard-eyed look of parents who'd been shepherding their children all day through a resort and were ready to leave. Their kids dragged oversized stuffed animals behind them, bedazzled with cheap necklaces that blinked incessantly. The younger party crowd and serial dice rollers had come in behind us, ready for a night on the town.

It was noisy, and air scrubbers in my helmet filtered out the smells, but I could only imagine. The primary star was below the horizon. The nighttime air felt charged with excitement. Rubicon pushed me forward, another pair of anonymous drifters in the foot traffic crisscrossing the spaceport until we finally reached the exit.

Sliding glass walls parted before us, and we stepped outside between palm trees potted along the sidewalk with a light breeze rolling in from the ocean. A roundabout with elaborate gardens in front of us clogged with hover vehicles waiting to pick up and drop off more tourists.

"Move it, you bjorek," Tess snapped behind me.

I tensed. That was our code phrase. I snapped the cuffs on my wrists and wheeled around, catching her helmet in a left backhand. I pulled the punch, but my partner sold it, flopping to the side like she had been hurt.

I grabbed the carbine from her hip and gave her midsection a kick to create distance. My kick sent her to her back on the sidewalk, and I winced, hoping she was okay, but she was well-trained, so there wasn't any reason to worry. Making sure the blaster was set on *STUN*, I shot her with an energy bolt.

Her body twitched once and fell still.

Several people around me shrieked, so I spun on the

crowd of onlookers on the sidewalk, pointing the blaster's muzzle at them and barked out, "Anyone else want to join her?!"

No takers. Anyone who had been gawking at us quickly returned to what they were doing. I needed to move fast, though, before someone alerted security.

There were two ways that I could run. At my twelve, weathered steps descended sandy embankments to a fence posted with Tiki torches to mark public entry onto the beach.

The wind carried distant notes of new music and people's laughter, punctuated by the hover traffic that drew my eye to the frenetic flashes of nightlife downtown.

I waved down a bullet-shaped taxi. It pulled up to the curb, suspended there over the asphalt on repulsor lift tech. Whoever was inside it hadn't seen my scuffle with Tess, so it stopped with a pneumatic hiss, and I climbed into the back seat, where I found a young couple of twenty-somethings.

I yanked them out through the open door and dumped them together on the sidewalk, careful not to do any serious damage, then dove back into the car. For the coordinates, I punched in a district of downtown Oathel Beach that would get me away from security and be a good place to start causing trouble.

I waved my quantum pad across its sensor, and the car zoomed away.

Walls of yellow and blue, pink, and red streaked by on either side of the street from advertisements as saturated as Times Square from Earth's New York City, if the lighted displays of those blocks had gone on for kilometers in every direction. Oathel Beach was a teeming metropolis on Caldera Island. It raked in billions of credits per cycle (their rough equivalent of our year), whose economic boon had originated from the natural beauty and grandeur of their very active volcano, an iconic site that drew visitors in the hundreds of millions each cycle.

The volcano, west and inland of here, may have been the original draw for travelers, but League of Desai king-pins who were suspected to own most or all of the island through shell companies and investments in legitimate enterprises and financiers had exploited the scrat out of that pristine wonder and built Oathel Beach into what it was now, a sweaty, bloated tourist trap of easy delights from restaurants and hotels to casinos and attractions where there was legitimate fun to be had.

But gullible visitors could blow their life savings with dazzling speed on anything from a night at the tables to prostitutes or narcotics sold at jacked-up prices to take advantage of addicts on holiday.

It was a crazy amalgam of glitz.

"What's next?" Tess asked on my internal comm.

My eyebrows rose. "You awake already?"

"You're not a good shot. That bolt glanced off my armor."

"Well, it made enough of a flare, that I don't think anyone could tell. Even fooled me with that acting of yours."

She blew out a raspberry. "Yeah, right. Our cybernetics give us perfect aim. I know you pulled that shot on purpose."

"Hey, now that you're awake and all perky, there's this really cute place on the corner... "

"Gage, be serious. What's your plan to track down the gangsters?"

I shrugged, sensing the grin in her voice. "We don't have to track down anyone," I said. "With what I'm planning, they'll find me and have no choice but drag me in front of their boss."

"Same kind of reckless behavior as usual?"

"More or less," I said. "Over and out."

I stopped at a quick mart, the kind of drugstore you'd see downtown that stacked necessities of life on top of every kind of impulse buy, all crammed into a very limited retailer footprint. The flashing neon on the glass advertised candy, alcohol, personal hygiene, and lotto codes.

But I paused at the entrance.

A conversation outside on the sidewalk had caught my attention. In front of the bakery next door, two very large men were roughing up a third guy who, I could tell by his white apron, probably worked inside the establishment.

The baker was Asian, in his mid-twenties, and was a lot smaller than the ones making threats. I could tell by his shoes that he didn't have money, since they were coming loose at the seams.

"I can't afford to pay any more!" he pleaded, shaken by the encounter. "Otherwise, I'll have to close up the shop!"

"Why don't you let us worry about staying in business?" the bald one demanded who'd scrunched up the baker's sleeve in his fist. "That's not your job description no more. Thing is, if you can't pay for protection, me and Artis here can't guarantee nothin' bad will never happen to you. You know how dangerous this neighborhood is. It would be a real shame—"

"Guys, guys," I interrupted. "Maybe there's been a misunderstanding." I placed an armored hand on the left dude's shoulder just to get undivided attention, while I stuck the butt of my carbine in the ribs of the one on the right, well, where his ribs would be located under the copious layers of fat.

He was the bald one. He was the talker.

The other guy was just physically imposing. The tatted up arms exposed by his dark, sleeveless jacket were knotted with muscle, and he actually had an axe blade pressed up against the baker's neck.

"An axe. Really? Okay, Paul Bunyan, if you get any ideas, my carbine is all up in your partner's stomach."

Baldie shot me a look of death. "Who the void are you? This is business and not your concern, ronk."

"It became my concern today, because this person isn't making protection payments to you anymore."

"Look, back off. What do you know about it, son of a bjorek? I never seen you before in my life," said Baldie, more impatient than anything else.

Clearly, he wasn't getting the picture.

"The reason he can't pay you for protection anymore is that I'm taking that job off your plate."

This announcement finally made the Lumberjack look back at me with a hard, creased face scorched by the sun, an effect that had aged his Irish complexion, despite the shocks of red hair in his mohawk. He let out a squinty-eyed growl to show his annoyance at the interruption to his sadistic art of making someone smaller feel pain.

Baldie stared at me a moment to gauge whether I was serious and found what he saw disconcerting. Finally, he spoke. "Don't know who the void you think you are, but nobody else will, neither, if you don't get that voiding gun out of my side and lay it down on the sidewalk, chump."

He'd been working his fingers around to the sidearm holster on his right hip, hoping I wouldn't notice when he'd let go of the baker's shirt if he moved ever-so-slowly.

"Your gun—Don't grab it," I said. "This will go worse for you if you do. Let me explain how this is going to work. You two are going to lay down your weapons, slowly, on the ground, then lace your hands behind your heads. Then you're going to turn right around and walk away. I want you to deliver a message to your boss for me, okay? Can you do that? Here's the message, Paul Bunyan—I'm counting on you! Stryker has taken over protection for this whole block. That's it. Just deliver that message, and no one gets hurt. However, if you don't follow my instructions, your only territory for a while is going to be the intensive care unit at your local hospital. But we don't want that, do we, Paul Bunyan? Really, guys, this is your last chance. Be smart, and just do what I say, and nobody has to get hurt."

The Lumberjack threw an elbow. I knew it.

I was worried he'd try that. My stomach dropped, because his sudden motion would've slit the baker's throat with that axe if he hadn't fallen at the same time. His elbow slammed into my chestplate, where it absorbed most of the impact.

The kinetic energy knocked me back enough that I had to regain my footing to keep from losing my balance.

I didn't want to kill these two, since I needed them to deliver that message, so I fired a round into Baldie's calf muscle. He collapsed, grimaced in pain, and groped for his sidearm immediately.

But I couldn't deal with that because the Lumberjack got up from where he had fallen and swung his axe in a wild arc.

I grabbed its handle. Pulling hard, I drove the axehead into Baldie's chest, because he'd managed to rise to one knee so he could aim his gun and shoot me. The axehead clipped his weapon, stoving his fingers, and knocked him back in an awkward folding of limbs that must've broken some bones.

If you could avoid its blade, that part of the tool made a good blunt force instrument.

I threw it into the Lumberjack's forehead. It struck with the sound of metal on meat. The big man collapsed with a heave, unconscious.

"Are you okay?" I said to the baker.

He had the lean physique of someone who worked too many hours and didn't get quite enough to eat. Working his square jawline, he grabbed his shoulder-length mane of black hair.

"I—uh, yeah, um, how did you do that?" He stuttered, glancing around. "We need to get out of here—there's going to be more of them."

"What's your name?" I said, pulling the baker to his feet.

"Zihan," the Asian man said. "What's going to happen to my shop?"

"Well, if you want, I could get you out of harm's way, and then you can take some time to decide if you want to return here. What do you think?"

"Yeah," he breathed. "Okay, I guess."

I flagged another hover cab, and we climbed into the taxi.

My main objective was to create enough distance so we didn't get murdered before I did what I'd come here to do.

CHAPTER TWELVE

I PROGRAMMED the self-driving taxi to take us to another quick mart like the first one, since I'd just been trying to make a stop at the convenience store to pick up some essentials when I'd gotten distracted by the guys making unrealistic demands of Zihan on the sidewalk. Tess and Bond would be tracking my location, ready to close in when we needed it.

More garish neon displays flashed by the windows of our cab as our car hummed down the street of Oathel Beach buzzing with hover vehicles. I wanted to ask the young baker more about the protection rackets.

I already knew The League of Desai had been known for protection rackets, extortion, and bribery and that these tactics were especially effective in industries that were driven by tourism.

Tourists, especially those well off who wanted to enjoy the various sundries of entertainment on Caldera Island while avoiding the seedier side of crime rumored to infest the streets were often willing to fork over paper credits for the promise that they'd be protected.

But it was the local business owners who took the brunt of the damage. That much was clear from the intel packet the Centurions had given us on Caldera Island.

The League of Desai would command dues for "protection" from theft or vandalism, and if the business owners refused, they could expect random acts of property damage or violence to themselves and their workers. That's what had made my hair stand on end when I'd overheard the young man being threatened.

The practice was so rampant on this world that a better term would be extortion.

It was like the League was taking a page right out of the mafia's playbook in Las Vegas during the 1960's when legitimate businesses from hotels to casinos were owned by the leaders of organized crime. Caldera Island thrived as a bastion of tourism the galaxy over. And the League profited from it all with impunity and freedom from prosecution.

Sure, there was a democratic system of government here that conducted affairs with some effort of decency and the rule of law. When that benefited the League, they had no reason to interfere.

But just like the American mob in its heyday, on planets like this that were their strongholds, the League of Desai was untouchable, due to their economic and political leverage. If law enforcement sniffed around too much, League enforcers would bribe or threaten whoever they wanted until the dirty status quo pushed out the good ones, or the good ones quietly disappeared.

"Tell me about your experience," I said to the young business owner on the chair across from me. Since all of the cars were driverless in the future, most bucket seats could swivel, so you could either face other passengers and socialize or take in the view out the window, unless you wanted to read or watch a vid on the gal-net. "What's it like to own your own business here?"

He scoffed and rolled his eyes then shook his head quickly, as a look of resignation consumed his expression like a dark shadow, which I found incredibly sad for a young man who should be excited about his future. But instead, he was dealing with this.

"It's the same method over and over," Zihan said, glancing out the window as ambient light from the neon ads danced over his face. "Most businesses anymore are owned by the League, although it's hard to tell. There's so much corrupt money and investments, shell corporations— it all gets a little hazy and hard to distinguish after a while. But there were a few businesses independently owned. Like my bake shop. Got it from my Dad when he passed away. My mother worked there until—well, we won't get into that. But those guys who you saw talking to me would come around and collect 'dues' for protection, said it was for my own welfare and that of my family. It starts to get hard to turn a profit after a while when they keep increasing their rates. Eventually, you start to go under and you can't make the books work. What happens then? A miracle investor shows up on your doorstep at just the right time to offer a loan, that little bit of liquidity to get you through to the end of the year. I told my mother that I could handle it, that I wouldn't let it get away from us. Just a little to get us into the new year, and then our profits would be back on track."

"Let me guess. It didn't stop there," I said, leaning forward, intent on his story already, disturbed by what he'd explained.

"The loan officer promised they were sending one of their small business experts to help out around the bakery, optimize things and make me more profitable. To be honest, it sounded like a good thing. Well, this woman they sent started giving orders, changing my product line and revamping displays, all kinds of stuff without my permission. I was like, 'Hey, these recipes are family traditions passed down from my grandparents from their territory. You can't just change everything around, because I know what my customers like—and this is my company.' And you know what she said? 'Not anymore.'"

Zihan shook his head.

"How can they get away with that?" I asked.

"It was in the terms of the loan, or at least, that's what they claimed, though I never saw any copy. But from that moment on, they'd taken control of my family bakery and kept me working there as the front man so they could benefit from my accounts that were in good standing. They started funneling so much money through me, forcing me to make these deposits and withdrawals through my business bank account—crazy sums of credits. I don't even want to know what they were for, but they had nothing to do with the bakery. That was it, though. I couldn't get out of there. They told me I was helping the company, that I was guaranteed a position the rest of my life, but the money I took home dwindled more and more until it's like I was just existing at that place to legitimize all the withdrawals and deposits they were moving through my accounts."

"Mmm, that's terrible," I said. "Look, kid, I'm going to do what I can to get you into a better situation."

Our vehicle pulled up to the curb in front of the quick mart, and I climbed out. Zihan followed me into the store, staying close on my heels after what had gone down already outside of his bakery.

Skittishly looking around, he cracked his knuckles, wiping his hands on his apron nervously. Bells chimed as we entered the convenience store.

I grabbed a package of playing cards, a black permanent marker and adhesive tape, along with some snacks and water to last us, since I didn't know the next time we'd get a decent meal, especially now that we were on the run.

Things would get worse here before they got better. I had a feeling about that already. The League of Desai maintained control over all public transport, something else I'd learned from the Centurions.

That included taxi companies, car rental agencies and bus services providing tours. It was only a matter of time before I was on the mafia's radar.

Good thing I was somebody else.

I picked out a tactical backpack, an interesting item for a corner store, but it underscored the reality of crime in this area where people needed to make deliveries or be able to pack up and leave at a moment's notice.

Something was wrong here. You know that feeling when you step into a room and can tell there was an altercation but no one is talking about it?

You can almost smell the bitter resentment and when someone fears for their life, there's a sharp quality in whatever follows that my gut had learned to detect.

Intuition pays dividends for bounty hunters even more than the credits we earned.

I put my items on the checkout counter. A Senchkin clerk started ringing me up. Her alien race resembled humans but with larger heads cloven in two bulbous halves with pointed ears and a pattern of birthmarks along their temples and brows.

Most people wouldn't have seen anything amiss in the

face of this Senchkin at the counter, the subtle twitch at the side of her mouth, since her race had a reputation for being extremely hard to deal with.

But there was a logic to their interaction, however foreign to our sensibilities.

And this one was very afraid.

Senchkins were ruthlessly honest and frank. They didn't engage in flattery or even what we'd consider polite. They were very objective. They didn't like metaphors, abstract thinking or even displays of emotion.

They framed every concept in a "yes" or "no" fashion, and if something you said didn't fit those parameters, they'd just fall silent and stare back at you without any clarification. At that point, your conversation was over.

They also never introduced or ended interactions with a greeting or expression of kindness.

Naturally, that put some people off.

They just stated facts. And if there were no facts to state, talking to them was like talking to a wall. But once you understood that their silence didn't necessarily mean mal-intent, it was easier to not get offended.

This made them great for some situations, like gathering intel about a fugitive, which is how I'd become familiar with them and their style of communication. Senchkins were great for that sort of thing—better than humans, in my view—to be honest.

So, when I saw her ringing me up, there was something that she wasn't saying. I didn't know why they had sentients performing these functions instead of machines at the corner drug store, but guessed she probably didn't get paid very much in a job like this.

"Who do you pay for protection?" I asked, remembering to avoid salutations or greetings.

"Protection of what?" she replied.

"Who do you pay to protect yourself and this business from potential vandalism, theft and violence?"

She blinked and said nothing, just kept ringing me up.

I'll have to find another tack.

"I can offer you that kind of protection for a much lower cost than the person who's providing it for you," I said.

"To make that statement, you would have to know who is offering me protection now, which you do not. Otherwise, you wouldn't have asked me that."

"That's not necessarily true," I said. "Not if I offer it to you for free."

"The man offering me protection would not allow that," she said.

"How do you know?" I said.

She blinked.

That's when I knew I'd caught her. "You just made a statement that you cannot prove, therefore you've brought shame on your ancestral clan if you cannot prove its veracity," I said.

She wouldn't be able to resist that challenge, even at personal risk to herself, because doing so would be tantamount to what I'd suggested. They were forbidden to make a statement they could not demonstrate with objective facts. That could get her disowned by her clan, which for them meant permanent banishment.

She dropped my items into the backpack, which I handed to Zihan.

"Hold this," I said.

Then, as I expected, she picked up her quantum pad and made a call. I heard a male voice connect on the other line, and the Senchkin asked him, "Would you allow me to receive your services of protection from another human for no financial fee?"

"No!" he barked. "Why would you even—"

I snatched the quantum pad out of her hand and cut off the man by stating into its speaker, "You *will* allow it, you son of a bjorek, because I'm taking over Protection of this store immediately."

"What?!" the man snapped. "Who is this?"

"Call me Stryker," I said and then disconnected the call.

The Senchkin woman's eyes were wild with fear, but she didn't speak.

"What's your name?" I said, breaking through the ice of the moment.

She swallowed with difficulty. Her voice came out in a choked whisper. "T'Amira," she said.

"How much do you get paid to work here, T'Amira?" I asked, since I hated to intervene if doing so would take her away her sole source of income.

"There is no remuneration for my employment. I am a slave of the men in the back. They've provided protection until now." Her voice broke off on the last syllable, and she fell quiet.

The admission felt like a stab in my chest.

An ominous clatter of footsteps sounded from behind the back wall of the convenience store. I hadn't paid any mind to how deep this building extended when we'd arrived, because sometimes these types of establishments had residential apartments attached.

But this wasn't that.

It was a front for something else.

"They're coming," she said, fighting back tears.

CHAPTER THIRTEEN

I SWUNG my N-50 into the ready position, and my finger tensed on the trigger, tracking the door behind the counter that led to the back.

She was right. The Senchkin's "masters" providing "protection" shoved through the doorway into the store, dressed in the fashion typical of people I'd seen here, black and gray western-style pants, shirts, and jackets, trimmed with a hollow piping along their outer seams that undulated with some kind of iridescent liquid, almost like what would be in a lava lamp.

Blaster pistols, and in some cases, slug-throwers, were already drawn.

I exhaled, the reticle of my carbine already pasted above the left eye of the man in charge.

"Who the void are you?" he demanded, a thick gangster of Middle Eastern origin. Dark circles rimmed his eyes, and he was more insulted than scared.

"I already told you to call me Stryker." My voice came through steady in my helmet's speaker. As did my breath. "All it takes is a tiny bit of pressure on this trigger, and I'll be looking at the scumbags behind you through a little hole in your skull."

The muscle fibers twitched on his jawline. "You do that, and you're dead within seconds. You're outnumbered here, my friend."

"Really?" I said with a cock of my eyebrow that he wouldn't see behind my faceplate. "You think your coherent packets of plasma and bullets are going to punch through this armor?"

His mouth twisted. "Battle suits have gaps. All armor."

"You want to test that theory?" I challenged. "Your bozo minions versus the non-lethal gaps in my armor? Or your soft, fleshy forehead against one pull of my trigger—who do *you* think is going to last longer?"

The Adam's apple in the man's throat bobbed, and sweat glistened on his upper lip. "Okay," he said to the men behind him, his eyes still locked on my helmet's visor. "Lower your weapons. It's not us this outlander needs to worry about, right, guys? He's not going to make it far without answering to Braddock, so let's humor him for right now, and see what he wants."

"No," I said, unsatisfied with half-hearted compliance. "One at a time, I want each of you to step aside from the others, unload your gun, then place it on the floor slowly and kick it down the snack aisle to my friend, or I will kill your leader and you'll have *that* to explain to Braddock."

One by one, the gangsters did as they were told.

Zihan deposited their guns in the canvas backpack, and everything was going according to plan. After we'd collected their weapons that had been visible, I made them line up along the glass wall, because their concealed sidearms were my next concern.

Eight pairs of hands pressed up against the glass, and

frisking them down would be a dangerous proposition, because that would mean I couldn't keep my gun trained on any one of their number.

They'd certainly know this. They weren't that stupid and were probably waiting for me to reach the inevitability of this decision.

When I'd be vulnerable.

I could ask Zihan to search them, because at least then they'd know I'd be ready for the first man who made a sudden move.

But did I really want to ask him to do that? That was risky for both of us, especially him, and probably a bad idea.

"Zihan, did I ever tell you the story about that time I hunted for foxes in the woods when I was a teenager?"

"Um—no, no, you didn't so far—but I just met you an hour ago, so you really haven't told me about much of anything—"

I cut him off before he could make a fool of either one of us. "Well, I should. I should tell you about that some-time soon."

"Uh—okay, yeah, sure! Anytime," the baker said awkwardly, his vocal tone shaken with nerves.

Gritting my teeth, I was trusting Tess had picked up my code words *fox* and *soon* in those sentences, because I couldn't let on that I was trying to communicate with anyone outside of this store, since that might mean one of these goons who survived this encounter could make a case to Braddock that Tess and I were working together.

"Acknowledged, Stryker," I heard in my ear. "We have run into trouble with local law, so stand by. There will be a short delay on that fox maneuver. About three or four minutes."

My stomach dropped. *Three or four minutes?* That was an eternity in this situation.

The leader swung around, brandishing a handgun from his back waistband. Dropping to one knee, his gun's report combined with the jolting clang of metal bullets hitting my armor.

I charged him, because there wasn't cover in the convenience store to repel bullets. Movies are full of it that show good guys taking cover behind a wall, as if simple drywall is going to stop nine millimeter lead cartridges, whereas if I charged him, my battle suit had a pretty good chance of protecting me during the few seconds between trigger pulls and my driving shoulder.

Drive him into the air, I did, grabbing his gun hand so he flipped over the fulcrum of his own arm, which snapped on his way down. *Bad choice for him to shoot at me.* I tossed his gun to Zihan, but the kid was doubled over and covering his ears, so a lot of good that really did besides getting it away from the other gangsters.

The odds were definitely not in my favor if I'd been the Tyson Gage of old before I'd left Earth, even with decades of martial arts training. Seven against one just isn't fair.

A well-muscled gangster slashed out with a knife. I caught his wrist and snapped it, forcing the blade to drop from his contorted hand and clang to the floor.

I picked it up. Here in close quarters was where bioengineering upgrades to my body through nanite enhancements had changed the equation, because I wasn't the Tyson of old.

I was something these men should fear, if they knew what was good for them. But they didn't. So, I would teach them.

Slashing the knife through the air, I warned them. "Did

I say you could turn around?! Get your hands back on that glass—you—now!"

Three of them complied, but another one drew a blaster from a holster within his jacket. I threw the knife into the meat of his shoulder as he fired.

His energy bolt glanced off my armor and he grimaced, until his adrenaline subsided enough or his brain registered that there was a knife sticking out of his flesh. He reached for it, but I stopped that with a roundhouse kick that only made the knife rake across the soft tissue of his deltoid.

I yanked out the knife and sliced it across the thighs of two men coming to tackle me. The point was not to murder anyone. The point was to make them stop what they were doing and reconsider life choices.

They didn't seem to notice the cuts but did come up short when they saw the blade. Kicking one in the groin, I stabbed the knife into the other one's kneecap.

But this thing was too dangerous, so I withdrew it and tossed the sharp-edged weapon behind me. Enough knife-fighting. The next guy swung at me with his fist, but I parried.

I caught another one raising a gun. He fired, and bullets ricocheted over my head. I grabbed the two of them, each one by the scruff of his neck and slammed them into each other, face first.

Their skulls bounced together with enough force to make me wince, and they slumped to the floor unconscious.

The final guy wrapped his arm around my neck to choke me out, but I pulled down so hard that he flipped over my shoulder and in the process, wiped out another gangster with wild swings of his boots.

I leaned on my knees to catch my breath, and Tess

spoke up in my comm. "Orb inbound now for fox maneu-ver. Two minutes until arrival."

"Not now!" I said, removing my helmet and wiping the sweat from my hairline. This biomask made perspiration weird, because sweat only gathered along its edges. The rest of my face covered by the mask's rubbery faux skin just itched. Well, I'd have to get used to it, because I was Henry Stryker.

Tess would have to wait for more information, because I couldn't blow my cover in front of the gangsters rolling around and groaning in pain on the floor of the quick mart.

"Zihan!" I shouted. "Are you okay?"

I found him curled up in the fetal position, clutching the bag with the guns, so at least he hadn't lost those. "Hey, it's over. We've got to get out of here," I said. "Come on."

The baker squinted up at me like I'd just woken him out of a thirty-year coma, like he was freaking Rumpelstiltskin or something, like he didn't even recognize the planet he was on, even though he'd lived here for years.

"Hey," I said. "We've got to go. Now. T'Amira, do you want to come with us? I'll do my best to find a new home for you, somewhere safe where you can make your own choices and live your own life. Maybe return to your home planet, I don't know. That's up to you."

She was standing so stiff behind the checkout counter, her shoulders bunched up in a sort of cringe like she was bracing for impact with something. The Senchkin blinked.

"Do you want to come with us?" I asked her.

With eyes wide and her lips pursed, T'Amira nodded, and that motion, that little acknowledgment of her own volition brought something back to her cheeks where all color had drained before now. "Yes," she said simply. "I'll go with you."

Snatching the backpack from the death grip that Zihan had on it, I pulled out the playing cards and black marker that I'd purchased earlier from T'Amira. "You gave me very good service here tonight, T'Amira," I said, flashing her a warm smile. "I always compliment great customer service."

I wrote one thing on each of the first eight playing cards that I drew from the deck. The letter, "S." Walking around to each of the gangsters who were moaning in pain on the floor, I slipped a playing card marked with my initial into each of their breast pockets.

"Make sure you tell your boss when he asks that Stryker sends his regards. Can you do that for me? Okay, great— thanks, guys!"

I replaced my helmet and led a wobbly-kneed T'Amira and Zihan out to the sidewalk, where we waited for a taxi.

"Rubi," I said on my internal comm, before a taxi arrived. "Tonight, I met two people who've been victimized by the League of Desai—and they deserve better. They don't have anywhere else to go, you know? They're both from tragic situations. Both got the raw end of a deal. Could you escort them back to the ship and see what you can do for them until we can find some permanent accommodations?"

"Absolutely," she replied. "I'm four blocks away."

"Thank you," I said. Placing a hand on Zihan's shoulder, I told him, "Tonight, you made that first step. There's going to be many more—and each one will require courage."

He looked down and nodded, glancing back up at me with a flash of recognition that told me he would be okay.

Or at least, he'd have the opportunity. What he did with that opportunity, well, that was up to him.

I nodded at T'Amira, knowing she wouldn't acknowledge the gesture, then headed off down the block to make sure I wasn't there when Rubi arrived so we wouldn't be seen together.

It was time to get something to eat and give Braddock a chance to respond.

"Wait!" Zihan called. "I want to come with you."

I turned around. "Are you sure?"

He nodded vigorously. "Yeah—I'll keep up."

CHAPTER FOURTEEN

ZIHAN JOINING me meant T'Amira was back there all by herself. I was confident that none of the gang members who'd been controlling her life would be getting up and making any sudden maneuvers in the next five minutes, so there was every reason to believe she was safe. However, I couldn't resist glancing over my shoulder just to make sure.

Thankfully, Rubi and Bodega arrived right on time to escort her back to our ship. That also meant I wouldn't have them to back me up until they returned, so I had to avoid any more confrontations that could get out of hand until that point if possible.

As we started off down the block, soon the baker and I had been camouflaged already by crowds of pedestrians strolling against neon backdrops of glass edifices and vaunted skyscrapers.

"Do you think it was safe to talk about your experience with the League's protection rackets inside the taxi earlier?" I asked, starting to second guess my request. "Maybe I shouldn't have asked you."

"I doubt it would matter one way or another," said

Zihan. "From what I've heard, they bankroll cab companies, but I don't think they'd waste their time listening to
the conversations in every car. Why would they? All the
League cares about is making credits—and there are much
easier ways to do that around here. Plus, the League oper-
ates with impunity. They don't see people like us as a
threat, because of how they control the economics."

"True," I said. That was why I was working so hard to
get Braddock's attention.

The mobsters' relationship with the locals was complicated. If the League of Desai packed up and left, the local
economy would go bankrupt. In a sort of dysfunctional
partnership, the people who lived here depended on them
because of how many jobs and employers they'd established
around serving the booming tourist spot. And the gangsters' involvement in tourism was not limited to illegal
ventures. They held investments in real estate development
and partnerships with local establishments like hotels,
restaurants, nightclubs, and casinos.

Their economic stronghold of the area allowed them to
generate billions in revenue by skimming the profits from
small businesses like the kid's bakery. They made even more
by selling tourists legal and illicit products and services,
then using the more legitimate operations as fronts for
their criminal activities.

A typical restaurant might serve as a front for money
laundering, drug trafficking or a meeting place for senior
League members. There was corruption wherever you
looked, and it made me uncomfortable.

Zihan and I climbed into a taxi three blocks away. I
asked him when we got on the road if he'd recommend any
places to eat.

"Have you eaten here before?" he asked me.

"This would be my first time," I said.

"Central Fusion is pretty good," he said. "They carry some items from my bakery."

"Oh yeah?" I said, leaning back in my seat. "Well then, we've got to go there."

A short drive later, and we pulled up in front of the restaurant. Central Fusion took up the whole block. Behind its wall of solid glass, hanging spheres of various sizes cast the tables and walls of mahogany wood in chill amber light.

It looked inviting, and when we walked inside, the serpentine network of dark wooden booths were abuzz with muted conversation, as an alien crab-like chef tossed a saucepan of sizzling morsels over the open-faced grill behind glass.

That was for show and really not necessary, because the printers could make any type of food imaginable at this point, either in people's residential homes or in restaurants like this one, but having an in-person chef on hand was considered the white glove treatment that added that little extra bit of luxe to eateries who wanted to position themselves as high class in a crowded marketplace like Oathel Beach.

Live waitstaff had been phased out long ago in most cases. So, we seated ourselves, and I scanned my quantum pad over the sensor in the center of our mahogany table to reserve our place and open the tab, resting in the knowledge that the task force had rebooted my quantum pad with my new identity as Henry Stryker as the new user.

"You going to order anything from the grill?" Zihan asked me.

I sniffed. "What makes you think I'm that rich?"

"You're not afraid of the League," he pointed out. "So I

figured you must be. Either that, or you work for the government."

"I'm an independent contractor," I said. That much was true. "And I'm perfectly content with feasting all night from the printer, so that's us. I'm hungry."

We stood because the sensor light in the middle of our table was pulsing green, indicating that our number was up to approach the counter and order our food. I'd learned in my three months living in the future that this was the custom, to approach the printer with the other diners at your table.

To go by yourself without them was considered rude.

The counter was a dark wood affair with a marble countertop in keeping with the gourmet decor. The dispenser window was illuminated by blue recessed lighting and wasn't any bigger than it had to be for a five course meal, because the inner workings of the food printer itself weren't anything to write home about. I'd seen the apparatus one time when, after being here in the future for a couple weeks, I was so fascinated by the entire process that I talked the in-person chef on a space station to let me get a peek behind the curtain, so to speak, and trust me, there was nothing of note back there except for a sterile-looking, room-filling machine that a guy like me from the twenty-first century would expect to see on some documentary about how microchips were made in Silicon Valley.

Not appetizing.

But the food that came out on the other side was surprisingly good and authentic. The steak, for example, came from real cows.

Well, okay, it came from cells biopsied from a real cow in a process that was much more humane than what we'd done in the twenty-first century, cells which then were cultivated in a lab and divided into muscle and fat in the perfect proportions to achieve any possible cut.

And, voila!

The raw material was shipped out to vendors, and numskulls like me could push a few buttons and get a mouthwatering filet mignon printed, layer by layer, in less than a minute while you stood there.

I liked mine with cracked pepper and butter.

Amazingly, this process, believe it or not, was already underway before I'd left Earth in 2024. We'd even pioneered cooking with lasers, but exotic techniques like that had a long way to go at the time before they'd become the trusted norm that they were now anywhere I'd ever been in the galaxy.

Then you had primitive ranchers who did everything the old fashioned way—subsistence living—in the Protectorate, but they were exceptions to the rule, not the standard, kind of like Amish populations in my day.

Who was I to say which was better? Civilizations in the CMC ran the gamut, but I wasn't here to think about the morshgur ranchers in the Protectorate. We had enough to worry about with Yakuza's fleet and convincing Braddock to give me a ticket before I tried to take on that project.

Right now, I just wanted a steak.

I tapped my order on the counter's touchscreen—my tried-and-true ribeye with a baked potato, seasoned crostini, and Caesar salad. Grated parmesan. Okay, brown gravy.

Zihan entered his order, too, and a minute later, the chime announced that the metal tray with all my dishes was rolling down the conveyor belt into the dispenser window.

The kid ordered sweet and sour pork. His plate came out piled high with tenderloin on a bed of rice slathered in the fragrant orange sauce that it was known for and a dash of sesame seeds.

We returned to the table with our serving trays and got started.

"What inspired your family to open a bakery?" I asked him.

"Well, my ancestors were from Hong Kong, and the way our shop came to be was my grandparents had the idea of opening a traditional Hong Kong-style bakery in Oathel Beach."

"Was that before the League controlled everything?" I asked him.

He sighed. "They were here, but it wasn't this bad. Back then, you could still open a business and pretty much steer clear of the League of Desai and their activities. A lot has changed over the years."

I could tell everything his family had endured was weighing heavily on him.

"You said this place carries your products," I said, trying to lighten the mood. "So, what do you recommend? I want one of each!"

"Well," he said, his expression brightening with that change of subject. "If you've never had classic Hong Kong-style, I'd probably start with a pineapple bun or wife cakes, and maybe egg custard tarts."

"I'm not a big fan of pineapple, so that first one is out."

"They actually get their name from the crunchy, sugary crust on top of the bun. It forms a crisscross pattern like the skin of a pineapple—but there's no pineapple in it—so you may like it. It's like a sweet roll served with a slice of butter or bean paste inside it."

"Bean paste?" I asked, trying not to show my trepidation. "That's not a flavor I'd expect in my pastries."

"It's good!" he insisted. "You really should try it. But if you're looking for a different flavor of fillings, you could try wife cakes."

"Wife cakes?" I asked. "Do I want to know how that got its name?"

He laughed. "There are several humorous legends that may have led to it, mostly about a husband and wife showing their care for each other by baking these cakes. We use this glutinous rice flour to make a flaky crust and fill it with sweet winter melon, almond and sesame paste."

"Hmm." I was starting to wonder if maybe I should've asked for a list of ingredients before I'd promised the kid that I would buy one of each—because the two desserts he'd listed so far each sounded sort of strange.

Come on, Gage. Try to keep an open mind, here. He's been through a lot.

"The husband cakes are made with minced meat, garlic, salt and egg yolk," he added.

"How about those custard tarts you mentioned?" I asked with a sidelong glance, hoping it would be closer to flavor combinations I'd recognize.

"Egg tarts are delicious," he said. "I make the short-crust pastry dough every day, then form it into molds and fill it with egg, butter, sugar, and milk. The best part is that all of my bakery items are low glycemic and high protein."

"Really?" I asked. "I know a guy back home with diabetes who'd appreciate that."

"Where's home?" he asked, examining my face for any clues about my origins. It was uncomfortable being scruti-nized when you knew your physical appearance had been forged, though maybe this was a good proof of concept for my biomask, since every interaction after this point would be so much more consequential. There'd be no room for error or detection.

I hesitated.

Zihan seemed harmless, but still, I hadn't known him for long enough to give away my planet of origin, especially with the classified nature of this op. "A long way from here," I finally responded. "But that egg tart sounds great. My grandmother made that kind of pie when I was little— and it was like the best pie I ever had."

He shrugged. "Well, let's order some!"

We returned to the counter. The desserts didn't need to be printed, since Zihan's bake shop delivered them from scratch, but they slid out through the same dispenser as our entrees had earlier.

The egg custard tart collapsed in my mouth with a sweet custard and incredible crust. I finished it before we'd returned to the table.

The kid cut off a bite from his pineapple bun and slid it onto my plate. "Try it."

The warm pastry melted in my mouth. "Mmm, that's incredible," I said. "What's the filling?"

"That's bean paste!" he said, now chuckling at me.

"I'm going back to order another one of those," I said before even swallowing the warm confection.

I walked back to the counter to place my order and stood there, drumming my fingers, but before my dessert popped out, hot breath raised the hairs on the back of my neck and the muzzle of a gun pressed into my ribs where there was a gap between my armor's panels.

"Take your weapon from its holster, Mr. Stryker, nice and slow," a velvety male voice spoke into my ear from behind. "Lay it there on the counter, now."

A flick of my eyes in their direction revealed the heavies

who'd sidled up on either side, two mafia enforcers in business suits who looked like they could be identical. Both were from a bipedal species built like a truck, covered in gray leathery hide with flat, noseless faces and ponderous eyes.

Calcified ram's horns curled around the sides of their heads.

Swallowing hard, I drew my carbine from its holster and laid it on the counter. The confrontation didn't surprise me. In fact, it was all part of my plan. That didn't mean my plan would succeed.

"They told me about you," I said to the leader who had his gun pressed into my side. "Your gang I beat up. It's funny, they said the only reason you carry a gun—since you don't really need one—is to make up for deficiencies in other areas."

He laughed, a slow, sadistic deep-throated sound. "What deficiencies are those, Mr. Stryker? Careful now, remember your place—where I'm standing and what I could do to you."

"Well," I said. "Where do we start?" At this point, I barked out a laugh so obnoxious and protracted that the gangster had to bore his gun a little deeper just to convince me to shut up. "The first thing they mentioned was your intellect, but that's pretty common for your species, isn't it?"

The assailant behind me grabbed the collar of my armor and yanked me backwards. He was strong—I'd give him that—which was the first theory I'd wanted to test by insulting him. Had I done enough to earn some attention from the brains of their organization or was this just the next level of brawn?

I knew it was the latter when he pushed me hard

enough that I wiped out into an unoccupied table. That hurt. It sent one of the wooden chairs sliding across the marble floor of the dining room. I winced.

He picked me up again and spun me around, then pinned me on my back against the table, and for the first time, I caught a glimpse of his face. I'd been wondering what species they'd send after me next, since I'd made quick work of their humans.

The answers? Not good news for me.

A bipedal monster like the two twins, this one, their leader, had the head of a jaguar or something close to it, the burning golden eyes of a predator, spotted fur, pointed ears, and a feline snout that retracted across yellowed fangs.

His Jagulen race shared one chilling feature with their genetic cousins, jaguars from old Earth—the same unorthodox means of killing, which for big cats, was unusual. Their jaws were so powerful that they could collapse the skull of their mammalian prey with a single bite, delivering a fatal blow to the brain.

But they weren't particularly smart. It wasn't surprising that the League had deployed a Jagulen and two Rammodors, because could I physically overpower all three? Not without some kind of weapon.

And each of the ram's-horned aliens had one of my arms pinned to the table.

Murder burned in the eyes of the cat. He removed my combat knife from the carapace of my armor, slowly, as if relishing my unease, and then my utility belt along with the pieces of gear attached to it.

A drop of saliva slid into my eye from the jaws of the Jagulen. Now unarmed and completely helpless, I needed to think of something, because his hot breath was making me squirm and wonder what lengths he'd be willing to take.

CHAPTER FIFTEEN

"WERE THEY RIGHT?" I asked, fighting against my gag reflex, trying to hold my breath under the oppressive snuffs of the Jagulen who tested the air inches from my face. "Was your gang right about your intellect?"

A growl issued from deep in his throat. He actually licked my face. "I am superior in every way, including my cognitive abilities," he said. "Because I have been enhanced."

"Ha!" I barked, trying to sound incredulous. "So, you're what, now? Only half as dumb as a human being?"

He roared and smacked the table so hard with one of his fur-covered fists, each of which was about the size of my head, that the wood cracked upon impact. "I am superior to you and every other human in ever way!"

"Hmm, that's funny," I said. "Because if that's true, I wonder why you're doing grunt work like this instead of being promoted to a Caudanum Mathum, or even a sergeant. Because my guess is, you're what? A private-level soldier in the League of Desai?"

"I will be promoted soon," he growled. "You will see. It's only a matter of time."

"I haven't heard anything about him being promoted, have you guys?" I asked, turning to each of the Rammodors pinning down each of my arms.

They just kept frowning.

"See, they haven't heard anything about that, either. Complete radio silence. That doesn't sound like such a good sign for you, Whiskers, I mean unless you know something that I don't. I could be wrong."

"This is foolishness!" he roared. "What gang are you in that you think you know so much about who is promoted and who is not?"

"Well, I'm reporting directly to Emin Braddock today, if that tells you anything, so I don't mean to brag, but—"

"That is impossible!" He snapped. "I have served the League faithfully for three years and never received a personal invitation from the Caudanum Mathum, and you, some voiding outlander who's just arrived is meeting with him after one day? No."

I grimaced as if admitting an uncomfortable secret. "That's what I mean, Mr. Whiskers. He *would* invite you, but I don't think he sees you as sharp enough to keep up with people like me."

The Jagulen roared again. "I will challenge you in *any* test of intelligence, and then we will see who deserves an audience with Braddock!"

"Any test?" I scoffed. "Surely, you don't mean—"

"Any. Test. You son of a bjorek, kerlanzi scum. See, you're bluffing! You wouldn't dare to challenge my intellect."

"Fine," I said. "I challenge you and your two buddies here to a game of poker at the Bay Casino. If you win, then you get to kill me. You can decide what to do with my body —just don't tell me about it ahead of time."

He chuckled a little too much at that. I drew in a deep breath.

"If I win," I continued, "then I get my blaster and other weapons back, but don't worry, you still get to kill me."

"You're just trying to get your weapons back so you can shoot us before we can kill you," he instantly recognized.

"Well, if you don't like that outcome, then why don't you just win?" I balked. "I mean, unless you're getting cold feet because you know that you can't, because you know that humans are superior, which is what I've been saying all along—"

"No!" he said. "We accept your challenge. Come on, Frantosia Bay Casino it is."

"One more thing," I said. "I need that kid at the table to come with me. What was your name?"

"I am Jorgendar," said the Jagulen.

"Right, Jorgendar. Meet Zihan, my poker coach. Zihan, meet the guys."

With that announcement, I don't think a muscle moved in the young baker's body, except for his eyes which had gone wide and were darting everywhere, looking for some means of escape. For his sake and for mine, hopefully I could pull out a win on a game that actually wasn't all based on intellect—because for all the strategy involved, another determinant of who might win could be nothing more than a stroke of luck.

That meant I could lose just as easily.

But I'd chosen a contest at the Casino because tensions were escalating in my feud with the League of Desai, and I couldn't afford another confrontation. This scrat was getting too dangerous.

My intel had told me that Emin Braddock had been known to frequent the rarified air of the Frantosia Bay Hotel and Casino, Oathel Beach's crown jewel attraction, whose upper floors entertained the wealthiest and most powerful visitors to the tropical paradise.

I didn't know if he was there today. But trying to make something happen at the Bay could be my best shot of drawing his attention. The hard part would be doing enough to accomplish that feat without getting myself shot in the process.

Jorgendar and the Rammodors forced us to walk in front of them to the train station, keeping one hand on the hilt of their weapons inside their jackets.

After purchasing tickets, soon we were gliding across the bridge spanning the crystal clear water of the bay inside a mag-lev passenger car. The Bay Hotel and Casino complex gleamed from its narrow inlet in the distance, its most prominent feature being its three towers of glass and permasteel that rose seventy stories into the sky from sea level.

The towers were unique in that they were capped by a 2.1 hectare (over 5 acre) sky park offering 360-degree views of the island from a seat in its restaurants, gardens, or the largest rooftop Infinity Pool in the Commonwealth of Member Civilizations.

The entire complex was nearly three hundred meters tall and the most iconic landmark of Caldera Island besides its volcano. I'd seen images of it on the gal-net and in our intel packet but had never been here in person.

When we entered the atrium on the first floor, it was clear that it had been meticulously designed with a level of grandeur to wow even the most cynical guests.

The atrium was an expansive six stories in height. The

top five levels wrapped around and looked down on the mezzanine floor where we were standing, guarded by gold-plated guardrails. The main casino area we'd entered was over four-hundred thousand square feet, a sea of gamblers gathered around tables separated by gilded arches and statues depicting a common theme. Fashioned in gold, they depicted winding sea serpents that must've been regarded as almost sacred in the local culture.

The Rammodors pushed us into the passerby milling around, tucked in behind us so close that they could keep the butt of their guns pressed into our backs without anyone really noticing, not that anyone was paying attention. Everyone was into their game or contest of choice. People and aliens hunched over roulette tables, sat along rows of bright slot machines or gathered for one of many card games with drinks in their hands and credits to burn.

"Go get us a table," Jorgendar ordered one of his meaty ram's-horned assistants, and the brute quickly obeyed. Bypassing the waitlist, he approached an employee and made it clear with a few simple gestures that our party needed priority billing.

Next thing I knew, we were being led into a vast poker room, and I caught the tail end of an interaction between the manager and a group of players where he was ordering them to vacate their places before they'd even finished a hand.

Because League gangsters got what they wanted—no questions asked.

I'd challenged them to poker, because unlike most games, we'd only be pitted against each other, not against the house, so I felt that gave me a better chance to control my own destiny in the casino. But I walked in there aware of all the things that still could go wrong.

Texas Hold'em could be played with anywhere from two to ten people, but most casinos kept games to a maximum of six or eight for the best experience. Although they used a different name for it, the form of poker here had some of the same rules, with a few differences, of course.

Jorgendar ordered Zihan to sit on the right end of the table, then sat between him and me, with one of his goons scrunched in on my left. He posted the other Rammodor alien opposite us next to the dealer.

Maybe he is enhanced.

I started to wonder, because this was a pretty smart arrangement on his part. He'd ensured I had a guard on either side of me and couldn't grab the kid to make a quick getaway if things got hairy.

Plus, the Rammodor with his gun under the table would notice if I made any quick moves. *Might be more difficult than I had hoped.*

Jorgendar made me sit in what was called "the big blind" position, meaning I had to put in chips before any cards had been dealt.

The other players would have to call or raise the size of my bet to stay in. Rammy decided to match my bet with chips of his own. Zihan also decided to match it.

I winced, feeling a twinge in my gut, hoping the kid knew what he was doing. I hadn't really figured on him in this game, but that's how Jorgendar had insisted we play it.

"I take it you're admitting defeat?" I said, leaning back in my chair and crossing my arms as I leered over at Jorgendar. "Here we are in the first round, and you already know that you're done for."

"You really think I'm that stupid, outlander?" he replied.

"That's my prevailing theory," I said. "If you were actually *confident* in your abilities, you'd put my gun on the table, because you wouldn't be afraid of losing it."

Shooting a scowl that flashed with yellow fangs, he slammed my blaster down on the table, not to be outdone.

When the dealer got back around to me, I decided I'd better not raise the bet. This game called for conservative strategies.

A few minutes later, Zihan surprised the whole table by throwing down a flush that won the round. Laughing nervously, he glanced around.

My plan was to create mass chaos that would require top levels in Braddock's leadership to intervene. Trying to antagonize the mobsters so I could turn this into a scene and hopefully get some attention from upstairs, I laughed at Jorgendar and mocked him so much that he lost it.

But instead of lashing out at me like I'd been expecting, the monstrous gangster sprang to his feet and choked out the kid in his powerful, fur-covered grip. Zihan's eyes bugged. Blood vessels bulged from his neck as the alien shook him like a rag doll.

His airway was being cut off, and Jorgendar's snout twitched with malice and cold resentment. He was enjoying this.

Snatching my gun from the table, I lurched backwards to get a clean shot. "Drop him!" I ordered. "Drop him right now."

But primordial instincts took over. Jorgendar's irises narrowed like the aperture of a camera. His jaws opened wide enough to snap the kid's skull. The mammalian lunged in for the kill, now given over to the dark act.

I fired right through the side of his cranium, sending a slosh of blood and gore across the card table. Jorgendar dropped. The poker room erupted into pandemonium, everyone rushing for the main exit, creating a bottleneck as the other mobsters were also caught up in the mad rush of bodies.

The Rammodor screamed at me, "Drop the gun!"

The second one was backing him up. Assuming that they were both half-decent shots, pulling my trigger wouldn't end well, so I laid the carbine down on the floor.

By that time, the poker room had evacuated and security was being called. One Rammodor tackled me to the polished floor hard enough that my head struck the marble and my ear started ringing from the sheer force.

His heavy body nearly suffocated me, and the breath had been knocked out of my lungs. It took a few seconds to breathe again, at which point, it registered that I'd been restrained, and he hauled me back to my feet.

Helpless in the shock cuffs, I stumbled forward, being pushed by the alien. He had started to confer with security, now that they were on scene, so, I'd either made the most brilliant move of my short time on Caldera Island or ensured that we'd never leave and our bodies would never be found.

There was a brief conversation between the Rammodors and security and some parties they consulted with on their comm links, until they finally decided what to do with us.

I breathed a sigh of relief, because by this time, Zihan had returned to consciousness and assured me he was okay, although he rubbed at the bruises around his throat and kept trying to swallow through the uncomfortable feeling that remained.

They put him in shock cuffs, as well. For better or worse, we were in this together. *Well, I gave him a chance to duck out,* I thought to myself.

The imposing twins were stoic who escorted us through the casino into a maintenance lift they had to unlock with a key. As we entered it, their solid black eyes set deep in their skulls betrayed no emotion. Their profiles stood leathery and flat like an axehead, their ram's horns scarred, calcified, and damaged like the ears of an MMA warrior set apart from commoners around them by the marks of battles gone by, and we descended the maintenance shaft into the bowels of the basement.

The Rammodors pushed us through a vacant tunnel to a service exit out back. There, in a dark alleyway blocked off between trucks, they forced us into the trunk of an air car and slammed it closed, cutting out light and leaving the kid and I crammed into the confined compartment in awkward contortions for the lonely hours left before dawn.

Neither Zihan or I had much to say, and being crammed into that trunk gave me plenty of time to think.

I wondered whether Tess was okay and what I'd gotten my whole crew into. Hopefully, they'd fared better than I had. I wondered whether, if I survived, anything between us would change. Our group dynamic seemed strikingly similar to how I was already feeling with Zihan.

Knowing I couldn't do this myself and needed allies, I was grateful for their involvement but had been pushing them for so long on a quest that was everything to me—the search for my son.

I wondered if the point in time would come that I pushed everyone too far, and when it did, would I have what it took to keep us together?

If Celin-Ohmi and Steinbreaker hadn't been one in their hatred of Yakuza, we may not have even made it this far, and we couldn't even agree on the best way to handle that. I needed to find a way to rally them. Hopefully, I wasn't alone in that sentiment, and we could still find some way forward.

That was my last thought before drifting off into a rest-less slumber that wasn't restorative but was less than conscious, a place where voices kept calling my name from soupy darkness that I couldn't cross.

CHAPTER SIXTEEN

SOMEONE CRACKED OPEN THE TRUNK, nearly blinding me in the piercing light of morning from the primary star. The Rammadors had returned and now were hauling us back to our feet and back inside the first floor.

I blinked and stretched out the kinks in my back from being crammed in the trunk with the kid. Taking in the Bay Casino as if for the first time, I realized how easy it would be to get lost in its luxuries.

Our glass elevator ascended through the hotel's open spaces, giving Zihan and I picturesque views of the complex's sun-drenched amenities.

Many rich patrons didn't want to flash their famous faces all over the city where they could be bothered by paparazzi or reporters, so the Frantosia Bay Hotel and Casino had a multi-story shopping mall awash in natural light from the ample skylights above.

Maybe I was so taken with it because we were still alive. The fact that we were being taken anywhere had to be a good sign. Zihan and I exchanged a grin.

A canal ran the length of the mall's hallways so visitors could take a leisurely boat ride or explore it on foot, featuring the best luxury brands and retailers, and an art and science museum housed inside an aluminum dome also shrunk in our view as our lift continued to rise.

We passed four arenas hosting live entertainment from theatre to dance to top music acts. This entire property was maintained and serviced by thousands of employees, and all of the attractions in the Frantosia alone were responsible for bringing in a whopping three billion credits per cycle.

Our elevator continued to climb, and I noticed the Rammadors seemed to relax the further we got from the ground floor casino. We were nearing the sky park on the roof. That made me uneasy, because I knew it was the most exclusive spot on the entire island.

Heavy security made sure that only the most rich and important VIP's ever entered its cluster of posh restaurants and lavish nightclubs. The roof was a hotspot for celebrities, diplomats, business tycoons. But our elevator kept climbing until we reached that height.

The guards led us down the upscale garden path of the sky park dotted with butterflies and sculpted shrubs amidst aristocrats who glanced at us with looks of disdain in evening gowns and tailored waistcoats.

The long Infinity Pool at the top of the towers was a sight to behold. At four hundred meters in length, the troughs that collected falling water along each edge created the illusion of an artificial horizon between the rippling pool and the skyscrapers beyond. Built of stainless steel, it held hundreds of thousands of gallons of water for the guests who frolicked in it under the light of the primary star.

It was so beautiful that I almost forgot how all of this profit and opulence came at a morbid price for people like Zihan and T'Amira who did the grunt work but never got to reap the rewards.

No matter what happened from here on out, I'd have to watch my six.

The guards led us to a hacienda ranch-style house, yes, a house, built on top of the hotel at one end of the sky park. They took turns having their retinas and faces scanned in the biometric scanner by the door, and then the AI welcomed them each by name and asked them to state their intention for coming.

"We were told to bring these individuals up here directly," one said.

The baker and I glanced at each other, tense and not certain how to take that.

"One moment," the artificial intelligence said. Shortly, the AI's female voice announced that we could all come in and the front door, which looked like it had been carved from an expensive type of wood, swung open automatically, then closed behind us after we stepped inside.

"You've certainly got my attention, Mr. Stryker," said a middle-aged man, approaching us from the lavish modern furniture of the spacious room. "So, why am I not killing you right now?"

He walked across the room, wary but not scared, not facing us directly, as if he just happened to notice us standing there.

"Because I have what you want," I said.

Maybe five and half feet tall, he was a human man in his fifties, if I had to guess, balding and unremarkable in appearance except for the garish colors of his outfit that contrasted with his ordinary looks, a lime green oversized suit jacket, gray tweed pants and a silk fuchsia shirt with a scarf that tied the strange colors together.

He snapped his fingers and one of the Rammodor guards kicked me in the back of my knees so hard that it drove me to a kneeling position. I chose to stay down, because of who I suspected this was. Now was my time to earn credibility, which in time, would become trust, but it had to begin with respecting his position and also not sounding like anyone's patsy.

"Wasn't my choice to land on this flea-bitten rot of the Kkoradian abyss," I said.

"Hmm, yes, I've already seen security footage of you assaulting the fugitive recovery agent who took over your ship," he said. "In fact, the crowds were so dense outside that spaceport entrance that we seem to have lost track of her after that. You wouldn't know anything about that, would you? My people weren't able to recover her body, so kudos to you for keeping it clean. I like a man who doesn't leave loose ends behind. Especially not on my planet."

He'd been walking my way slowly, his polished shoes tapping across the tile until he now stood inches away from my ear. "It's bad for business," he whispered. "Are you a businessman, Stryker? Clearly, you're not trying to disrupt my ventures here on Caldera Island. If you were, you wouldn't have gone to such great lengths to get caught, that whole dramatic bit with the playing cards. Ha. You were seeking an audience. I'll admit you've got talent, but I've got people with similar skills—so what's your pitch? Tell me why I haven't killed you."

"Because I have what you want," I said.

"And what do you, a thief and two-bit pirate have that I'd possibly want?" he said, leaning forward with a patronizing grin from ear to ear and his arms spread wide.

STAR CENTURION   157

I rose to my feet. "Physical proof of how Yakuza has been successful in their recent acts of sabotage on the Antrydium supply chain. I know how that's hurt your organization's biggest investments—and the balance of power in the entire Commonwealth of Member Civilizations."

He frowned, his eyebrows shooting up briefly, before he started rubbing his chin. "Not a small claim, not a small claim at all. But you didn't seriously think I'd take an offer like that at face value, did you? I don't make a habit of working with people that I don't know. Do you have any idea how much one hour of my time's even worth?"

I cleared my throat. "Maybe a vague idea, but it's probably more than I'd guess," I said quietly.

He chuckled. "More than you'd guess—more than you'd dream! More than you'll ever make in your entire lifetime. You have to show me that you can be an earner in this organization before I let you infringe on that hour. Plus, you haven't been very nice to my people out there. Now, you mentioned a trade, so I assume you're looking for work. Most people are who come to me."

"I'm offering you proof of how Yakuza is committing these acts of aggression against your investments. In exchange, all I ask is one thing. Access to a seven-day sightseeing trip in the Free People's Protectorate on Samudra."

Emin Braddock burst into laughter for an entire minute. Finally, he sniffed, wiping his eyes. "You know why I haven't gotten rid of you? You've got skills and you take initiative. Two things I look for in new recruits! You can't teach someone to *want* something in life, you know that, Mr. Stryker? Either they do and they fight to get it, or they don't and they get run over in the stampede of people who are more ambitious. I can't use unmotivated people. Just toss them in the meat grinder—that's all I can do! Vedana's not a good place for people who don't want something, but getting into the Free People's Protectorate? Now, you're operating way outside your strictures."

"Fine," I said, knowing if I could just earn his trust enough to give me his undivided attention—which would take time—he would be very interested in the evidence I had of the Quonella's role and how we might use that together to turn the tables on Yakuza. I saw it. It was so obvious. Yakuza was the League's biggest rival.

But we weren't there yet. Braddock didn't know me from some random guy off the street. Like he said, I'd been here less than a full day and had been nothing but a royal pain to his business dealings so far, really.

I had zero credibility and couldn't even use my victory in the arena of the Battle Mech Tournament, because I was posing as a petty criminal. My only chance was to find some goal or unmet desire, something really important to him where he wasn't getting the results he needed from other sources.

Then, show him how I could fill in that gap. A job with no downsides to him, only upsides.

Where I could prove my potential.

"What do you need?" I asked him. "What's the one job that no one else will take because it's too dangerous or risky or expensive?"

Braddock, who had previously seemed casually disinterested in anything I'd said until then, met my gaze. His eyes narrowed at me, appraising.

Bingo. Now, we were getting somewhere. The change in his facial expression had been subtle, but it felt like I had a tug on the line. Now, I just needed to reel in that fish.

"Name it," I said. "I'll do it for free if you promise afterwards to take a look at my evidence."

Braddock opened his mouth and closed it. He pursed his lips, weighing his options, before glancing down and showing a hint of what? Regret? A tinge of sadness or pain. Well... that was unexpected.

When he made eye contact again, the flashy bravado he wore on his sleeve like the bold outfit and ostentatious surroundings, all the trappings of power, were gone.

"Each of my brothers is a Caudanum Mathum in the League, like me. They're both older, and they came here to visit a week ago. 'We want to see all the sights,' they said. 'See what our baby brother's been doing.' Well, they disappeared five days ago, and I've had my best people on it. Not a trace. I keep asking them, 'Did you check the caverns and minor islands? If they were abducted and the kidnapper is getting ready to demand a ransom, those would be great places to hide them!' But no, those voiding bjoreks are all too scared of Owari worms to go anywhere near the volcano regions."

The man scratched his forehead and smacked his thigh with a flash of anger that faded so quickly, I wondered whether it had smoldered so long that all that remained of that fire now was a cold ember of despair.

However ruthless and evil he was, clearly, family mattered to Braddock. Now he was facing the one thing all the credits in the galaxy couldn't solve. The loss of his older brothers.

"If I find your brothers, will you let me explain the evidence I have on Yakuza and what that has to do with the Antrydium freighters?" I asked. "I need your word."

Emin Braddock reached out and shook my hand, patting it with his other one. "They're wearing medallions like this around my neck, see? Whether alive or dead, get me that evidence, and I'll pay *three* million, plus my full attention for ninety minutes."

I drew in a breath. Now, that was an offer. "Thank you. I'll get you the closure you need, one way or another. I will find out."

Braddock patted me on the shoulder and smiled. "One more thing, Stryker. Your ship's in the spaceport until you do. Only fair for the property damage and medical bills you caused my employees," he said.

"So, you're saying we're not allowed to leave Vedana until we bring you results."

He shrugged. "You can leave if you need supplies or additional crew members. I don't care—just get it done. But I'm keeping the ship you arrived in as collateral to make sure you don't do anything unprofessional," he said with a grin.

"My ship has an Ectocraft in the hold—can I use that for the job?"

"Ah," he said with a look of recognition. "From that fugitive recovery pig you disposed of? Heh, very nice. Normally, I'd say 'no,' but in this case a street-legal personal law enforcement craft would give you that extra layer of credibility among the locals and help you shake people down. So, sure! See, I knew I kept you alive for a reason. That siren still strikes fear into the locals. Everyone here's got a bounty on their heads. You've got one week. After that, I'm not responsible for anything that happens to you. I'm expecting big things! Can I count on you? Are you an earner like I hoped you were—or are you the kind of man that I need to get rid of to make room for those who are?"

"You can count on me, sir," I said.

Because what was I going to say? He ran the economy

of this entire planet and had already grounded my ship. The verdict was out on whether he'd order our execution before this was over, because one week wasn't much time to find missing persons, when the previous searches hadn't found bodies.

This job hit too close to home for the gangster.

We had to deliver.

Braddock snapped his fingers twice more with a nod, and the Rammodors roughly pulled us outside. They escorted the baker and I down the pathway leading back to the main elevator, as if our existence in the upscale sky park had insulted everyone there.

"Well," I said, "looks like we've got our work cut out for us."

"You mean *your* work, not mine," said Zihan. "I don't want any part of this scrat. Not after what he did to my family."

"Right," I said, wincing. "Sorry, I get it."

The kid fell quiet as our elevator dropped through the hotel's bright seventy stories until we reached the bottom where Vedana's desperate could blow a few credits in their attempts to outsmart the house.

All of their lives were real, like Zihan's and T'Amira's. They all put a face to the brutal hierarchy that ruled over this planet. But I couldn't deny that Emin Braddock was affable, even charming.

There was something fascinating about that kind of wealth, that kind of prestige. For a fleeting breath, I wondered what it would be like to be one of his colleagues, hanging out literally on top of the world, enjoying drinks in the Infinity Pool where servants catered to your every need and money wasn't an object.

Hopefully, my crew wouldn't mind joining me on this job, but I bet the offer of three million credits would put to rest whatever concerns they'd have... because that was more than we'd ever earned on any bounty hunting operation outside of the Battle Mech Tournament.

CHAPTER SEVENTEEN

BRADDOCK'S HIRED muscle released the kid and I outside the main entrance of the hotel and casino with orders to go somewhere else, which was fine, because I needed to touch base with Mercedes.

She was waiting for a status report, but the Caudanum Mathum had just introduced a wrinkle to the plan that we hadn't expected. If anything, I figured she would be happy, but it wasn't clear how her superiors would react. That kind of worried me.

It was too soon to return to the *Lizard King*. I didn't want to explain to my crew what had happened until we had clarity on what to do next. Hopefully, Mercedes would give me the green light and we could start looking for those missing persons.

I'd need some privacy to make the call but didn't have anywhere to send the kid. He didn't strike me as a security risk, and I'd promised to protect him, so my only option was to keep Zihan with me, as I purchased tickets for the volcano park.

The two of us boarded a mag-lev train car outside the

Frantosia Bay complex. It whisked us away on a breezy ride across the water to the island's interior. Plumes of steam and gas rose up from the active eruption as our train climbed the volcanic rock leading to the caldera's summit.

It surprised me how close we could get to views of the natural wonder without being exposed to its heat because of the cavernous outer walls of the caldera plunging so deep in the ground, keeping the cauldron of molten rock a relatively safe distance away, though there'd always be some aspect of danger. You could never completely eliminate unpredictability from natural environments.

We disembarked in the train station at the entrance of the tourist area and made the hike the rest of the way. The kid and I peered over the outer rock rim into lakes of lava that bubbled at depths of four hundred meters below our feet.

A holographic tour guide explained how lava flows emptied into the churning waves of the ocean kilometers away. I excused myself to make the call, while Zihan leaned on the guardrail, listening to a lesson from the hologram that he'd probably heard a thousand times.

Hiking across a jagged edge of hardened magma that had formed land in a matter of hours, I called Mercedes on my quantum pad and decided to leave out the part about the mobster threatening to whack us if we didn't complete his task in one week, because I didn't want her to get too concerned and try to take us off the job. I needed this.

I didn't want to endanger my crew any more than I already had, but I needed this inside connection to get me into the Protectorate, so I could figure out what they'd done with my son.

We'd come too far to back out or leave it all up to the Centurions. I was his father. It was up to me.

"Are you safe?" Mercedes asked me when she picked up my call.

"Yes," I said, "but I've got an update. I met with Braddock, and he's not buying the fact that I have evidence for how Yakuza's sabotaging the shipments."

"In your first meeting?" she asked.

"Yeah."

"Well, that's understandable. This is the first time he's even met you. It'll take time to build up rapport."

"About that," I said. "I asked him what I could do for him, you know, jobs that nobody else wants. Well, turns out he's got two brothers, each a Caudanum Mathum. They came to visit him recently then subsequently disappeared, and he thinks they might be dead but never got closure one way or another. He wants to me join the search. If I find them, he's already promised ninety minutes of undivided attention so I can explain what I've got on Yakuza."

"Gage, that's fantastic! You got him to agree to that in your first meeting?"

"Yeah. I know he's going to freak when he finally gives me the chance to explain. It's a good opportunity. I can feel it. We've just to got to build some rapport, like you said."

"Just focus your search on one of the continents or in Oathel Beach proper—stay away from the rural environments along the island coastlines and especially the volcano," she said.

"Braddock actually recommended the opposite," I said. "Mentioned something about how other guys he's had working on it gave up too quickly on parts of the island because they're too scared of Owari worms."

"That's what I mean," said Mercedes. "Mature Owari worms are a handful, not something you want to come across without a larger team who's been professionally trained to deal with them. Even then, they're extremely dangerous. That's why I'm saying, stay inland, either on one of the continents or in the city of Oathel Beach—away from the rural environments on the coastlines and especially the volcano."

"What do they have to do with the volcano?" I asked.

"Its eruptions make the water nearby too hot and acidic for most animals, but Owari worms need a very specific environment to flourish," she said. "The high acidity and presence of certain microbes in the ocean around volcanoes makes those regions one of their perfect habitats. That's why you're safe as long as you're on land. Even the ocean out there should be safe as long as you're at least two hundred kilometers from any volcanoes, because the worms are drawn to the waters acidified by their lava eruptions."

I frowned. "How large are these Owari worms, then?"

"Adults can reach ten or fifteen meters," she said. "But they have, on occasion, been observed even larger than that. I don't think we really know how big they can get in the right environment. They're very dangerous and hard to kill. They have multi-pronged mouths that can latch onto your face and suck the liquids right out of your body, so yeah, this is not a species you want to mess with. Just promise you'll stay away from the danger zones."

"I appreciate you letting me know what to watch out for," I said. "Our search for his brothers can start on dry land, but I can't promise we won't search the caverns and minor islands that Braddock brought up, because from the way he described it, those regions around the volcano seem to be some of the only ones his people haven't even explored, and I told him I'd be willing to do any job he needs—even one that other people aren't willing to take. That's the only way I made it this far. Since he's not interested in Shintox's ship yet, I've got to offer him something he values, because—well, he is already making some threats."

"Gage," Mercedes said in a level tone. This was how she spoke when she was trying to redirect my attention to a different plan. I didn't like it. "Your job is not to take Braddock on in a head-to-head matchup. Your job is to earn his trust, and then offer him Shintox's corvette and video of the Quonella you found dead inside it, in exchange for access to the Protectorate for one of our Centurions to perform recon. Your role is clearly defined. I think you'd better let us take over now, because I'm not sure you understand the risks."

"I do understand the risks!" I growled. "But you know what's worse than taking action even when it's risky? Doing *nothing* and losing more time! My son may not have another three months to waste while your bureaucrat bosses circle the mini-fridge in their office chairs and work their way up to making a decision!"

I looked around. Thankfully, the crowd of tourists was thin this late into the wee hours, but a few of them shot glances my way because of how I was raising my voice. I lowered my volume and picked up the argument where I'd left off. "Look, I'm a few steps away from getting this done. How often does that happen for you guys? Just think—the man's brothers. I'm telling you, Mercedes, I saw it in his eyes. This job is voiding important to him. If I can pull this thing off, he's going to give me the time to explain about Yakuza and everything else. I know it."

"No, Gage, the longer we talk, I think it would be better for us to send in a team to take it from here and pull you out. It's just too dangerous. I'm responsible for the health and welfare of you and your team, not in an official capacity, but that's how I like to conduct my work. You've served your purpose in this operation, and I thank—"

"Mercedes, I can't back out now!" I said, unable to believe what I was hearing. "If you send someone else to replace me, Braddock's going to get cold feet. Then, we won't be able to get anyone access to the Protectorate, and that rescue mission is dead on arrival."

"Gage, I said that's *enough*. You and all of your crew will be compensated—"

"I don't want to be compensated!" I roared. "We're talking about innocent lives. I'm telling you, if you send someone in to replace me after I already met with him, he's going to get suspicious and stop playing ball. He already shut you out once before, remember? That's why you sent me to see if I could reestablish contact, and I did. But you've got to let me finish the job!"

"Part of *my* job is to enlist the help of consultants and independent contractors as needed for my team to complete our missions," Mercedes said. "I am responsible to manage those teams, and you—I mean, we—this... I think this is no longer working."

I couldn't believe it.

She was firing me.

"That's your right," I said, trying to steady my voice and remain civil. Losing Mercedes' trust altogether wouldn't be good for my future prospects. I needed her. "You can hire whoever you want to. But Mercedes, I'm tired of all the delays and having to watch this from the outside in. I know you're doing everything you can, but I want to speak to whoever is responsible for your Centurion training and certification program or recruiting, depending on how all that works."

"That information's not available to the public," she said.

"Well, *someone* is making a decision on who to let in and who to reject. Let me talk to that person, and then I will leave you alone and let you get back to work. Simple question. Who makes those decisions?"

A pause. She was losing her patience—and I was losing her. I could tell.

But, miraculously, she answered anyway. Mercedes had always liked me. "Mavgardon Rexlin is who you're looking for."

"Okay, great," I said, my brows wrinkling, because I'd heard that name somewhere before. "How can I reach him?"

"I don't have the authority to give out his contact."

"Well, certainly you know where he lives or works."

She let out a long breath. "He doesn't answer to me, that's for sure. The best I could say is his last known location. He's been spending time on Ethos, the namesake for the private military company behind us. That's all I can tell you. Goodbye, Gage. The compensation we agreed upon will show up in you and your crew's accounts within twenty-four standard hours. I truly hope you find what you're looking for."

With that, Mercedes disconnected.

Maybe, it was for the best. I was tired of dealing with the Centurions' scrat as an outlander, being siloed and sidelined by them every time I made any progress. I hadn't risked this much and come this close to earning Braddock's trust, just for some government spooks to come in and ruin everything.

I wouldn't stand by and let that happen. It was time to take over this op.

Now, if I can just get this Mavgardon Rexlin person to help me.

It came back to me where I'd heard his name. Mav Rexlin was the master swordsmith who'd fashioned the plasma blade for Hidalgo, the one my mentor had passed on to me.

If nothing else, I wanted to thank him and meet this figure who'd made such an impression on the hunter who'd taught me our trade.

CHAPTER EIGHTEEN

"You work in the food industry—is there a butcher shop you'd recommend?" I asked Zihan.

He frowned and scratched his face. "A butcher shop?"

"Yeah, there's something I need to pick up on my way back to the ship," I explained.

Twenty minutes later, we pulled up outside the shop the kid had told me about and climbed out of our taxi. A purveyor of real meat like this place catered to very rich clientele since any meat not produced in a printer was sold as a delicacy, but of course, they had to cater to everyone. After wolfing down cheesesteaks printed by their machine, I worked out a deal with the manager on my next purchase over the harsh glow of the display case.

He grinned, asking me to come back again. "I don't get many people coming in here asking for a cow's bone," he said, wrapping it up for me in white paper.

"Well, it's for one special hero," I said. "And she's pretty picky about her treats."

Zihan and I returned to our air taxi that was elevated and waiting at the curb. We took off through the neon city, zipping above the light-drenched asphalt until we got to the spaceport. The two of us disembarked and walked the rest of the way to our ship.

Right away, when I opened the *Lizard King's* cargo ramp, I could hear Steinbreaker screaming.

"Back, I command you! Away from me, ravenous beast!"

Rolling my eyes, I rubbed my temples. It had been a long night and morning. What in the stars was his problem, now?

The little engineer was plastered to the overhead of the cargo bay, kept aloft by the nitrogen-gas jets of his backpack—technology originally designed to help astronauts maneuver on space walks in the absence of gravity—but in Steinbreaker's case, designed to help him access hard-to-reach places in the craft for his duties as ship engineer.

On the deck below him was my German shepherd, reared back on her haunches and barking incessantly.

"She's trying to eat me!" he cried from above, pointing a little accusatory finger with one hand and wielding an oversized wrench with the other. Obviously, the wrench hadn't increased his confidence much against the poor dog, since he'd retreated to a corner of what amounted to the cargo hold's ceiling.

"Steinbreaker, how many times do I have to tell you? She's not trying to eat you, okay? You're conditioning her to get stressed out by the way you act with that jetpack," I said.

Kneeling down for her to lick me, I cupped Maggie's jowls in my hands, and she bucked with excitement, her tail beating the air in a frenzy since I'd been gone overnight. "Is Steinbreaker antagonizing you?" I said to her. "Look, I got you your favorite treat because I know it was hard putting up with him while I was gone. Maggie, look what I got you!"

I unwrapped the treat from its paper package in my backpack and she wrestled it out of my hand, then pranced around the deck with the thing like she was gloating over everyone else. Hey, whatever made her happy. She didn't have to know that nobody else on the ship had any interest in her bovine reward.

Most dogs would be happy with a typical biscuit or maybe rawhide. Not Maggie. She turned her nose up at every kind of conceivable treat, except for one thing—a genuine cow's bone. So, I saved them for special occasions, like putting up with Steinbreaker's scrat when she had to stay in the ship for extended periods. And she loved it. She'd probably keep me up half the night, gnawing on that thing for hours.

She wouldn't pay him any mind now because she already had it between her paws, working on it with her incisors. But the engineer still looked wary.

"Steinbreaker, it's fine—she doesn't even care about you anymore," I tried to reassure him. "Can you please lower the jetpack and power it off?"

Reluctantly, he lowered himself to the deck and cut his jets' power. "Okay, but I'm keeping one of these things nearby at all times for when she turns wild."

"What? You mean a cow's bone?" I asked, scratching her fur.

"No! My nitrogen jets," he said.

"She doesn't seem to bother me, Hedgehog," Bond said with a shrug, "But then again, Roftamorians are probably just more soft and juicy than Oshwellians."

I snickered at that.

"Not helpful, Bodega," Tess interjected.

At least, that's who I assumed she was.

We were still calling her Rubi, since I hadn't needed to use her call sign before she'd switched identities from the bounty hunter persona to a criminal member of my crew, a transformation which now had granted her appearance a new set of features, most notably a boxier forehead and a scar over one eye.

She'd supplemented the biomask with a curly, pink wig and dark brown contacts to change her eyes from their native blue. It took me a minute to realize it was her. That is how well she'd pulled off the disguise.

In fact, enough doubts lingered in my mind that I decided not to address her in case I was wrong. The last thing we needed was to blow our cover, especially in front of our visitors.

The woman I assumed was Tess sauntered up to me and pulled me into an embrace, nuzzling my neck with her face.

That caught me off guard, and I wished I had some way of knowing whether the gesture was genuine or just part of our collective ruse to make sure I knew who she was without needing her to come out and say it.

"You okay, Stryker?" she asked tenderly, pulling back and stroking my cheek. "I was starting to worry about you."

I grinned. "Doing well. I've got news and a visitor! Everyone, meet my new buddy, Zihan. He owned a family bakery downtown before the League of Desai took control of his business and forced him to keep working there for next to nothing."

The kid nodded at everyone and flashed a half-hearted wave.

"So, I told the goons trying to shake him down that we'd provide his protection from now on, so I want everyone to make him feel welcome," I said.

"Thanks," said Zihan in a muted but grateful voice.

"Let us know anything we can get you!" said Stein-breaker, his arms spread wide in a magnanimous gesture.

"Is this all it takes to make you a nice person?" I said with a scowl. "What do I have to do—rescue someone new every day?"

Steinbreaker's face fell, taking on a darker, more sinister expression as he pulled a cigar butt from his coveralls' front pocket and lit up the half-used stub. If the habit wasn't bad enough already, he reused old ones. It seemed that due to his small size, he usually tried to get five or six days out of each.

I didn't understand it, nor did I want to.

"So what happened?" asked Bond. "Did you accomplish what you set out to do?"

I hesitated, trying to decide whether to include T'Amira and Zihan in our secrets. This starship was small enough that the only way we could keep them onboard and prevent eavesdropping would be locking up in the cargo bay like one of our bounties. That just seemed wrong.

What was the point of rescuing them from one form of incarceration, just to throw them into our brig?

"T'Amira, Zihan, you both have a choice to make," I said with my hands on my hips.

The female Senchkin was standing next to Rubi, who mercifully had given her a change of clothes. Even through the stoic facade her race used to face the world, she defi-nitely looked a lot more relaxed and refreshed than the last time I'd seen her face outside of the quick mart after I'd beaten her captors to a bloody pulp.

"I'm not going anywhere," said Zihan. "At least, not on Vedana. Though, maybe if you finish this job Braddock gave you, you can put in a good word for me and they'll give the bakeshop back to my family?"

"If that's what you want when the time comes—sure," I said.

"So, you *did* meet with Braddock!" said Rubi, making a clapping motion in her excitement.

I held up my hands to slow everyone down. "I'll explain everything, but first, T'Amira, how about you? I need to add that we can't tell you anything about our past or where we came from, because it's safer for all of us that way. You both can decide whether that's a dealbreaker or not, as far as whether you want to come with us. But if you do, you should also know that we're not delivering radiators, here. Our business dealings are dangerous endeavors, and we can't guarantee your safety anytime you walk off this ship, but we're not going to hold you here, either, unless you prefer staying on board. Basically, the next steps are yours to decide. I just feel responsible to let you know that as long as you travel with us, anything you hear or find out on board must be kept confidential for the rest of your lives. Understood?"

"I understand your statements and will remain on your ship until we reach my homeworld," said T'Amira.

Tess squeezed her arm and smiled, apparently gratified that the Senchkin had made that decision.

"Zihan, are you good with those terms?" I asked him.

"It's not like I really have a choice, but yeah, I'm good with it," he said.

I breathed a sigh of relief. At least, we could keep our real names and identities under wraps. They didn't have to know we were in disguise.

But there were three things I wouldn't be able to hide any longer from anyone on this ship.

Braddock was threatening to execute me if they didn't deliver the goods. Mercedes had cut us off from future support or funding. And I somehow needed to convince her boss to make me a Centurion.

I rubbed my jaw. Scrat, this wasn't going to be easy.

CHAPTER NINETEEN

"LET ME GET THIS STRAIGHT," said Bond. "Task Force Cyberblade is going to still pay us the same amount they agreed upon originally, and then, effectively immediately, they're cutting us loose. But the mob leader of this planet has offered to pay us three million credits to find his two missing brothers, dead or alive?"

"That's right," I said. "If we don't get results in one week, we need to find a quick way off this planet, because he could try to kill us before we even get back control of this ship."

"But you want to seek out Mav Rexlin first to see if he'll make you *a Centurion?*" asked Tess. "Because it's not like we're not under enough pressure already in the next seven days!"

I steepled my fingers over my mouth. "I know. That part's crazy. I get it. In fact, I could just go to Ethos myself and let you all start the search for the Braddock boys without me if it makes you feel better."

"No, that doesn't make me feel better at all," she stated.

"Why don't you wait on the trip to Ethos until after we finish this job?"

"Because, when we finish this job, it's going to set things in motion with the Caudanum Mathum. Things could progress rather quickly. When he finds out the dirt we have on Yakuza, he's going to want to take action, so we need to be ready at that point to plan my insertion into the Protectorate, not for some kind of attack just yet, but to do recon, to scope things out."

Rubi crossed her arms and chewed on her lip, a tell of hers even in the disguise. I glanced around at the others gathered around Aerial's tank of water in her dedicated compartment.

"None of us wanted to be in this predicament, but here we are," I said. "Let me reiterate that everyone's involvement is and will continue to be voluntary. I understand if you want to back out. Now, the search for Braddock's siblings may be dangerous because of a number of factors and conditions like local wildlife and criminal elements. He's decided the *Lizard King* has to be grounded here as collateral until we can get his job done. So, let's not disappoint him. My offer will be different than our usual split, because Hedgehog's and Aerial's responsibilities for this job should be very limited, so I'd like to pay the two of you fifty-thousand credits as a living stipend during this mission. For T'Amira and Zihan, we don't expect you to do anything except for some errands and admin work while on board. Your food and lodging is free, as long as you're with us. The rest of the three million would be evenly split between Rubi, Bodega, and myself. Like all of our missions, this one's completely up to you guys. What do each of you want to do?"

"So your only interest in becoming a Centurion is to get

into the Protectorate at some point," Steinbreaker considered over his cigar.

"Yes," I said. "We know they have some kind of proprietary tech that can get us past the DNA scanners at the Protectorate's border and some other tech that makes them safer *inside* it, although I can't get any more details on that as long as I'm just a bounty hunter."

"How confident are you that Braddock will help us set my people free from Yakuza?" asked Celin-Ohmi.

"He'll do it," Bodega interjected. "Think about it, Aerial. Of all the business ventures they're involved in, the League of Desai makes the most credits on their investments in FTL technology, specifically, Antrydium. You see what Yakuza's been doing to the supply chain. The League can't let that stand."

"Exactly," I said. "I totally agree. Braddock just doesn't know whether I'm reliable, because we just met, and I had to cause a lot of trouble to get his attention in the first place. It's going to take time to build up our reputation. Thankfully, in this case, he's not asking us to do anything that goes against our ideals."

"And for a lot of money!" said Bodega.

"And for a lot of money," I agreed.

"What about your disagreement with Mercedes?" he added. "Couldn't that be a problem with Rexlin if he's in charge of the program?"

I winced and tugged a bit at my collar. "Not sure how we can get around that part. If we followed her orders and stood down from this job, we'd be back to square one. I'm just now finally making progress with Braddock after being stiff-armed by him for the past three months. I just couldn't give up that opportunity."

"Well, it's not just an opportunity," said Steinbreaker

around his cigar, before tapping it out in the ash tray. "It sounds more like a threat! If he's holding the *Lizard King* as collateral and it sounded like he couldn't decide whether or not he wanted to whack you."

"I agree, not every aspect of this is ideal," I admitted.

"Not ideal? Ha!" Steinbreaker grunted. "I need an extra fifty-k hazard pay if I have to sleep in this ship with this unsupervised animal until you're finished."

"Fifty-k, seriously?" I asked.

"Yeah! Seriously," he said with crossed arms.

"I can do thirty-k 'hazard' pay. How about you, Aerial? Do you need hazard pay?"

She just laughed. "Please. Watching Hedgehog run away from that pup is its own reward."

Rubi burst out laughing at that. "Wow, Aerial, I didn't know you had a sadistic streak in you."

"Not sadism," said the Quonella. "Justice."

"It's the cheese crackers, isn't it?" Bodega asked.

"Mmm-hmm," the mollusk intoned.

I smirked. "Don't think you told me that story."

"Here we go," Steinbreaker groused with a dramatic roll of his eyes.

"Perhaps a more appropriate time, I will fill you in," said Aerial.

"Do you think you'll be safe here by yourself, Aerial?" I asked, squinting and swallowing hard. "I don't want Braddock figuring out that your race is the key to how Yakuza's been attacking those shipments until we're here to protect you."

"Yeah," said Tess. "What's to stop him from taking her from this ship and forcing her into giving up Yakuza's secrets? How are we going to keep that from happening if you, me, and Bond aren't here?"

"I can speak to that," said Steinbreaker. "I don't think a mob boss or any of his cronies would know anything about her species. Sometimes I think you people forget that I'm the xenomarine biologist who discovered the Quonella when I was working on a government research grant to study the coral reefs on their planet."

"That's right," I said with a snicker. "I remember how surprised I was that you were both an engineer and some kind of oceanic scientist when I first met the mollusk."

Tess giggled.

"It shouldn't be *that* surprising," Steinbreaker replied with a scowl.

"He's right," said Celin-Ohmi. "Steiny was the first one to ascertain our superintelligence, and as such, he was keen to protect us from those who might try to take an advantage. Our special gifts of multi-track cognitive processing, as he likes to call it, were only shown to a small number of parties who were vetted and had to sign an NDA for the privilege of using our services. They were motivated to keep everything about us under wraps, because sharing those things wouldn't serve their own financial interests. They viewed us as a trade secret, a way to get a leg up on the competition. And the first truly nefarious people—pirates—who caught wind of our abilities were already linked with Yakuza. Their organization has kept our distinctives, even our existence itself, a closely guarded secret ever since then, keeping us hidden away as their slaves."

"But if Braddock's guards come on board, they're not going to miss your water tank sitting in the middle of this compartment," I said.

"It's okay, we've encountered this situation before, and we're prepared," she said. "To the untrained eye, my species looks pretty similar to several aquatic species that do not share our intelligence—and certainly aren't capable of piloting ships. People who've spotted me over the years just assumed I'm a dumb fish. Somebody's pet. As an extra precaution, Yakuza's guys used to put a fake shipping container over our tanks when they had to be gone for an extended period of time for two reasons. One, it made it hard for us to try anything with the computers since *we couldn't see,* but it also made it look like we were just over-sized cargo."

"That's terrible," I said, shaking my head. "Before we go, I'll pick up a shipping container. We just need someone to stay behind so that they can put it over your tank in case security starts nosing around or tries to force their way on board for an impromptu search."

"Well, I'm confident in my ability to keep the *Lizard King* on lockdown so that no one will be able to board her," she added. "Remember, this ship was heavily modified, so you don't have to worry about anyone breaking in here unannounced. But if they do, they'll just think I'm a delivery for someone's aquarium."

"Good to know," I said with relief. "Protecting my crew has to come first. Rubi, Bodega, you guys in on taking Braddock's job?"

"Tracking down the brothers? Void, yeah," said Rubi.

"Count me in, too," said the Oshwellian.

"Now, if we're going to go to Ethos to find Mav Rexlin, we're going to have to charter a flight—a private one, so we don't run into any DNA scanners—since Braddock says this corvette is grounded. I don't want to ask any of you to pay for it. This is just something I need to do. Anyone's free to come with me, but I'm prepared to make the trip alone."

Steinbreaker narrowed his eyes and glared. "You'd like

that, wouldn't you? Leaving me here, AGAIN WITH THAT DOG?!"

"Actually, I was planning on bringing her along, Hedgehog," I said. "Since it seems like that's what's best for everyone."

"On second thought, you know, I'd better stay here because there are a lot of maintenance subroutines I've been putting off, and—"

Rubi put her hands on her hips. I could tell she didn't like it but was coming around to my reasoning. "I understand how once we show Braddock the evidence, he may want to move quickly, and at that point, being Centurions might be our key to survival, and I do think we're better off on their task force. This path we're on is becoming too big for our little crew. Plus, I really liked Mercedes. Maybe, if we can talk to Mav Rexlin before the divide between us gets wider, somehow, we'll be able to patch things up."

"Well, Ethos is *amazing*," said Bodega. "You guys ever been there? You owe it to yourself to make that trip at least once in your life."

"I'm not staying here by myself," said Zihan. "This spaceport is a creepy place."

"T'Amira?" I asked. "What about you—would you rather come to Ethos with us or stay here?"

"I will stay and gain knowledge from the Quonella," the Senchkin replied.

"Okay," I said. "Don't worry, Aerial will make sure this ship is secure, so you should have nothing to worry about while we're gone, as long as you don't mind putting the shipping container over her tank in the event of an emergency. But she'll let you know."

"Do you like soaps?" the swimming mollusk asked

T'Amira. "I have twelve seasons of *General Spaceport* on holovid."

The Senchkin did not reply.

"That should be fun," I said under my breath.

"See, Hedgehog, you've been voted off the island," Celin-Ohmi said. "T'Amira and I are having a girl's night."

Our engineer stiffened and blinked, suddenly uncomfortable, and I knew exactly why.

Celin-Ohmi was kicking him out, so he'd be stuck with my dog.

CHAPTER TWENTY

"Honored guests, we're now approaching the village of Katafygio where the local time is 08:00 standard," the stewardess announced as our passenger shuttle entered its final approach toward the private spaceport on the planet of Ethos. "Please take your seats and make sure restraints are fastened. At this time, all quantum pads must be stowed away and hand luggage stored in your overhead locker or under the seat in front of you. Thank you."

"Don't you find it ironic how we can cover light years in the blink of an eye, and then sit for hours waiting for traffic control to give us clearance to land?" I muttered to Rubi, after slipping my quantum pad into my go-bag and stuffing it under the seat in front of me.

I'd been watching a holo vid on this planet.

"I know," she said with a yawn, pulling her seat beside me into its upright position and stretching after the announcement had wakened her from a nap. I'll admit I'd glanced over at her a few times while she was sleeping, in this case, because I was trying to get used to her disguise.

It was surreal to be next to someone you knew when

they looked so different that until you engaged them in conversation, you'd be convinced they were someone else.

"But there's a lot of things they have to consider like the volume of traffic and weather conditions," she pointed out.

"Traffic? Have you seen any ships since we left the wormhole and got in range of this planet?"

Rubi shrugged. "No, but I've been asleep for a while." Her curly pink wig was teased up in the back from being pressed into her pillow.

Not me. I'd been sitting here, drumming my fingers and trying to find ways to pass the time. I shook my head. "Well, you've got more patience than me. Though I could understand weather," I said, craning my neck to get a view of the surface from my window seat.

We'd just broken through the thick clouds, and that revealed high peaks of a mountain range penetrating layers of mist. "Okay, so there's a blanket of fog. Looks like that must be the reason."

"That and the fact that, as a small village, Katafygio didn't run a bustling operation. Apparently, they weren't concerned with becoming a hub of galactic tourism anytime soon, which seemed like a missed opportunity to me because of the natural beauty of Ethos.

It was renowned.

As we descended, the terrain that came into view was enthralling. Massive mountain peaks, the highest among them over eight thousand meters, towered over a picturesque valley carpeted in a lush bed of green dotted with charming square houses and coniferous forestry.

The Katafygio Valley had been shaped from its sedimentary layers over eons of time by glaciers up to two thousand meters high that carved out the breathtaking vertical cliffs of stone encasing it and terraces covered in fir trees, framed by the snow-capped peaks that now stood sentry and made the place so surreal.

Although Ethos was vested by the huge private military conglomerate that shared its namesake, the planet, at least where we were landing, didn't strike me as a corporate center and didn't have any manufacturing facilities on the scale of what it would take to construct Randall-Sundrum drives or laser batteries.

No, this seemed like a getaway from anything that remotely resembled either corporate trappings or industrial factories. It was more like peaceful retreat tucked away in the grandeur of a rugged wilderness.

After we landed, I collected my luggage and disembarked the small spaceport with Rubi, Bodega, Zihan, and Hedgehog. Maggie's tail beat the air, and she strained on her leash, eager to explore the new world.

Like most or all of the village's inhabitants, our tour guide was a Yemahtavan, a race with tanned yellow skin who streaked by in open-air transports hovering along the winding road, their cloaks of burlap and leather flapping carelessly in the wind behind them, almost human in their appearance except for their glowing eyes.

Our guide was so old that he approached us with the aid of a carved walking stick. "Greetings, I'm Sojihontra," he said with a knobby hand and signet ring over his heart in salutation. "You can all follow me."

He led us down the sidewalk out of the spaceport through a concrete archway into our first incredible view.

Beyond the village's chalets and fir trees, a rock face rose thousands of meters high. Local sunlight glinted off its rugged surface streaked blue and gray with mineral deposits from the waterfall cascading nearby. Ninety waterfalls like that sparkled from cliffs that encircled the town so high that their peaks got lost in the low-flying clouds.

"Wow," said Rubi. "I say we go hiking!"

"Would be a shame not to!" I said and glanced down at my feet.

I could tell my crew was ready for a break from the grinding pace we'd maintained without letting up since the Battle Mech Tournament. Most of that time, we'd been on the run from the *Hantakira*, and the crisp mountain air of this valley invoked the welcome relief of a world where Marekk-Thuul and his destroyer would never find us.

My German shepherd probed the air with her nose. A short walk from there behind Sojihontra led us into the chalet we were renting. Its bright interior had exposed rafters and timber elements from local forests.

"I'm looking for the man who made this," I said, pulling the hilt of the Reckoning from its cold fusion scabbard I'd hung on my belt enough that our guide could see the insignia inscribed in its metal.

"The Master Swordsmith," he said with a nod, rubbing the drooping skin on his neck. "He's on a personal retreat. Mount Rhema, due north of here."

"Do you know when he'll be back?" Rubi asked. "We've come a long way to see him."

"Maybe a couple days," said Sojihontra. "Sometimes he goes up there by himself to get away and shut off communication. The Luminance has a lot of responsibilities, you know. He owns several private military companies. There are many demands on his time."

"The Luminance?" asked Bodega.

"What you'd consider his alien race," Sojihontra said matter-of-factly.

"How high is Mount Rhema—is it something like one

of those cliffs?" I asked, squinting out our chalet's window at the base of one of the mammoth rock formations that would be impossible to scale without a shuttle in one day.

"Much less steep," Sojihontra said. "It's over four thousand meters in elevation, but we can only take you to the trail head by hover vehicle. Elevations above that aren't safe for hover vehicles because of the snowpack, so you could charter a ride, but once you got to the trail head, you'd have to make it the rest of the way by snowmobile."

"Uh, can't we rent any jetpacks or shuttles or some other way to get up the mountain?" I asked.

"There's nowhere to land a shuttle up there," the tour guide answered. "And jetpacks were banned here eighteen years ago when a gang of kids flying up and down the mountain triggered an avalanche that killed thirteen people. The steep slopes combined with all that heat and vibrations from jetpack exhaust can be a deadly mix for all of that snow if too many people use them at once. So the village decided to issue a ban. I'd recommend waiting, personally, because making that trek can be dangerous this time of year. The warmer temperatures make the snow unstable. You can get buried up there in a heartbeat."

"Well, we can't wait here for Mavgardon Rexlin, since we're under a deadline. We've only got a week to complete Braddock's job, so it looks like we'll do this the old-fashioned way," I said. "Snowmobile."

Then, I turned to my dog. "You're staying here."

At that, Steinbreaker unzipped Rubi's rucksack she'd dropped on the floor and pulled out her clothes, tossing them under a chair.

"Hey!" said Rubi. "What are you doing? That's my stuff, ronk!"

He climbed inside it and pulled both zippers snug to his

neck so only his head and voluminous ears stuck out from the rucksack's opening. "I'm ready!" he said. "When do we leave?"

Smirking, I turned to Rubi. "I'm not carrying that."

She rolled her eyes and said to Steinbreaker, "You could've asked, you little freeloader!"

He just gave her a sheepish grin, and I shook my head.

"If it's all the same, I think I'll stick around here," said Zihan.

I nodded, and our tour guide reluctantly led us to the shop in the village that outfitted travelers. We rented the gear, including snowmobiles, winter clothing, and crampons —spiked metal plates fixed to snow boots for gripping frozen surfaces. I made sure our vehicles had winches with cables and grappling hooks in case of emergencies.

On that note, the store owner also recommended a piece of equipment that was new to me—the avalanche airbag—a backpack with a rip cord that could be pulled to rapidly inflate a large airbag that could lift a person above the snow, decreasing their chances of getting buried and suffocating in the event of an avalanche. That seemed like a good safety measure. So, we each purchased one with our order.

Like Sojihontra suggested, we chartered a hover vehicle to take us up the incline around the base of the mountain until we reached the start of the snow line.

That got us as far as the trail head. We unloaded our snowmobiles from the back of its cargo ramp, one for me and a second that Bodega and Rubi mounted. Hedgehog was zippered tight in her rucksack.

No doubt that was his punishment.

Before we took off, I zipped up the parka I'd rented a little tighter and adjusted my gloves, because the temperature had dropped more than I'd realized, the more we'd climbed in elevation. We bid our driver farewell and gunned the motors of our snowmobiles, a little thrill I hadn't expected to experience in my travels through space.

The skids of our vehicles dug into the snowpack that had covered the trail, and we scooted around the mountain's perimeter on our way to visit the Luminance.

"I gotta stop and use the facilities," Bodega spoke up in my internal comm, breaking the trance-like state I'd entered in the gorgeous snow-swept environment. "Too much chagra back at the village."

"Roger that," I said with a snicker, shifting gears on my snowmobile until I brought it to a complete stop.

Glancing over my shoulder, I saw the kid climb off his machine and start trotting down the path to find a private spot to relieve himself. I breathed and my breath fogged instantly. Little ice crystals had formed in my nostrils, making me glad for the biomask, which actually lent my face some warmth.

A frightening roar caught me by surprise. By instinct, I grabbed the end of the winch on my snowmobile, holding the grappling hook for dear life. Fear seized me as the snowpack gave way. I dismounted my vehicle and started stumbling to my team members stranded behind me.

The whole world turned white, as the heavy impact of an avalanche cut off my visibility. Tumbling forward, end over end, I pulled the rip cord on my backpack, and a mechanical whine announced my airbag's deployment around my shoulders. It buoyed me to the crest of the avalanche.

I slid down the mountain, out of control, skidding on top of collapsing snow. Flying off a bluff, my legs kicked through empty space. But the steel cable I'd grabbed before it all started caught me and slammed me against the rock.

That hurt. I began to climb up the cable, using the superhuman strength programmed into me by my engineered nano-tech.

I reached the edge of the cliff. Sliding onto it, I gasped, out of breath from the shock of the situation. "Bodega! Rubi! Are you okay?" I said over the comm channel that we all shared. "Bodega! Rubi! Respond."

"I'm here," said Rubi, sounding strained, a bit dazed.

"Where are you?" I asked her.

"Trying to find Bodega. I don't think his airbag deployed."

"Scrat," I said, trying to raise him again on the comm.

A few minutes later, a shadow fell, and I heard the roar of engines as a puddle jumper came into view. A space-capable craft often used within atmosphere for its maneuverability, its boxy hull had black and yellow warning stripes under its side-entry hatches and four maneuvering thrusters that enabled it to hug the mountain while it dropped me a tow line.

I got my legs into the line's harness, and it pulled me up into the reaching arms of two crew members in flight suits who helped me into the craft. They yelled into my ear over the roar of the engines with the bay hatches still open something about whether I knew where the other two were. I shook my head and we kept searching.

We found Rubi first, mostly on top of a pile of snow, buoyed by her avalanche airbag. Bodega proved more difficult. When we finally recovered him, he was unresponsive but thankfully breathing and two medics went to work on him on the puddle jumper's deck. I sat beside him, watching and waiting and shivering, now soaked to the bone.

Ten minutes later, we made a landing that could only be executed by an expert pilot flying a craft with this nimble of handling.

It struck me how private Mav Rexlin must be that the tour guides of the village below didn't even know what assets he had or that there was a landing pad up here, although I realized, that wasn't surprising. It wasn't like rich CEO's to divulge that kind of thing to a tour guide. We were relying on his good graces, and that may have already saved Bodega's life. They carried him down metal steps in a stretcher, up a cobblestone path leading to a rustic lodge with heavy eaves and smoke pouring from its stone chimney.

Rubi and I exchanged a glance and followed the crew inside. The lodge's interior was warm and inviting, decked out in woodgrain and stone, and a whole retinue of personal assistants bustled about, one of them bringing us changes of clothes to get out of our freezing wet garments and others at work in the kitchen.

They led us each to a personal bedroom, although Bodega was still laid out on the stretcher, absorbing the warmth of the blazing fire under the hearth. I stripped down and toweled off with a towel from the stack of bed linens, then dressed myself in the corduroy pants, thermal shirt and socks they had provided.

All these little points of kindness had caught me off guard, as upon returning to the great room, I was handed a bowl of hot turkey stew. It came with a baguette that was fresh from the oven.

The personal assistants were all Yemahtavan. Their glowing eyes were mysterious and arresting.

CHAPTER TWENTY-ONE

I TOOK a seat by the fire and was joined by Rubi, wearing her pink wig again, having kept it dry in a pouch in her rucksack, and Steinbreaker in a fresh outfit like ours. We ate our soup, warming ourselves at the hearth and watched our unconscious crew member, alarmed.

It was colder than we'd realized out there, and the three of us had only narrowly missed getting frostbite because of being bundled up from head to toe in the winter gear we'd rented in town. But when the puddle jumper had airlifted Bodega, he'd been stripped out of his snowsuit before falling asleep. We all agreed that was strange.

"Why do you think he'd do that?" I asked our group seated on the floor and the medical technician busy checking his wounds. "Take off his snowsuit before he was rescued?"

"Cerebral edema," said Rubi.

Sometimes, I forgot she'd been a doctor.

"It's a severe form of altitude sickness that causes swelling in the brain. It's scary for a number of reasons, one of them being that it can lead people to do irrational things, like take off their clothes in sub-zero temperatures and can also lead to a drunk-looking gait, hallucinations and, eventually, death."

"Scrat," I whispered.

The blue skin of his cheeks seemed darker than normal and leathery. Bodega stirred. His yellow eyes opened.

"Do you know where you are?" Rubi asked him.

"No," said Bodega.

"Can you tell me your name? We're among friends here, so you don't have to use your call sign," she clarified.

"Actually, none of us do," I said. "That might help with his confusion."

"My name's Bondranamir."

"Good," she said, and we all exhaled with relief.

"Where is this boat going?" he asked, sitting up on the cot. Bond sprung to his feet.

"This boat?" said Steinbreaker. "You're not right in the head!"

"He's hallucinating," Tess breathed, and I stood up to stop him, because he tried to bolt across the room but was unstable and crashed into a chair.

"Whoa, buddy, let's get you laying back down," I said.

One of the assistants brought him some turkey soup and bread. Listlessly staring into the distance, he lowered himself down to the cot and accepted the meal. "Here, drink some water," she said.

Bond took a shaky sip.

"As he gets some water and calories in his system, we need to get him into the AutoDoc immediately to prevent any amputations," said the technician.

"Amputations?" I asked.

"From the frostbite," said Tess with gravity written in her expression.

I rubbed my neck and watched him finish the soup. A Yemahtavan assistant took him by each arm and helped him to the back room that was outfitted with state of the art medical equipment, a fortunate privilege of the super-rich. It underscored just how dangerous crossing these mountains had been.

"That's why the tour guide had tried to warn us," I said, running a hand through my hair. "I hope he's going to be okay."

Tess nodded. "It looks like these people are well equipped and prepared for emergency cases," she said. "They sprung into action right away."

"I'm guessing it's going to take time," I said. "Who do you guys work for, anyway?"

"Mavgardon Rexlin, who else?" said one of them.

"Just making sure," I said.

"These changing temperatures are making my biomask itch," Tess said. "Since our visitors aren't here and these people work for *him*, do you think we could remove them?"

"Yeah, good idea," I said.

So, we did, and our skin could finally breathe. It felt right to be back to our natural selves.

"Can anyone tell me where he is—the CEO? We came all this way to talk to Mr. Rexlin if he's able to see us," I said.

"Check the forge," said one of his assistants.

Assuming I'd find the forge on this compound, I nodded to Tess. "You coming?"

"Why don't you try to talk to him, and I'll stay here with Bond to see how he is progressing?"

"How about you, Steinbreaker?"

"I'm good," said the engineer. He was sprawled out on

the floor on his back, his fingers laced behind his head, his feet being warmed by the fire.

"Good enough," I said and returned to the bedroom I'd been assigned in the mountain lodge to retrieve my plasma sword called the Reckoning.

The least I could do is thank him for it, and it certainly couldn't hurt our rapport for him to know that Hidalgo had given to me before his death.

Walking outside, I found a trio of industrial buildings. Above the entrance of the one in the middle was a sand-blasted sign that bore the same insignia as that on my sword.

"That looks right," I figured and took the liberty of cracking open the door when I reached it, hoping I wouldn't be disturbing anything. So far, no one had tried to stop me, and time would tell how far *that* strategy lasted.

The worst thing he could tell me was, "No." Okay, that wasn't the worst thing, but I didn't expect him to use any violence.

Then again, to be honest, I really didn't what to expect. Mav Rexlin had been a mystery, like the stuff of urban legend, but I wasn't going to stand in my own way. Something was going on inside of there.

Something loud, involving brute force.

Inside, I found a large man striking a piece of metal with a hammer on a well-beaten anvil. I could tell that his workpiece had just been withdrawn from the fire, because it was so hot that it glowed under the heavy blows of the swordsmith. He drew a well-muscled forearm across his brow to wipe away sweat.

To say that he was intimidating would be an understate-ment. Mavgardon Rexlin, who I assumed was standing before me, was built like a champion bodybuilder, but dressed like a poor peasant, with a jaw so square, illuminated by the flames of his forge, that he made Jocko Willink look like a schoolboy.

Although, there was a resemblance.

"Excuse me, I'm looking for the man who made this sword," I said, presenting the Reckoning in what I hoped would be a respectful gesture.

He set the hammer down in acknowledgement, but his gaze remained down at my knees.

"I take it you're Mavgardon Rexlin."

"You can call me Mav," he said, examining a workpiece of iron.

"I won't beat around the bush," I said. "I know you own private military companies, including Ethos who partners with the CMC to run Task Force Cyberblade. I'm here because I was told you select their candidates, so I'd like to submit myself for consideration on the basis of my service record and years of experience in the United States Marine Corps of the twenty-first century."

Mav squinted at me and pursed his lips. "I have a project."

He disappeared down an aisle of industrial shelving and returned with something I hadn't seen for months— the body of an acoustic guitar in a state of disrepair. The neck, back, and sides were intact, but its top was badly damaged.

"How did you know I was a luthier?" I asked, grinning, invoking the technical term we used in the industry for expert guitar makers, as he handed the instrument to me.

"I have Earth's entire internet on file as part of the annals of history my father constructed, *The Chronicles of Lower Worlds*," he said. "Including your service record."

"So you know everything about me already," I said.

"Would you like to test that theory?" he asked with a raise of his eyebrows.

"Not really. Look, as much as I love working on guitars —I've missed doing that a lot since arriving in the CMC—I can see right now that this thing's going to need some work that would take me a couple days. We need to get back to Vedana, because I'm already contracted with Emin Braddock, our contact in the League of Desai that your operator Mercedes assigned me to, so we can do our first job. He's threatened to kill me if I don't get results for him within one week. I'm just here because I was hoping to schedule the necessary examinations and training programs when I'm done with that to join your special forces unit."

I handed him back the guitar and watched him set it aside.

He was either using it as a way to break the news that he'd never select me, or maybe like some kind of hazing or version of scrat duty because of my interpersonal conflicts with members of his staff.

His next sentence provided some clarity.

"You had friction with Oxhorn. You had friction with Mercedes. And now you're here because you want the privileges that come with being a Centurion without embracing our values. How am I doing?" he said with a squint, finally returning my eye contact.

My shoulders slumped. "So am I disqualified? I'm willing to learn. You need me to shovel scrat for your workers or what? You name it."

He just picked up the hammer again and went back to work.

I shrugged, extending my hands and had to walk up right next to his hulking frame and shout to be heard. "I'm just trying to understand the process. How does everyone *else* get in? We had special forces units where I came from. For example, in the Marines, we had the Fleet Anti-Terrorism Security Team, or FAST, warriors trained with state of the art weapons for rapid deployment when government installations needed additional security worldwide."

He mercifully paused and put down the hammer.

I continued. "We also had ANGLICO. The only fire-power control team in the Department of Defense that operated full-time, fully equipped to coordinate fire support from air, on land, or at sea. We didn't operate in space in the twenty-first century, as you know. We had the MARSOC Raiders, part of Special Operations Command. They did special reconnaissance, internal defense in foreign environments, counter-terrorism, information ops, and unconventional warfare. Those guys were highly trained to operate in fast-paced, remote, and complex environments."

"You forget that I have your whole internet on file," he said.

"Please," I said. "I'm going somewhere with this. There were special forces units in the other branches of my country's military, too, like the Green Berets or Navy Seals, to name a few. And there were private military outfits. Every one of these units was trained to perform certain duties but each of them had a *definable path* to joining their unit. Sure, they had lots of hoops to jump through. I get that. The public had no idea about everything that went into it. But there was a path. So, what do I need to do to be part of Task Force Cyberblade in the rank you call a Centurion? I can't seem to get any information."

"Information is not what you lack," he said.

"Well, are you looking for someone who's already served in your Navy or Marines? Do I have to pass a physical fitness test with a score of 235 and a GT with a score of 105? Maybe you do something like the AS&S Phase 1 and 2 to test for physical and mental stamina? Help me out here— what are my steps?"

"You've already proved yourself in such areas. I've reviewed your physical and tactical exploits and seen how you perform under pressure, first on Earth in the USMC, then in the Battle Mech Tournament and as a fugitive recovery agent here in the CMC," he said, then looked down and actually chuckled. "But because you lack patience and tact, you came to my personal residence unannounced and almost got yourself killed on my mountain. Now, your friend Bond has severe frostbite and cerebral edema. He's going to need a few days to recover in my AutoDoc."

I winced. "A few days?"

If we lost that much time, we'd be under even more pressure to locate Braddock's brothers when we got back.

He turned up his chin. "I thought you American service members left no one behind. I'm giving you something to do in the meantime."

"I can't leave Bond behind—I need him for this job on Vedana," I said. "Plus, you're right. That's not who we are. I got him into this situation, and it wouldn't be right to leave him here." I drew in a deep breath. "So, you're asking me to fix this guitar for you while Bond's in there getting better."

"No," he said with his hands on his hips. "I'm asking you teach Tess and Steinbreaker how to fix it with you as a team."

My eyes went wide. That sounded horrible. "Do you ever want to play it again? I mean the guitar."

He shrugged and looked annoyed. "Do you?"

I groaned. "If I do this, Mav, can you promise we can start training after that to become a Centurion?"

"What makes you think that we haven't already?"

I opened my mouth, but before I could protest, he placed the guitar in my hands. "There's a workshop next door with every tool and species of wood that you'll need," he said.

"Well, considering we almost died on our way here if your puddle jumper hadn't airlifted us, and now I finally have your attention, I'd rather not risk this trip again and maybe not even catch you," I said, trying to warm up to the idea.

"I'd rather that, as well," he said. "Now, move. You're burning daylight."

I shook my head and got out of there before he could see my scowl. "What kind of Mr. Miyagi scrat is this?" I mumbled. "They don't know how to fix a guitar."

Apparently Mav wanted to observe my leadership skills or something. What that had to do with instrument repair was anyone's guess, but we were *stuck here* until Bond recovered, so I had to make the best of it.

CHAPTER TWENTY-TWO

THE PRESSURE WAS on to impress Mav Rexlin, and the clock was ticking.

While Bond recovered inside, we were stuck here, after Mav had been forced to send his people to rescue us from frostbite and death on the side of his mountain and I'd burned my bridges with his operators then asked if he'd pick me to be on their task force.

Basically, everything was going great.

If fixing his guitar would somehow help ease the tension between us, I was happy to oblige. He gave us free reign of the two other buildings on either side of his forge, both of which were impressive workshops with a variety of tools and materials, including an impressive array of hardwoods.

It turned out that Mav liked to build things, and his property was well-stocked with what we'd need. Now, it was time to teach Tess and Steinbreaker how to repair a guitar.

I paced through the thin film of sawdust on the floor where I'd gathered them to figure out who would do what.

There weren't *any* parts of this project I was excited about delegating, because due to their lack of experience in ever doing anything like this, it wasn't a stretch to assume I'd do it all better by myself than a surgeon from Portland or an alien from the twenty-ninth century. But, Mav had made it clear that he was expecting me to treat this like a team-building exercise.

So, here we were. Whoop-de-doo.

Tess was hanging on my every word, bright eyed with her brown hair pulled back and the sleeves rolled up on her thermal.

"Each member of our crew has strengths," I said. "Let's play to those as much as possible. Steinbreaker, I'm not expecting you, at your size, to clamp things or work with a saw, but you do have excellent hearing, right?"

He crossed his arms. "Don't forget about my engineering skills."

"Right. I think I have a perfect job—and Tess, I'm guessing as a surgeon that you'd have really precise fine motor control and be used to time-consuming, meticulous tasks."

"I'd better be. If not, I wouldn't get many patients," she said with a laugh.

I smiled. It was cute how enthusiastic she was to help out with this project. I couldn't tell if that was because of how she'd always been interested in the work I'd done before leaving Earth—or if she was just eager to contribute in any way possible to rebuild our rapport with Mav.

She *had* brought up several times since arriving how she was hoping to become a Centurion. If she'd felt that way for long, she hadn't told me about it before now, but I think that working with Oxhorn and Mercedes and even just being aboard *Excalibur* had left a mark on us all.

"How would you like to make the rosette?" I asked. "Come here, I'll show you. The rosette on a guitar is a decorative ring set into the top around the sound hole. It can be made with a number of materials—mother of pearl, plastic, or wood."

"Ooh, let's do mother of pearl," she said.

"A personal favorite of mine, as well. Only thing is that we don't have any in Mav Rexlin's workshop. I checked. We don't want to go all the way into town just for that, you know what I mean?"

"Wait," she said. "Doesn't pearl just come from inside of an oyster?"

"Yeah, when it gets an irritant or a parasite in its shell, it secretes a fluid to protect itself. That fluid builds up in layers that form the outer shell of a pearl."

"Couldn't I ask at the lodge if they have any oysters in the kitchen and just use them?" she asked.

"I don't know. Even if they do, that's going to be a lot of work. You'd have to clean them, cut them down and sand them into little pieces for this project."

"That's okay!" she said. "I'll do that while you're working on the other things. Don't worry, if I get started and it doesn't work, or they don't have any seafood in there, or I can't get them cleaned properly, I'll just use wood, instead."

"Okay," I said reluctantly.

It made me uneasy because there was so much work to do in the time we had left. So, I wouldn't be able to check back with her all the time to see how it was going. "I'm trusting you to let me know if you run into any problems," I said.

"Gage, I can handle it," she said. "Relax."

"Okay."

After leaving her with the measurements to start the rosette, I hurried into the other workshop to start on wood for the top. Working alone on something like this was the only way to preserve my sanity. If I tried to work with the two of them, it would be a constant distraction. I'd be constantly trying to hover over them and correct what was being done wrong. It's like Mav was trying to make my life difficult and then acting like I was the one who needed to change.

We needed to finish this in record time, so that just in case Bond recovered faster, we would all be ready to leave.

They didn't have my top pick of Italian Spruce on an alien planet. No surprise there.

But the Katafygio Valley was a mountainous region where the trees had to thrive in a harsh climate and cold conditions, so they did have coniferous evergreens that would yield a similar wood. He also assured me that the boards he'd pointed out on the shelves had been air dried for over nine years, since Mav was a master carpenter.

Wood like this was planted on the north side of their slopes so that indirect sunlight and good drainage produced dense, slow growing trees well suited for musical instruments based on what I said I was looking for: something dense that rung like a bell but also remained stiff against the torque produced by the tightly-wound strings.

After cutting, I glued the halves of the top together, holding up the joint to the window. This seam between pieces had to be so tight that no light could escape through it. Perfect.

Mav had glue that dried faster than anything I had back on Earth, so later that day, I glued and clamped the top to the base and because of our compressed time frame, had to glue on Tess' rosette that same evening while the other parts were still drying.

"I thought you were going to use mother of pearl," I

said, noticing that she'd made the ring out of wood, instead.

"Oh, well I changed my mind," she said. "You don't like it?"

"No, I think it looks good. Everything seems to be moving along, so we should be ready for Steinbreaker's contribution to the project in the morning," I said.

I wish I could've just basked in that moment before everything turned to scrat.

"That's right, thump the top gently with this rubber tool," I said to Steinbreaker. He looked kind of like a kid in high school marching band on the bass drum who was having trouble staying in sync with the other musicians. He just had that look.

But he had a very keen mind, so I had to be patient. "This microphone will pick up and map those vibrations in a frequency response curve on the screen of this quantum pad," I explained. "That will give you a visual map of the sound for this guitar, but you're also going to be testing the thickness of the wood all over the top with this magnetic gauge. Does all this make sense?"

"I'm following," he said. "If a region of the top doesn't sound uniform or the way it's supposed to, then what do I do?"

"You take this planer tool and gently shave off a *very* thin layer of wood in that area, and then you test it again," I said. "Just work on that until I get back."

I ran back to my building to finish working on some other elements. The clock was ticking. When I returned, Steinbreaker announced that he was done.

I tapped the top and it made an obnoxious thump in reply. "That's not the tone we're looking for," I said, my face screwing up.

I tapped it again, and when I did, Tess' rosette sprang loose from the wood, but the adhesives here were so strong, that the separation formed a hairline crack through the top of the instrument.

My stomach dropped. "Tess! Can you come over here, please?"

She ran over from the other side of the workshop. "What? Oh! Why did it come loose and crack like that?"

"Did this wood you used for the rosette come from Mav's woods that have been properly dried?" I ground out, trying to remain sympathetic.

"No," she said, "I just put a piece of the firewood through the saw because I liked the way it looked."

"Any wood you use on a guitar has to be dried for long enough to reach the moisture level of the surrounding environment. Otherwise, if there's a sudden change in humidity, it can contract and pull away from the instrument or even crack."

"Don't get mad at me!" she said. "How was I supposed to know?"

Fearing I'd lose it if I kept talking, I stormed off into my private workshop and started one from scratch.

Mav Rexlin stood in front of Tess and I in his private forge, surrounded by blades of every size and shape and the sooty tools of the trade.

I was trying to make my case. It wasn't going that well.

"We ran into a few problems on the first model, so I tried to start one from scratch and stayed up all night to finish it but didn't get to, well, because of the truncated timeline," I said.

"Which guitar's farther along?" asked Mav. "Just show me that one."

Tess presented the original that we'd worked on together. The top had splintered because of her rosette debacle, and it was imbued with a strange tone because of Steinbreaker's ignorance of the style of music that a guitar was made for, which predated him by hundreds of years.

"What happened?" asked Mav.

"That's my fault," Tess quickly interjected. "I got some oysters from your people in the kitchen, but they smelled, so I had to clean them out really thoroughly, and the cleaner I used must've been too acidic, because it stripped away the color from the mother of pearl."

"Why didn't you tell me that?" I asked. "I could've helped you pick out a piece of wood to use instead?"

"I was afraid you'd be mad," she admitted. "So I tried to take care of it without getting you involved. When I got a piece from the firewood, I didn't realize it had to be dried for a certain amount of time before it was safe to use."

"Well, you made a valiant effort," Mav said with a grin. "What did you learn about yourselves in the process?"

We both fell quiet.

"Okay, I'll share a few thoughts of my own," he said. "As

a Centurion, if you're not transparent and direct with the members of your team about challenges you face on a mission, it can put people at risk."

Tess looked down, her cheeks turning red.

"Others don't communicate enough with their team to empower them for success—and when that inevitably doesn't go well—they dive in and try to make up the difference, because it's hard for them to give up control," he said, shooting me a hard stare. "These aren't easy lessons, but until you learn them, I can't use either of you in my program."

Why did those words feel like a gut punch?

Mav tossed me a crude-looking rod from his smithing materials.

I caught it.

"That may look rough, but someday, it'll make a nice blade," he said.

"Like the plasma sword I got from Hidalgo?"

"No. Plasma swords involve a much more intensive process, because they require the metal Evridian. The one in your hand is high-carbon steel. After it's purified, I will heat and shape it with a U-shaped channel for a strip of low-carbon steel that also must be heated and hammered to fit into that channel. The material on the outside is prized for its sharpness. The low-carbon core is prized for its strength. Two metals will be forged into one. But those are advanced steps in the process. First, I must fold it and hammer it dozens of times at extreme temperatures."

He lifted an intricate sheath from its display and drew the sword from inside it. The blade was a study in elegance and lethality, honed and polished to a mirror finish.

"Turning a crude instrument into a work of art takes

months of practice," he said. "Only time under the fire and hammer can purify steel."

"So, where am I in the sword-making journey?" I asked him.

"That unrefined piece that you're holding right now? That's you." He flashed the mirror-finish blade through the air with blinding speed. "*This* is what you'll become," he said, "if you commit to the process."

"What process?" I asked, exasperated. "That's what I mean."

The master swordsmith returned the showpiece to its display case. "Show me the hilt of the Reckoning," he said.

When I did, he pointed out the insignia of the Luminance carved into its grip—three intersecting rings superimposed on a leaf with three fronds. "These rings represent the Eternal Paths—Dedication, Solidarity and Defiance." He traced the first one with his finger. "You have plenty of Dedication. That's what got you this far in your journey to rescue your son." He traced the second ring. "This is where you are now—the second path."

"Solidarity?" I asked.

He nodded. "It's the unity that comes not by controlling others, but by gathering around a cause that's fueled by your common ideals, a cause that each individual believes in so strongly that each would be willing to die for it."

"So, you're saying I need to master that next."

"No," he said. "It needs to master you. That is hindering you from learning the Third Path. Until all three become who you are, you're not ready to become a Centurion."

I released a breath. This was not what I expected to hear. *Just give me some external metrics, man!* That's what I really wanted to say.

But when I thought about how I'd worked with—or

hadn't worked with—both Oxhorn and Mercedes in his organization, maybe he had a point. "I don't have a problem working with people," I said, "as long as I can be in control."

Mav just stared at me in a silent bid of encouragement to think about my own words.

"What's next?" Tess asked, finally breaking through the tense silence.

"I'll be watching how you both lead yourselves and work with the people around you."

"Okay," I said, not sure how I felt about being *watched*. Maybe that explained the spherical drones I occasionally caught on the edge of my vision when I was planetside or buying supplies at a space station. "Here I thought Marekk-Thuul from *Hantakira* was the only one who was watching us. Maybe, we should be flattered."

Tess elbowed me in irritation. "He's trying to *help*, Gage. We both have things to work on, here."

I exhaled. "I'll give it some thought."

"I'll send the written materials you need to complete to become candidates for the Centurion program," Mav said. "You can fill them out, and I'll keep you two in consideration, but I'm sorry. Right now, neither one of you is ready."

He slid the Reckoning back into its scabbard and gave it to me. "Bond has made a full recovery. I'm sending my personal contact information to your quantum pad. Don't make me regret that decision."

With that, the meeting was over, and Mav brushed past me, leaving me to wonder if this excursion had been a good move—because now we'd have to return to Vedana to complete the job I'd promised Braddock in three days less time than we had before—with no more resources than when we landed.

CHAPTER TWENTY-THREE

TESS AND I WERE INCOGNITO. We'd activated our biomasks and resumed our false identities as Stryker, Rubi, and Bodega—who'd made a full recovery from his frostbite —before leaving the mountaintop with our snowmobiles in the puddle jumper.

By the time we met Zihan at the chalet, our transformation was complete, down to our way of talking and backstories. Soon, we were boarding the shuttle, on our way to Vedana but had to stop at a spaceport to catch a connecting flight.

That seemed innocent enough.

Nothing seemed out of place.

This kind of thing wasn't uncommon with private outfits like the one we'd chartered—mainly due to their limited fleets. The company transferred the luggage, but the passengers had to drag their sorry hides through the spaceport to board the new craft. They were constantly shuffling flights in order to book as many trips as possible.

So, Bodega, Rubi and I were on our way through the concourse to our connecting gate, Steinbreaker in Bodega's backpack, since we were taking turns, when I caught the first sign of danger.

The first sign that something was off.

My companions had only mildly complained when I'd insisted we change into our armor in the spaceport restrooms. But I wasn't one for taking chances. There were too many variables at work.

And I don't like too many variables.

"What's taking her so long?" I asked offhandedly to Bodega.

Rubi was still in the bathroom, changing, and her comm link was muted.

"I don't know, but we have a suspicious character at the flower shop on your six," he responded. His voice had gone taut.

"Just caught something in the picture-in-picture from my helmet's rear-mounted camera," I said, just above a whisper. We powered on our N-50 carbines in unison, their capacitors warming up in high-pitched hums.

The something I'd seen was a young man in a black leather jacket and drab cargo pants. It was the Japanese characters that caught my attention under his ear when I zoomed in and snapped a photo.

Not everyone with a tattoo in Japanese was suspicious, but not everyone chose symbols for their ink job from a particular musical act. It was easy to pass off the songs of *Midori No Shi* as self-expression. When anyone accused them of inciting violence, they could always just say it was art.

Well, I supported freedom of expression just as much as the next guy, but this group was financed by Yakuza and made that clear in their lyrics.

Fanboy was talking with a woman at the ticket counter,

probably claiming to be with our party, when she leaned forward and searched the stream of pedestrians before pointing our way.

Fanboy looked directly at us, thanked her, and left, receding into a cafe tucked in from the main hall. Suddenly, the crack of blaster fire erupted from the gangway above us.

Either the first two persons of interest were a diversion, or maybe they were setting up an elaborate trap. Bond and I turned on the source of the assault, finding a gunman on either side of us, shooting down on the crowd from the railing.

Returning fire, we lit up their positions, in a panic to stop the indiscriminate lines of plasma from tearing through innocent people who'd started screaming and rushing for cover, but some of the bystanders' body parts were scorched by heat damage caused by coherent packets of plasma fired at velocities faster than sound.

It was a madhouse.

A staccato burst from my muzzle sent the gunman fleeing before I even got close, since he didn't have any good cover, and I assumed Bond's had done the same.

Someone, probably the guy he'd spotted at the flower shop, was calmly walking our way in the concourse with his head and torso hidden behind a massive arrangement of roses. He wasn't fleeing with everyone else, just methodically striding our direction, but we couldn't engage him since he hadn't revealed any weapon. I hated situations like this.

By his behavior, it was so obvious that he was a threat. I fired the tow line from my armored vambrace and lassoed his ankle, then gave it a jerk to the right. He wiped out in a mess of rose petals, and when I saw his face, I knew. It wasn't a man—it was a robot and hidden inside the bouquet was a bomb. It looked like a standard time-delay fragmentation anti-personnel hand grenade.

"Get down!" I screamed, hoping people would hear me above the racket of mass hysteria. My helmet's external speakers amplified it, so that helped.

Bond and I hit the deck, along with ten or twenty percent of the people around us just before detonation. The explosion disintegrated the casing and expelled nasty fragments into the flesh of those walking in the vicinity. Dozens of metal fragments blew into the bodies of those unfortunate enough to be within range.

Yakuza must've gotten to security, because they were noticeably absent.

It was like no one knew what to do.

"Looks like they've taken over the whole port," I said, giving Bond a whack beside me to make sure he was okay. We were lying in the prone position with our carbines ready to fire. "You good?"

"I'm good," said Bond.

"How about you, Hedgehog?"

"Well, I'm going to need to change my coveralls, but other than that, just peachy," he said, wild-eyed, hanging from Bond's backpack.

"Get him moved under your chest," I said. "He's liable to get picked off back there."

"Roger that," said Bond, and he did, orienting the backpack to protect our engineer.

"Rubi, do you copy? Report," I said.

My answer came. Not how I wanted. The door to the women's room burst open less than a minute later. Out strode an armored bounty hunter with Tess pinned to his chest in a headlock.

She was in her tarnished battle suit but was missing her helmet.

"Drop your weapons," he barked at us through the vocal modulator in his front grill. His tan armor had a coat of arms emblazoned on one corner of the chestplate, and his gun was pressed into her temple.

"Don't listen to him!" she growled then flipped him over her shoulder, splaying him out on his back.

He must've been stunned by her countermove, because he didn't resist her fast enough for Tess to steal his firearm and shoot him, point blank, in the thigh.

Gunmen reemerged on the gangway, but Bodega and I delivered suppressive fire to keep them pinned down. "I'm calling Braddock," I said, "because we don't have any good options."

Surprisingly, the kingpin picked up right away. "You have any news for me on the search?" he said, sounding upbeat.

"Not yet," I said. "Right now, I'm getting shot at by Yakuza at a private spaceport. I'm calling as a last resort. Could you please send us a pickup? Otherwise, my team may not make it to finish your job. Neither of us want that, do we?"

There was a stifling pause, making me wonder if I'd come across as too commandeering. *Well, I'm getting shot at, so maybe he can find it in his heart to forgive.* "Braddock! Do you copy?"

"Don't bother me again with your problems," he said.

The bounty hunter under Tess was talking. She'd straddled him in the ground-and-pound position, having achieved what we called a low mount. She wrenched off his helmet and punched him with a heavy right and left hook.

The coat of arms on his chestplate was bothering me

because I knew it could yield a clue about his identity. Something about it looked familiar. But I couldn't put my finger on it. It wasn't like the Japanese tattoos I'd seen on street thugs in Yakuza gangs on bounty hunter runs. This was a European design from centuries past. That's what made it stand out.

Then it hit me.

The crest on his chestplate matched one I'd seen on a guard standing beside Marekk-Thuul when the captain had addressed me on screen from the bridge of his destroyer. So that confirmed it.

Hantakira was here.

Somehow they'd tracked us, which was disturbing because we hadn't been in our ship, so it couldn't have been our transponder.

"Frederick, call Mavgardon Rexlin," I said. "Ask for an emergency evac. Tell him there's an Ekibyo-class destroyer at our location killing civilians."

"Right away, sir," said my AI.

Fanboy tried to launch a sneak attack from the cafe with a crew-served rotary blaster, taking pot shots at Bond and me. My jaw clenched. His plasma riddled my armor.

I rolled. That weapon was too dangerous. Two taps of my trigger lit up the triggerman, and he pitched forward, dead on arrival.

Tess was engaged in a screaming match with the man she had pinned to the ground. The head under her bludgeoning fists lolled my way and made me recoil behind my weapon—because I *recognized* that face—but it didn't seem right because he was in the wrong place at the wrong time. But I didn't get time to process it.

Thrown from above, an anti-personnel grenade bounced across the floor meters away from Rubi.

"Rubi!" I screamed.

Scrambling forward, I dove for the bomb in order to shield her from its detonation.

I winced. The explosion pelted my chestplate and pauldrons with shrapnel, blowing me back. Metal fragments shot into the bodies of anyone still languishing on the floor.

Blood spattered. Sounds of agony echoed around me in the ear-ringing aftermath and confusion. I rolled over.

Smoke filled the air, and metal crunched under my battle suit. Thankfully, it had done its job. I didn't feel any major injuries beyond the shock of being that close to an explosion. "Bodega, call emergency services," I said with a grimace. "Don't stop calling until you get through."

"I'm on it, boss," he replied, grateful for an actionable task to staunch some measure of the suffering around us, young as he was and inexperienced with making decisions in the horrors of war.

I limped to my feet and hoisted up Rubi. She'd been knocked out cold and had rivulets of blood running down the side of her head, but my torso had protected her face from the shrapnel. My mind caught up to the chaos enough to process the identity of the bounty hunter that she'd been assaulting, as I heaved her over my shoulder.

It was Devon Fenstermacher-Dole, that pretentious wuss from Vancouver Island who I'd beaten up to take the last spot at Magnum on the day that Hidalgo had hired me.

What in the void? He joined Yakuza?

I fired at the remaining gangsters still shooting at us from behind cover. Bond and I backed out of the battle space into a maintenance corridor.

"What's next?" Bond panted.

I held up a finger, because my AI had started speaking. "Mavgardon Rexlin has sent me instructions," Frederick said. "There's a locked closet twenty meters ahead of you on the right. Break into it."

We did and found a hatch for waste disposal.

"So, it's the dirty way out," I said.

"I'm afraid so, sir," said Frederick.

I creaked open the rusty lid, then bear-hugged Rubi's limp body against my stomach and gingerly climbed into the tube that was slick with putrid organic waste. Bond followed me, and my heart dropped into my stomach for the slippery fall through the chute into a soup of nastiness that I didn't really want to dwell on. We kicked and swam to the edge of the vat and hoisted ourselves up over the side into the sand of the terra firma.

"Let's never do that again," said Bond.

"Just be thankful for your air scrubbers. Look at poor Rubi. She's got scrat on her face. Let's not tell her when she wakes up."

We let out a cackle, until Bond was interrupted by the zipper opening up on his backpack.

A trembling Steinbreaker slowly emerged, his one eyelid twitching. His mouth moved but didn't form words. "I should've stayed with that dog," he admitted.

That got me laughing even harder. "Steinbreaker had a near-death experience, and now he's wrestling with his life choices!" I slapped Bodega on the shoulder and we shared a moment there, shaking our heads at the ludicrous nature of the situation.

Sometimes, all you can do is laugh.

The hum of engines descended from an unassuming personal transport touching down in the sand. It wasn't military—this craft was tiny.

Its portside gull wing hatch swung open and the pilot waved from the cockpit then shot a thumb towards the stern in an invitation to enter. A second hatch slid open behind him. Carrying Tess, I strode to the craft and climbed inside. Bodega and Hedgehog were right behind me.

The passenger seats were in the same compartment essentially as the cockpit because of the compact size. The pilot was clad in gunmetal armor, and when he turned to give us a nod, I was surprised, because the man in the pilot's chair was Mavgardon Rexlin.

"Sir, I'm sorry, I didn't want to bother you personally. But I figured since we might have been tracked by Yakuza from your personal residence, you'd want to know right away."

"That's exactly right," Mav said. "For that very reason, it's best for me to be involved directly and keep this situation between us. If there's a security breach at my home, I need to know that right away, both for personal reasons, and for the threat that would pose to the balance of power in the galaxy. I need every one of you to give me your word that everything we discuss pertaining to today's events in that spaceport will be considered highly classified and held in the strictest confidence. Do I have your word?"

Bond and I both agreed.

"Is Tess still unconscious?" Mav asked.

"Yes," I said, "but she's breathing and her vitals look good."

"In that case, we'll wait to begin until she wakes up," said Mav.

"Sorry about the upholstery," I said, disgusted by my own appearance.

"It's okay," Mav said. "It's about time to scrap this thing, anyway."

"I only wish we could've seen what your forces did to *Hantakira*," Bond said. "I can't believe I missed that!"

"There wasn't much to see," Mav said, as he flipped switches and tapped commands into his controls. "Ethos came with the superior destroyer, and *Hantakira* jumped to another system as soon as their scanners spotted us. They know when they're outmatched."

"And I'm sure that's not the last we'll see of them," I said with a shake of my head, watching the starboard viewport as our ship lifted off. "But what really bothers me is how they found us, because it's like they're one step ahead."

"It's a really good question," Bond agreed. "We weren't in the *Gambit*—we were between connecting flights run by a private enterprise. How would they know we'd be there?"

"I don't know," I said, at a loss. "But we need to find out."

"I'll have to ask you some questions to narrow down the possibilities," Mav said methodically. All of this was routine for him as CEO of Ethos.

I could tell.

CHAPTER TWENTY-FOUR

RUBI STIRRED BESIDE ME. I examined her face. Her eyes were still closed, but she was breathing. I tapped her shoulder. "Hey, are you with us?"

After a slow moan, her lips smacked together and her pretty eyelids flicked open. "Where are we?" she croaked. Her voice was raspy, and she cleared her throat. "What is this on my face?"

"I don't know what that is," said Bond. "Maybe, *taste* it?"

"Stop," I said, holding her arm down. "Our escape route involved a waste disposal tube, so use your imagination."

"A—what?!" she snapped with a sour expression.

"Hey, we're alive, ain't we?" said Steinbreaker, swinging in the backpack now anchored to a bulkhead since he was too small for the seat restraints.

He was eating an apple.

"Where did you get that?" I asked him.

"This?" he said, nodding to the apple. "Found it outside of that waste—"

"Stop talking," Tess said, waving him off. "We really don't want to know."

"Mav Rexlin came for us personally, because Yakuza might've tracked us from his mountain lodge so he needs to ask us some questions, but I have one of my own. What were you saying to Devon?" I tested. "It seemed like you two were having a pretty lively conversation."

"Who's Devon?" asked Bond.

Her jaw jutted forward, and Tess looked down. "I'm not ready to talk about him."

"Did you know he was working for Yakuza?" I pressed, narrowing my eyes. She wasn't going to wriggle out of this that easily.

"I had a theory."

"You had—*a theory?!*" I balked. "What is that supposed to mean?"

Tess flushed red with anger. "We almost just died, and I have a pounding headache! So, can we please not talk about that, right now? Let's let Mav ask the questions."

"She doesn't want to talk about it anymore," echoed Bond. "So, why push the issue?"

I shot him a glare and removed my helmet, no longer concerned with the stench of our armor. We needed to get to the bottom of this. "Well, Devon is connected to Tess and me since we all came from Earth, so *yeah*, it's pretty voiding important, Bond! If you don't want to talk about that, let's start here. How did the *Hantakira*, which we now know Devon has been serving on for at least a few months as one of their crew, know that we'd be there in that private spaceport? Is that *connected* enough to be relevant?"

"I—I have no idea!" Tess deflected. "I thought they were using our transponder to track us, which is why I was arguing that we should go dark."

"Yeah, but he's right," Steinbreaker added. "Our transponder may have been what they used at first, but not anymore, because we hadn't come there in the *Gambit*. The only other thing that comes to mind would be a tracking device, but someone would have had to put it on our shuttle when we left Vedana and then tipped off Yakuza."

"That seems unlikely since Vedana's controlled by the League of Desai, right Mav?" I asked.

"Could their syndicate have any spies on that planet?" He shrugged. "It's certainly possible, but that's why my team gave you false identities and a refitted ship. Even if there was a spy on Vedana, there's no way they could've linked it back to Shintox. There had to be some other security compromise somewhere along the way."

"Guys, do you realize what this means?" Bond said. "If Marekk-Thuul tracked us there today, he's going to find us again."

"That means from now on, wherever we go, we're never safe from Yakuza," I said.

Rubi exhaled. There was something she was hiding.

I could feel it.

"I'll do an internal investigation on all of my people," Mav Rexlin said, but before we jump to any conclusions about Ethos being compromised, tell me more about this person named Devon."

"What do you need to know?" said Tess, eyes hard and fixed on some distant memory. Her thoughts were elsewhere.

But I wasn't letting it go. How could we not feel betrayed by the fact that she'd been withholding secrets with even a remote chance of hurting our crew?

Now, she was what? Hesitant about coming out with it?

No, this was not okay. I was the captain of this little crew, no matter what personal feelings I'd had for Tess in the past, and maybe still had—it was hard to know anymore—if she was going to pull stunts like this.

"Why don't you start with how long you've actually known him?" I said. "Because you told me on the day that we met in the pub that you'd only met him the evening before. Clearly, you two have some kind of history." I tried but failed to keep my frustration from bleeding into my tone. "If you don't want to tell me all your secrets, that's fine. You have every right to your privacy and to share whatever you want or don't want to. I know I can be a little rough around the edges. I get it. And I'm sorry. But it's not just me that we're talking about here. You are a member of this crew, and Bond and Steinbreaker and Celin-Ohmi and Oliver are depending on you. This even affects Mavgardon Rexlin, one of the most powerful men in the galaxy. Tess, you've got to be honest with us! We love you, but there's no more holding back about this, alright?"

She looked down. "When we first started dating, I thought things were going so well. It was flattering," she began with a shrug. "I'd never been with someone who gave me that much attention. He bought me something every day, always opened doors for me and wanted to be together every minute. He had a lot of money and took me on expensive trips. I thought everything was good until one night, we were having dinner and he invited me to his parents cabin by the lake the next morning. I was coming down with the flu and had a lot of studying to do that weekend, so I said, 'no,' and thought that he'd taken the news well enough, but I just remember before our date was over, starting to get very sleepy. The next thing I remembered, I was waking up in bed at his parents' cabin. He... drugged me and literally drove me there and put me into bed while I was unconscious, or maybe I was still conscious, but just couldn't remember. He was actually making breakfast and had a bouquet of my favorite flowers on the dresser."

"I hope that you broke up with him," said Bond.

"And I hope you pressed charges," I added, disturbed by what she'd told us already.

"Devon had mysteriously 'lost' both of our cell phones, and we were staying in the middle of nowhere, so I didn't have any way to reach the outside world. I couldn't find any physical proof. He had me convinced that he didn't drug me and that I should make an appointment with the neurologist since I couldn't remember what happened. I didn't have a way to prove it because by the time he 'found' our phones that night, whatever drugs may have been present would've already washed out of my system. He was perfectly nice to me at the cabin and had a whole story about how I'd changed my mind after dinner the night before and decided to come. That's the way that Devon is. He talks you into doubting your instincts, because he's so charming. I felt really uneasy, so that week, we broke up. But a couple weeks later, my brother, who was serving as a police officer, was shot on the job and passed away. I was working on a speech and slide show for his funeral that week after my classes in med school, when I came home one night and my laptop was missing. In its place was a card from Devon. It said, '*Sorry about your brother. Please call me. I have your computer.*'"

"How did he get into your apartment?" I asked.

"I'd given him a key when we were dating, and he'd returned it but must've made a copy. So he insists that I meet him that night. When I do, there's my laptop under his arm, but he won't give it back until we have drinks. I only had one glass of wine to appease him. My whole presentation was on that laptop for the funeral, and I needed it back. The next thing I knew, I woke up again hours later at his parents' cabin. But this time, I was wearing a diamond ring and his freaking family's crest was tattooed on my shoulder!"

"A real, permanent tattoo?" I asked, trying to wrap my head around it.

She nodded. "The only thing I can figure is that he must've snuck Rohypnol, Ketamine or GHB into my drink. Those initial drugs alone are capable of not only making someone lethargic and open to suggestion, but also giving them amnesia of the events surrounding that time. That's what makes these cases so hard to prosecute. Have to prove there was a drug in your system, maybe several, after your body's eliminated them—*and* you have to remember what happened. Otherwise, it's your word against his! It had become a fad at the time among celebrities to get tatted up under sedation, but obviously not without their consent. Devon must've taken me to a tattoo parlor run by thugs and forged my signature while I was semi-lucid to convince the artist that I was drunk before they gave me the anesthesia. The engagement ring probably helped. He probably paid the dude a fat bonus. Whatever happened, I woke the next morning with his coat of arms on my skin, so that, as Devon put it, 'I'd know who I belonged to forever.' Again, he claimed that he didn't drug me and had this whole convoluted story about what we'd done the night before that I couldn't remember and how the tattoo was *my* idea. All of that happened four days after my brother—and best friend—had been gunned down in the line of duty."

Tears streamed down her cheeks at the memory, and she licked her lips, looking down at her hands.

"Wow," I said, releasing a breath, rocked by the depths

of Devon's psychosis. It was much worse than I'd thought. "Tess, I'm speechless. I don't have the words. Everything you've been through with that man! That must've been the coat of arms on his chestplate."

"That's how I knew right away that he was on board *Hantakira*," she said. "Of course, I recognized that family crest the first time I saw him there in his armor, even with the helmet concealing his face. I had to see it every day on my skin! Paid a small fortune to have it removed with laser removal. That didn't work and left my arm ruined with scar tissue. The tattoo's still there. It's just a lot lighter. But Devon made sure he was always standing next to Marekk-Thuul every time the captain came onscreen, because he honestly thinks I still want him—still to this day! I'm telling you, he's sick."

"I can understand why you taught him a lesson," Bond said. "I saw what you did in the spaceport, and let's hope he got the message."

"Did you ever get your computer back?" asked Stein-breaker.

I winced, shooting him a look. Not the most sensitive question from our engineer or the right time, but Tess took it in stride.

"Ya know, Steinbreaker, that's the worst part," she said. "He gave it back to me, but when I got home and powered it on to work on my brother's memorial service, all of my files were gone. He had completely wiped all my files—not only those on my hard drive, but all of the photos from my social media accounts as well—every family photo, photos of me growing up, every image that I had put together for my brother's funeral. Gone!"

"He just erased it?" I asked.

"No," she said. "He didn't erase it. He put all that data,

all those files—including my banking spreadsheets and coursework for school, as well—he transferred all of it to a flash drive and then, putting his dermatologist skills to work, cut an incision in the subcutaneous fat of his stomach and sewed the flash drive back up right under his skin. Can you believe that? Can you freaking believe that some human being would even conceive of doing something that sick? Who does that?!"

I shook my head, because there was no answer. It defied logic.

"That's odd—what was he trying to achieve?" asked Steinbreaker.

"Blackmail," said Tess. "He said if I tried to press charges about the tattoo or make accusations of any crimes or misbehavior, that I'd never see any of my files again. The pictures of my brother! The memories from my entire life. I didn't want to get the police involved the week after Jay's murder! My whole family was in law enforcement—my dad and my other brothers. They had enough to deal with. That would've sent them over the edge. They didn't need that while they were grappling with Jay's death, and neither did I, so I caved. I caved and had to get photos from my Mom for the slide show, and the memorial service went on, and every day I took a shower, I had to look at his claim on my skin and remember what he'd stolen from me. That's how he wanted it. He still has that flash drive, as far as I know. He traveled here to the future with it. I know, because he was talking to me about it in the bathroom at that spaceport when he was trying to cut off my airway to make me helpless while he held me at gunpoint. He was talking in my ear about how much he loved me and how much I loved him, and that he had my photos. Then he started talking about how much Yakuza was paying him, that I could join their crew, that I'd make a lot of money, too. He's out of his mind. He's out of his voiding mind. You know what it is? He can't fathom that I'd ever want to not be with him! That idea just breaks his brain, like he can't imagine that it could be true."

CHAPTER TWENTY-FIVE

HER STORY WAS a lot to process, but a picture was coming together in my mind of the first day I'd met her and Devon. It filled in details about that day that I hadn't understood until now. "So, when I met you on Galiano Island—"

"I was there by myself," she said. "Devon had continued to stalk me for several years after Jay's death, even after I got a restraining order. He actually went to my favorite bagel place where I got breakfast every day and drew his family crest on the inside of the stall in the women's bathroom, just so I'd see it. Why? Because that's the kind of thing you can get away with if someone puts a restraining order on you. Little things like that to make sure I always felt like he was nearby, even when he wasn't. He called this, 'showing his love.' I don't know how he figured out I'd be staying at Galiano Island. But I'd gotten used to it. I knew how to handle myself if he ever tried anything. My dad had taught me how to handle a gun and self-defense, so I wasn't worried. When you invited me to sit with you and your son, I accepted. When he showed up, I lied and told you I had just met him because I didn't want to give him the pleasure of taking up any more moments of my life than he already had."

When Tess ended this vent of emotions, her lower lip trembled, and tears streamed down her cheeks, but her expression remained defiant.

There was a strength inside her that kept her pushing back Devon's psychotic influence for years without letting it deter her from the pursuit of her goals or living the life that she wanted. And for the first time, I understood why she'd never wanted to talk about it.

Tess was on a mission to reclaim her future—not fritter away the remaining years of it dwelling on the terrible things that he'd done.

"So, I take it he wasn't part of Yakuza back in the twenty-first century," I said. "To me, his coat of arms looks European, not like the tattoos I've seen their gangsters wearing on planets like Sudeni Minji."

"Right," she said. "He wasn't part of Yakuza back then. He was just sick and possessive. But I'm not surprised that he joined them at some point in the past couple months since we arrived here. He probably saw it as a way to gain leverage and get to me in the process."

"Well, the Battle Mech Tournament was televised, right?" I pointed out. "I'm sure he heard about that and how we killed Shintox. Yakuza's been after us ever since then, so Devon took that as an opportunity, like you said. He probably convinced them that since he knew us, he could help them to track us down."

"That still doesn't tell us how the Yakuza destroyer he served on was tracking you," said Mav.

"I was wondering the same thing," said Steinbreaker. "But a terrible story—and you have my condolences."

"It's okay," she said, wiping a tear. "I should've talked about it before now. I don't understand how he could've tracked us to that spaceport. I thought the only way they could do that was through our transponder. If I had any idea that something I'd done could've put the crew in danger—"

"We know, you don't have to say it," I said.

"There is one other possibility," said Mav. "Did Devon have your quantum pad contact?"

"Well, he had both of ours," she said.

"Yeah," I agreed. "The Immigration team on your Centurion ship who rescued us preloaded the new pads they gave us with the contacts of the others who'd come with us from Earth. I think they figured we could be a support system or something for each other, since none of us knew anyone here when we first arrived and were all in the same predicament. Personally, I blocked Devon's contact right away. Even without knowing that much about him, I could tell right away that I didn't want him calling or sending me any texts. He was annoying enough the first time I met him, so I can't imagine what you've been through," I added, glancing at Tess.

"I blocked him right away, too," she said. "Didn't want him calling me, either."

"But that just keeps him from contacting you at that number after that point," said Mav. "It doesn't keep him from capturing your number from his list of contacts before you *did* block him. Have you received any text messages from numbers you didn't recognize?"

She sucked in a breath and her lips twisted. "No. The only possible thing I can think of is one message I got from Steinbreaker a while back, because when I opened it, the message was blank."

"When was this?" Steinbreaker said with a scowl. "I never messaged you in my life!"

"Maybe six weeks ago?" she said. "I just figured it was a mistake—what we called a 'butt dial' on Earth, so I ignored it and went back to what I was doing. That's the only thing I can think of."

"Tess, can I scan your pad for malware?" said Mav.

"Please!" she said.

Mav placed it in a storage bin on his console so that it linked up with his pad. "Astrid, can you check this device for compromises?"

"Yes, one moment," the AI announced, as a status bar flashed across his screen.

"A tracking program was installed on this pad thirty-seven days ago at 09:00," the AI replied. "Would you like me to remove it?"

"You'd *better*," said Tess, her jaw jutted forward. She started massaging her forehead. "I can't believe this. Yakuza was tracking us for thirty-seven days because of me?!" Covering her mouth with one hand, she started to weep. "You're telling me all of this was my fault?"

"No," said Mav. "Don't look at it that way. Devon could've saved your quantum contact the moment he received his own pad, before you had a chance to block him. After the Battle Mech Tournament, he probably passed it on to Yakuza who later—when you didn't suspect it—had one of their hackers send you that message under a fake account in Steinbreaker's name. There's no way you could've prevented this. I'm just sorry that the Immigration officer shared all of your info with each other without asking for your permission. We don't have protocols for time travelers, because it rarely ever occurs."

Her trembling hands balled into fists, and she unleashed

a primal scream laced with several obscenities then buried her face in my chest and broke down. I gently patted her back and let her get it out.

"Do we have confirmation that Devon is dead or in custody?" asked Bond.

"It all depends on whether he was able to make it back to the *Hantakira* before they jumped out of the system," said Mav.

"Or some other escape craft," said Steinbreaker.

"Or some other escape craft," Mav echoed.

I winced, drawing in a deep breath, as Tess cried in my arms. "I don't know. She beat him up pretty bad, but with the medical wonders they can work these days, I don't think we can be confident..." I said, my voice trailing off, because it was no longer helpful.

"After that attack on the spaceport, we should have plenty of evidence to put a Red Bounty on Marekk-Thuul's head," Mav offered.

"Could you downgrade it to blue?" Tess asked with an edge in her tone. "Because, then we'd be eligible."

"In your little corvette?" challenged Mav. "That wouldn't be responsible of me."

"I've been working on an idea," I said.

"We can put our best Centurions on the case," Mav tried to reassure us. "Everything you've been through is terrible. But I can't put more innocent lives at risk by downgrading Marekk-Thuul to a Blue Bounty just so you can pursue a personal vendetta against him and his crew. That would be irresponsible."

"It's not a personal vendetta," Tess said. "I'm looking out for his future victims, because I know what Devon can do. I'm not the only one who's been affected. I found out conducting independent research into his personal history."

"You mean there's others who have that tattoo?" I said.

She nodded. "I've met them."

I shook my head, feeling like I might be sick to my stomach.

"You'd have to show me some plan that makes sense to consider it," said Mav.

"I don't want to run anymore," Tess said, wiping the tears and filth from her face.

"Me neither!" said Steinbreaker. "Forget going dark."

"So, we're all in agreement," I said. "*Hantakira* needs to go down."

"Look, I don't want to seem like the bad guy," Mav said. "My mother, Ellenai Rexlin, is a counselor. I'll send you her contact. Consider looking her up to see if talking to someone would help. But as far as downgrading that Yakuza captain to the level of authority you have to take as hunters for Zenith, you'd have to show me some plan that makes sense to consider it."

I rubbed my chin. "To do that, we're going to need to complete the job we've already signed up for, since we need additional assets. Are you swearing us off that contract for Braddock?"

"You're not on our *payroll* for that job," Mav clarified. "But what you do on your own time's your business. As long as you don't break any laws. Just remember that every decision you make has consequences."

"Void, isn't that the truth?" I said.

"I wouldn't bet against this crew," said Bond. "People who've done that have lost a fortune."

We all smiled.

I leaned back in my seat. "You know, he's not wrong about that."

CHAPTER TWENTY-SIX

I TURNED TO TESS. "Are you sure about this? We'd all understand if you want to sit this job out after everything you've been through."

"Are you kidding?" she asked me with narrowed eyes and her helmet propped on her hip. "There's nowhere I'd rather be. Devon's taken enough from us already. I won't let him steal any more."

Nodding in return, I clapped her shoulder. Tess was a warrior. That much was sure. Disembarking our Ectocraft, our boots clicked along the volcanic rock spire that rose thousands of meters above sea level. With a blast of heat, Bond piloted the compact ship away.

He'd be nearby if we needed evac.

Rubi and I stood alone like islands in a sea of industry, looking out over canyons so vast, the successive cliffs of stone grew more blue the farther they rose in the distance through the haze of atmospheric humidity that hung in the air at the top of the world.

The site? Vedana's major shipyards. Inland on their continent Vrawntilus. Keeping watch over the valley, capital ships roosted on the black cliffs like gargantuan birds of prey.

"Let's just remember what Braddock suggested, that we check the caverns and minor islands around the volcano," said Rubi.

"I know, but I still think we're best off starting with the last person documented to have seen the man's brothers, and that's our guy, Mikhail Harrison," I replied.

"Hey, you're the captain, I'm just saying—keep it in mind, so we don't get off track and follow some tangent that leads us nowhere."

"Rubi," I said. "Like I ever do that."

She snorted. "Um, yeah. Just remember, four days. That's what we're working with."

I almost forgot, but thanks for the reminder, I thought but didn't say it out loud, already looking around for who we could squeeze for some information.

A rusty bucket of an android crouched behind us, collecting litter, bipedal and claw-like, not easy on the eyes.

"Excuse me," I said to the robot, "we're looking for a worker named Mikhail Harrison. Do you have that name in your registry?"

It seemed clear from the fact that it was on trash duty that this was the low bot on the totem pole, meaning it had to oblige inquiries from anyone who approached it since it wouldn't have any seniority. And though it might not be a treasure trove of random facts, it would at least be able to tell me what department and sector in the sprawling ship-yard I could check for our man.

"I do see one Polariti employee by that name on this work site," it said.

"Great, can you tell me his current location? Where is he working?" Because it was so easy for one random slacker to skip out on their work in facilities this large that spanned many kilometers of land mass, it was cheaper to host a shared network with the location of everyone's quantum pad on every bot than to hire enough muscle to patrol every stall.

Ask the trash-collecting android, and you could pinpoint where anyone was—well if they made middling wages—not the upper management, of course.

"Mikhail Harrison is not currently working?" it said.

"Why not?" pressed Rubi. "Is he here today? It's the middle of the week, before closing."

"He is here today—in that cage that's hanging from the arm of that crane."

I scowled then followed the angle of the bot's copper-toned segmented finger. Sure enough, a thousand meters away, there was a construction crane with a, well, I guess you would call that a cage, dangling from the lower sheave that swung from the extended arm of the construction machine.

"What in the void—do you know why he's up there?" I asked.

That last question was for fun, because I could practically smell the circuits frying in the robot's cerebrum at a request that esoteric, and its answer was, "No."

"What do you think—I fly, and you cover?"

"Sounds good to me," said Rubi.

We both took off in our fusion jetpacks, her twin engines burning off plasma streams ice blue in color, as she took a trajectory under me to provide covering fire when I got into position. If needed. We weren't getting ahead of ourselves, but you had to admit, a birdcage? It was strange.

Not in his job description, I'm sure.

As I flew over the canyon, I had to dodge the occasional drone and wedge-shaped flying transports for slave drivers—I mean, supervisors. The giant frames of ships under construction were strung out in the valley like unearthed fossil records with robots and people milling around them and knobby-wheeled vehicles ferrying parts.

Reaching the cage, I hovered outside its bars. "Mr. Harrison? I can spring you out if you don't mind answering some questions," I said.

"Let me guess," he said, fuming with sass. Harrison, a picture of the overworked laborer, was past the point of caring about his disheveled dark hair and white tank top stained with slimy black grease.

He wanted out but distrusted me already. And we'd just met.

"Let me guess—this is some kind of test," he said. "You just want to see if I'll spill any intel about Braddock's brothers to any random jerk who flies up on a jetpack, so you and your gangster buddies can feel justified about leaving me up here even longer in the rain without food and having to relieve myself in front of the entire system! I have kids, man. Come on! You guys are driving me nuts!"

So, the League of Desai put him up here, I thought. Now, I felt bad.

But this wasn't a good time for sympathy, because someone was shooting at me. "Scrat!" I snapped, as sparks sprung from my vambrace so close to the liner between armor panels that the shock and heat bled through to my skin. Plasma hammered my armored thigh.

I seized the jib of the crane and used it to swing myself into a tighter arc and rocket the other direction than I would've been able to execute without its aid. Wind rushed over my helmet.

Three Rammadors were diving toward me in a V-formation in their own jetpacks, firing semi-automatic pulses of plasma from shoulder-braced auto rifles. Rubi lit them up from below, and the two on the outside peeled off, leaving the frontrunner and I locked in a collision course.

Chicken was a game that I kind of enjoyed, because that kind of lunacy ran through my veins, but not against the blunt trauma of his ram's horns. That wouldn't end well.

I fired on him, because he picked this fight when I was just trying to have a conversation with my new friend in the birdcage. My plasma bolts raked across the leathery flaps of his throat that squirted blood, and the Rammodor spun into a dive, dropping his gun and smashing into the crumbling rock face.

Rubi was engaged with the other two. We needed to keep this moving, because I knew there'd be more on the way, but if I stayed midair any longer, I'd be an easy target. Even worse, so would this innocent dude who was being held hostage.

"Hey! Harrison! How do I lower the crane and get you out of there?"

After he'd seen the League firing at me, now I had his attention, since he realized I was legit. The sincerity in his wide eyes testified to that, and he called back, "They have it locked. You have to get into the control room!"

"Where's that?" I yelled, barely evading more blaster fire. Scrat, we needed to get out of here. An idea flashed through my mind, so I jetted to his position and handed him my quantum pad. "I'm going to broadcast live video from my ocular implants to that screen. You watch it and tell me over the speaker where I need to go."

He nodded furiously, gripping my quantum pad with both hands. I shot through the air away from him, smacking into a Rammodor on my way who'd been targeting Rubi. The shoulder pauldron of my battle suit plowed into his midsection.

He grunted as I flung him from the black cliff where he'd been shooting at her with a crew-served weapon. The Rammodor flailed in free fall on his way down to new construction, and that was the end of that.

"Harrison, are you getting the video I'm streaming you?"

"Yes," he said through my quantum pad, the audio routed through my brain's hearing centers. "I can see it. Enter Hangar Bay 142, down, to your left. Not that far. Do you see it?"

My eyes scanned overhead labels on metal rims of the industrial box-like structures, stacked on top of each other like the cells of a honeycomb. "Got it," I said, darting into the bay.

"This might be a group effort," he conceded.

I scaled a wide metal ramp worn green with patina then hurtled a gap that bridged the next section. Sparks spattered from a welding project off to my left in an adjoining bay.

"Hang a right," he said, "two bridges down!"

The inside of the hangar was dark, and I didn't like flying in such enclosed spaces. One wrong move and I'd crash. Occasional flashes of welding torches lit up steel panels that formed the walls.

According to his instructions, I swung right and powered down my jets, because I'd entered a corridor that was too confined to maneuver safely, plus we needed to conserve fuel to make what we had last as long as possible. We were only forty minutes in. The *clickety-clackety* sound of my boots echoed across the deck, as I ran. Harsh LED lamps lit the way at regular intervals.

"Rubi, you good?" I asked with a pit in my stomach. I don't know why. Maybe it was all this bad news about Devon and knowing that he was still out there. Somehow, it made me worried about her.

"I'm good and in a secure position, had to hunker down after that firefight," she said in reply.

"Good," I said, now breathing heavily, taking another turn into a corridor and running at near-top speed. "The contact's guiding me to the control room so I can lower the crane," I said.

"Roger," she said. "Watch your six."

The floor ended suddenly since I plowed through the railing at a T-junction and started falling into empty space. "Harrison!"

"Sorry, this part's been rebuilt," he said.

I triggered a love tap on my throttle, just enough to propel me across the gap to the catwalk on the other side then wiped out in front of the door that he was pretty sure held the control room.

Scrambling to my feet, I tore off the handle and the door itself. I ducked inside. The hostage led me through a tutorial of levers and switches on the control board then alerted me with a frightened yelp that his cage was going down.

"Keep it at that pace," he warned, voice quivering. "Any faster, and you're gonna turn me into a pancake! Okay, get out here—hurry! The guards are going to be here any second."

I spun around and retraced my steps, running and leaping, skidding my way through the corridors and open spaces of the hangar bay, lighting my jets with fusion fuel when I reached the opening.

A retinue of guards took up firing positions intended

for us, as I soared over them. "Rubi, I need you to keep those gangsters busy. They're forming up at the base of the crane. We've gotta go!" I shouted.

Withdrawing the plasma sword from the scabbard on my hip, I sliced through the hook that was holding the cage and tried to carry it with me. That was a mistake. Too much dead weight.

I thought I could manage it, but it was creating drag, and I had to make an impromptu landing behind a capital ship perched on one of the high stone plateaus that surrounded the canyon.

I leaned on my knees to catch my breath. Now that we were on solid ground, I worked on cutting the man out of confinement and asked him what we needed to know. "Why did they have you locked up like that?"

"There's a particular gang in the League of Desai who runs the shipyards, and they want to be the ones to find Emin Braddock's brothers. By dangling me out there like a piece of meat, that got them two things. It prevented their rivals from being able to grill me with questions that could become leads. And secondly, as you saw here today, it drew out the competition they needed to worry about. Professionals. Obviously, people like you."

I rolled my eyes. "Nothing like making a dramatic entrance. Great, now these ronks are going to be tailing me. So what can you tell me about where to find them—the Braddock brothers?"

"Everyone keeps asking me that," he said, exasperated. "How should I know? They were here on a tour of the shipyards. I think that day, Emin Braddock, the baby of the family—well, you know him—had a prior engagement, so he couldn't make it. Anyway, one of his aides probably was taking them around, showing them everything. I was down in the cafeteria on my lunch break when they came in there, all smiles, looking around, and they asked everyone in there, including me, who knew a boat captain who'd take them on a fishing excursion at Caldera Island. I don't know why they didn't just check the gal-net, but I knew they were important people, real VIP's, so I piped up and told them about my cousin. He has a boat. And trying to build up his business, too. That was it—that's all I know. I really don't like to talk about it because I never heard from my cousin again. It creeps me out. His wife keeps telling me that he's okay, but then why can't I see him? It doesn't make no sense."

"Can you give me the name of his wife and boat and where it was docked? Also, anyone else he had working with them—any other details about his fishing business?"

Harrison gave me all the details, and I didn't bother to write them down, because my cybernetics recorded audio and video of what he said so that I could replay it later.

We had a lead already.

I radioed Tess and asked her to look for the best expert she could find on this planet's volcanoes since we'd be venturing back into that environment to follow this lead.

"Now, where can I drop you off?" I asked him.

The ronk just wanted to go home. I asked him if he thought it was safe, and he said it was, because he could just claim that I had abducted him by force.

At this point, he just wanted to see his children and take things from there. Not one to stand in his way, I flew Harrison over the shipyard to his trailer park thirteen kilometers from that place of employment and bid the man farewell at his stoop.

Then I thought better of it.

"Hey, since I sprung you out, could you do me a favor

and come with me to talk to your cousin's wife? Because if she's holding back information from you, I can't see her opening up to me."

"Naw," he said, his face screwing up as he lit a cigarette from a half-pack in the yard. "I'm not into your espionage scrat or whatever this is. Ask her yourself."

"Would you do it for thirty-thousand credits?" I asked.

His eyebrows shot up. "Half up front, and I'm in," he said, taking a drag.

"Okay, but you only get the second half if and when I've got some actionable intel."

CHAPTER TWENTY-SEVEN

BOND DROPPED me and Harrison off on his cousin's street before taking off with Tess in the Ectocraft, on their way to the *Lizard King*.

The house that belonged to the contact's cousin was a typical single family unit, white buildfoam construction, in this case streaked with stains from particulates in the air that drifted in from eruptions. Reinforced duracrete piers undergirded its foundation over the slope of hard lava beneath to provide a stable foundation.

A dilapidated hover bus was parked on the side of the home with the chipped logo of a delivery company. Maybe one of them was a driver.

The woman, the spouse of his cousin who answered, was an aging blonde with a sunken face, three missing teeth and a black eye as if she'd been hit.

I let Harrison do the talking, standing back and watching each detail and micro-expression of her responses. "I told you before, Absolom's fine," she said, closing her eyes as she voiced the sentence, which could be a tell that we'd broached a subject that she didn't even want to consider. "He's just not available right now. Took a new job in the city. He's gone a lot. Gone every night." As worn down as she seemed, she also had the patronizing look of someone who was telling a lie.

"Then why don't he answer my calls?" asked Harrison.

"He—" she shook her head, closing her eyes, again. "I'll let him know you called, but like I said, he's just busy with work."

The man stood there searching her face before finally conceding, "Okay. Let me know if you need anything, Helga. I'll keep in touch."

"I will—bye, now!" she said like she couldn't get the door closed fast enough.

He returned to me with a look of defeat. "What now?"

I studied the pier that led out to the ocean at the edge of her property two hundred meters away, the fishing boat that was moored there. "I assume that one's hers," I said, "You think it would have a camera?"

Harrison's face lit up. "Great idea," he said. "We could check the memory card for footage of their excursion."

I nodded, directing him to the sidewalk with an arm around his shoulder, so cousin-in-law Helga wouldn't get suspicious. "Now, we wait for the cover of darkness. Are you hungry?"

"I've been hanging from a crane for a week. What do you think?"

He led me to a diner a klick down the road. I nursed a mug of chagra after dinner in an effort to kill more time, making plans with the rest of my team through the quantum pad.

The first one I called was Steinbreaker.

"You were a xenomarine biologist. So far, my lead's taking me back to the regions that Mercedes had urged us to avoid because of an organism she called the Owari worm. I've never heard of it, but she was convinced these things are so dangerous, that we should call the whole trip off if it means we have to hang out near the coastline around the volcano."

"Huh," said Steinbreaker. "That's interesting. I've never heard of them either, but the species of aquatic life in the galaxy, as you might imagine, number in the tens of millions. That's one reason I loved the field. I never stopped learning and still only touched the edge of everything there was to know in the marine biology local to a single star system, much less the broader civilized and uncharted worlds."

"Well, let's focus on that one species this week, because apparently, they're dangerous enough that they seemed almost like the determining factor in Mercedes cutting us loose from her team. She didn't want to feel responsible for what happened to us out there."

"And you're just telling me this now?" he said, getting worked up.

"I had it in the back of my mind, but it wasn't urgent until today," I tried to convince him. "Tess and I needed to get our application process started for the Centurion program, then Bond almost died on the mountain and we got attacked by Yakuza, so maybe you could excuse me if—"

He blew out a breath to interrupt me. "Fine, fine. I'll look it up. Rest assured, I'll learn all about the Owari worms and have a full report when you get back."

"Thank you," I said, trying to sound more stern than I felt to redirect his attention away from the real reason I hadn't told him about the worms before now. If I had, he and the others might've flat-out refused to accept this job from Braddock at all.

And I couldn't take that risk. I needed their help—every one of them—because this was big, and Braddock was still my only hope of getting into the Protectorate where the gangsters were keeping my child.

I'd make sure my team was compensated. I'd taken good care of them until now.

But this environment was unsettling me. There was a lot I still didn't know about volcanoes and their ecosystems on this strange planet.

Braddock had claimed his best operatives had failed to track down his brothers. Why? For some reason, none of them would go into the caves or the minor islands, the places Mercedes warned me not to go.

I clipped one end of a pair of handcuffs—not the electric shock inducing variety—old school, to my wrist and the other to Harrison's. If the League had gone to such lengths to keep him hidden away, I'd feel better if he stayed close.

Harrison didn't appreciate this. "What am I now—a prisoner? I thought I was getting paid for this scrat."

"Look," I said. "We've got a long night ahead, and you're going to help me, so you'd better catch a few winks while you can." I leaned back into the diner booth's upholstery to fall asleep. Didn't need Harrison wandering off and getting us into trouble.

Just as I was starting to nod off, the crack of a blaster jerked me back to life. Dead weight pulled on my arm like a sack of concrete.

I blinked awake, refocused my eyes. Harrison slumped to my side and a trickle of blood ran down his forehead from the puckered entry wound in his brain. My own heart skipped as I checked his pulse and confirmed the testimony of his glassy eyes.

My contact was gone.

Sucking in a sharp breath, I cased out the gunman, Rammodor, in a trench coat with his collar turned up. His gaze averted. He was trying to slip through the traffic that had started to rush for the entrance after the first person spotted Harrison's murder and started screaming to everyone else.

He'd miscalculated his risk of causing a scene because of the diner patrons who were seated closer to the only door and had made it to the entrance in front of him. Probably, those tables were full when he got here, and the hit had to proceed.

I didn't have time to break free from Harrison's body. If I did, I'd lose him out the door, so I fired my tow line from my free vambrace and gave it a jerk when it sunk in his calf. His species was huge—too much in close quarters—but the barbed prong of my grappling hook hung up deep in his muscle tissue. It was sharp and designed for that.

Have you ever tried to run with a severed calf muscle? It doesn't matter how strong you are. He couldn't push off, only limp, dragging the compromised leg behind him with the weight of dark choices that had led him here.

He tried to swivel, intending to fire. But a hard yank from my monofilament cable slammed him into the floor before he could bring the gun to bear.

"Drop it!" I ordered, letting the bystanders glance back in horror as they clambered out through the door.

He did. Smart Rammy. I kicked the carbine away from his hand. That gave me just enough time to free myself and my contact from the handcuffs and take one more look down in regret.

Harrison wouldn't make it home, now, after all.

I slapped my shock cuffs around the heavy forearms of the Rammodor and ordered him to his feet. Their electrical charges leveled the playing field between me and his superior brawn, at least, that's what I hoped, because I was counting on him to take me to the head of the snake. Whoever this thug reported to would certainly have more details on what we knew so far on Braddock's brothers and their whereabouts.

Otherwise, they wouldn't be trying so hard to keep invaders like myself out of it.

I muscled him into an air taxi in front of the diner and set a course for the home of the cousin's wife. We had to hurry, because someone would be calling to check on his progress or maybe watching it from a secure location.

Within twenty minutes, we were outside Helga's fishing boat on the water in the pitch dark. I couldn't watch this thug 24/7, so I forced him into the prone position on the volcanic rock along the coastline, then attached another pair of shock cuffs to his ankles, so I could focus on breaking in.

I turned away from him and started prying the vessel's cab open with my multitool. There was something creepy about being out here on the coastline in the inky darkness, since it was overcast. The planet's moons were barely visible.

It was so dark that I had to keep the headlamp on my helmet focused on the boat cab's keypad. Otherwise, I kept losing track of my progress.

A loud splash sounded.

I paused.

What was that?

I had to chuckle at my own overactive imagination,

because I realized that couldn't be the gangster. If he'd thrown himself in, the shock cuffs would've electrocuted him instantly and ensured he would drown.

It must've been the crash of a wave, I reasoned.

Resuming my work on the boat's keypad, I struck up a conversation with the Rammodor to soften him up for when I needed to switch over to my bad cop routine.

"I bet you've got a pretty nice multitool," I said. "Something to help with all those fat fingers? Where I came from, it was the Swiss Army knife. That was the gold standard, when I was a kid. Even MacGyver—"

A scratching on the rock brought me up short. I bristled.

Chills ran down the length of my spine as the scraping was followed by a panting sound, then a low growl from somewhere behind me. I spun and my headlamp caught a flash of ravenous jaws.

It barked and bayed. It was an animal that looked vaguely canine, but not like a dog. Mangy and hump-backed, it looked more like a mutant combination of a wolf and wild hyena with three eyes.

The third eye didn't look natural, either, but was higher on the forehead and off-center. I didn't know if that was a feature common to every member of its species or just this one. But it lunged at me and snapped.

The first bite crunched down into my gauntlet, and the animal thrashed but couldn't penetrate the hardened material, so it slid off. The hyena's lips retracted over carnivorous teeth. It was almost two meters tall at the shoulder.

Muscles in its hindquarters bunched. It faced off with me, and I circled it, trying to anticipate the creature's next move.

It attacked me. This time, I fired because it seemed my

life was at risk. The blaster bolt hit its chest, and the thing whimpered, pawing the air as it slipped on the rocks.

The baying and howling that came out of it next was about to wake up the whole mountain.

"Shh! Shut up," I urged, but the damage had already been done, and lights flicked on from within Helga's beach house two hundred meters away.

Soon, the woman shambled onto her porch, the ambient light from the home lighting up her gingham nightgown and 12-gauge shotgun. "Hey, who's down there?!" she called, wheeling her weapon in my direction.

"Scrat!" I whispered and shoved the wounded wolf-hyena into the water so it didn't betray my position any more than it already had.

For a moment, it doggy-paddled, then it dunked below the surface and didn't return.

Helga stole down the path across the volcanic rock from her house toward the dock where I was hiding. Since I didn't want to shoot innocents, it put me in a very awkward position if she'd see me, because I'd be forced to surrender, and my activities weren't really legal.

The boat stood between me and her, blocking her view. But my headlamp leaked light all around it, so I shut it off and feverishly continued to work in the darkness.

"Come on, come on!" I rattled the keypad on the boat's cab, trying to break in without leaving evidence of damage that might trace this back to me. That was the hard part.

It still wouldn't click.

"I know you're out there—I seen your light!" Helga rasped into the darkness that engulfed us both.

I froze, because she'd gotten so close that any movement could tip her off. I picked up and threw a rock thirty yards down the coastline, but it was too late. She'd seen my light earlier.

The woman started edging around the side of the boat. I did, too, in the other direction, until she was on the ocean side and I'd quietly slid around its perimeter to the mouth of the walking path. My heart was pounding, so her scream turned the blood to ice in my veins.

A sucking sound followed by a slap of water caused my nerve endings to bristle. Drawing my carbine, I powered it on. "Helga?" I said. "I'm not here to hurt you. Let me explain."

Nothing. Silence.

Just the gentle lapping of the midnight tides against the wooden pier. It creaked, and I bounded around the boat with my gun at the ready.

Where is she?

The woman's 12-gauge was jammed between rocks on the water's edge, but there was no trace of her. She'd disappeared.

"Scrat!" I ground out, abandoning my earlier stealth. Some kind of crazy stuff was going on, and I didn't want any part of it, now.

I smashed an armored fist through the window of the fishing boat, setting off the alarm. It shrieked like a banshee, echoing across the hardened lava and alerting the neighbors for miles around.

I didn't care. I needed to hurry. League of Desai cops would be here any second. After everything else that I'd seen, there was no doubt in my mind anymore that they owned the police.

Fumbling around on the dash, I located the camera and ejected its flash drive then slipped the little storage device into the slot on my quantum pad, which I'd stored on my utility belt.

Once more before leaving, I scanned the mysterious expanse of ocean that stretched to the horizon. It shimmered in the haze of faded moonlight and provided no answers about where two beings and a giant hyena had vanished to moments before. Just lapping, that gentle, insistent rhythm of seawater against the moorings.

Beyond that, it was stillness incarnate.

I couldn't help but wonder about Mercedes' warnings to me.

In the distance, I could hear sirens. They were coming, so I turned and charged back up the mountain where I made an emergency call to Bond and asked him for a pickup before the League could take me into custody.

CHAPTER TWENTY-EIGHT

"GAGE, MEET DR. PORTINGA," said Tess. "You asked me to track down an expert on volcanoes in these islands, and Dr. Portinga's our man."

The heavy-set black man with dreadlocks and wire-rimmed glasses shook my hand in a mild-mannered gesture, and I smiled in return.

"Thank you for coming," I said. "Just tell me what you think's a fair rate, and we can pay you by the day."

"That would be fine. Right now, I'm just working as a tour guide between grants, so I can accommodate whatever you need," said the volcanologist in an accent that sounded close to Jamaican, sounding pleased with the arrangement. "Uh, within reason," he added with a smirk.

We all laughed at that last part.

"Within reason," he said, grinning quietly.

"We'll have lots of questions for you along the way," I said, as Tess led us from the front porch into the main room of the bungalow she'd rented for us to use as our temporary lodging and command center for our team for the remainder of our time on the island.

"This is great—thanks, Tess!" I said with hands on my hips.

The cozy home had a low pitched roof and open floor plan, which had worked nicely for briefings and setting up equipment. While I had the others working on tasks, I'd been toiling on my application to become a Centurion since before dawn.

That included many of the tests I had expected from my earlier knowledge of special forces, and I'd just gotten done submitting it over the gal-net when we'd taken a break for lunch. I was exhausted.

But since Tess was back with the volcanologist, it was time for our next mission briefing.

"Okay, everyone, gather around," I said. "Ran into crazy scrat last night trying to follow up with our lead which I'll tell you about, but first, I thought, why don't we watch the dash cam video of the Braddock brothers' fishing excursion? Because I have it right here on this flash drive. This should give us their last known location."

I brandished the little storage device from the pocket of my cargo pants and waved it in the air to a smattering of applause from my crew.

With a wry grin, I bowed. Tess inserted it in the designated slot in the holo bank on a table in the middle of the room.

We'd already cued it up to the Braddock's trip.

It began. We could hear them chatting with Harrison's cousin, Absolom Stewart, but couldn't make out much of what was being said over the noise of the outboard engine. The dashcam had the forward view of their boat chugging along through coastal waters for sixty minutes until the captain pointed at the mouth of a large cavern that had been shaped by lava streams over untold cycles of time.

Though it was hard to hear, the mood of their conversations seemed to grow more excitable. They made gestures toward the inviting chamber of rock and their party must've agreed to explore it, because the mouth of the cavern grew larger until it swallowed them up in its opening.

Their boat bobbed on the water inside it. The cavern was breathtaking—until the video turned static. And went black.

I tried to fast forward it, but all that did was skip to footage of the excursion with whoever hired the fishing boat after that. We scoured the contents of the flash drive but couldn't find any other footage with the mob leaders in question.

My mouth twisted.

I contemplated. "Okay, so we know where they went but don't really know what happened to them. Absolom Stewart made it back home, though it sounds like he could be missing, as well, according to Harrison. Either that or someone's silencing him from breaking his side of the story."

"Seems like a dead end," Steinbreaker grumbled.

"Ah, not at all," said Dr. Portinga. "That cave system was formed by old lava flows, and it is quite extensive, though some parts are underwater."

"Well, I guess we have a destination," I said.

"That area is very dangerous because of the wildlife," Portinga said, raising his voice above his mild-mannered demeanor to make sure everyone heard.

"Yeah, about that," I said, concern etched into my brows. "Last night on that coastline outside the fisherman's house, man, what in the void? I got attacked by some three-eyed hyena that must've been eight feet tall."

"What?!" said Tess, contorting her face in disgust.

"Yeah, counting its head, close to three meters!" I said. "And the thing attacked me. Would've bitten right through my arm if I hadn't been wearing the armor."

"That's a razgit," Portinga said. "Their species are scavengers who hunt in the rural parts of the islands."

"A razgit," I repeated, narrowing my eyes. "Can those things swim?"

"They're not suited for it like fish," he said, shrugging, "but short distances—sure, they can."

"Well, I pushed it into the water, and it went under but never returned to the surface, so I don't know if it was just too injured or..."

"Something else pulled it under?" Portinga asked me with a cocked eyebrow.

"And if you think that one sounds strange, I had the Rammodor who'd shot Harrison locked in shock cuffs on his ankles and wrists, right? I turn around for two or three minutes, and when I check on him again, he's *gone*. Then, the lady who lived there—this fisherman's wife—comes out after the razgit woke up the whole neighborhood, and she's like stalking me around her fishing boat. Suddenly, *boom!* She disappears, too. It's really making me wonder about these organisms Mercedes was warning me about, the Owari worms. She said they can be ten or fifteen meters, but maybe could get a lot bigger. That sound right to you, Dr. Portinga?"

The volcanologist's eyebrows shot up, and he nodded soberly. "Yes, they're very dangerous," he said. "People disappear on the rocks all the time. The government doesn't get involved, because they're run by the League of Desai, and all they care about is making credits—which they are, hand over fist."

"How comforting," I said. "Steinbreaker, what did you find out about these alien worm things to help us prepare? Enlighten us, please!"

"'Worms' is just local slang for them, not a scientific designation. Technically, the Owari are jawless fish like lampreys, except they can grow incredibly large."

"Lampreys?" I asked.

"Yes," said Steinbreaker. "They resemble eels but without fins. You're looking at scaleless, elongated bodies, six eyes, gills and a mouth that's wider than the Owari's head, which works well for hematophagy."

"Hematophagy?" countered Bond.

"Boring into the flesh of life forms to feed on their blood. They're giant parasites."

Tess moaned, giving voice to how we all felt.

Steinbreaker shrugged. "It's just biology. Blood's a fluid tissue rich in nutritious proteins and lipids that can be gleaned without much effort. Hematophagous animals have mouth parts and chemical agents for penetrating vascular structures in the skin of their hosts. This type of feeding is called phlebotomy. Once that is achieved, the blood's collected either by sucking it from veins or capillaries, from a pool of blood that escapes, or by lapping it up, like bats."

The scientist apparently wasn't very good at reading the room, because to me, most in our circle were looking a little queasy—but I didn't want to stop him prematurely, since we needed to collect all the knowledge we could about the Owari.

So, I took a deep breath and jotted down notes, mentally probing his descriptions for clues into potential weaknesses or vulnerabilities of the species that we could exploit in order to keep ourselves safe where others had failed.

"What can you do to survive an attack by one of those things?" I asked.

"The host's body will try to protect itself when its blood is being sucked out with coagulation, vasoconstriction, inflammation, and pain," he continued. "But vampiric animals like Owari pre-inject hosts with a chemical called lamphredin in their saliva. It prevents coagulation and puts the host in a dreamlike trance with an anesthetic, so you go limp and don't fight back."

"That's horrible," Tess said in revulsion.

"How often do they come after humans?" I reasoned. "We're not going to be out there to engage them—just trying to find the missing men. With most dangerous animals, it's usually just a matter of staying out of their way."

"These are aggressive by nature," said Steinbreaker, "They don't keep to themselves, and they're not afraid of humans. Some scientists speculate they must spend the earlier stages of their life cycle in a different environment then undergo a mass migration as adults, because we've only been able to observe mature specimens in the shallows close to volcanoes, where they seem to be drawn by the highly acidic waters inhospitable to other life. The fact that these acidic environments are low on the populations of prey they need for survival is why some believe they're so aggressive to humans, razgits or other animals that get too close to the shorelines. That's how they earned their other nicknames—bloodsuckers, vampire fish. "

A chill ran down the length of my spine. "That must've been what happened last night," I said with a shudder. "I didn't see any, but that would seem to fit what went down."

"Well, I've heard enough. How do we kill them? That's what I want to know," said Bond.

"Yeah, I'm with you," I agreed.

"You're going to have to get creative," Steinbreaker said, "because they're extremely fast in the water, and though the Owari haven't responded to the documented attempts we have of inter-species communication, they show all the signs of high intelligence."

"There's gotta be *some* way, Mr. Sunshine," I said, rubbing my whiskers. "We could check with the locals."

"Yeah, how do they deal with 'em?" Bond said. "They've got to know what's worked in the past."

I nodded. "If these things hang out in the shallows and we find ourselves mucking through caves, chest-deep in the soup, plasma's no good. Ever see someone fire a blaster into the water he's currently standing in?"

"Not anyone sober," Bond barked with a laugh.

Everyone shook their heads, their eyes wide.

"You guys never saw that viral vid?" The Oshwellian said. "That poor guy electrocuted himself along with all the fish in his pond. They floated to the surface, but he didn't!"

I rubbed my forehead. "Traditional slug throwers wouldn't work either, if we're shooting at them as they're diving. Why don't you ask around, Bond? I hope these locals have supercavitating rounds! We need to know what caliber they've found effective against vampire worms and those big razgits. Pick us up the best guns you can find."

"Roger that, boss," the pilot said.

Four hours later, he called me from town on his quantum pad, as I finalized other preparations for our mission in our makeshift command center.

"Okay, we've got two choices that accommodate super-cavitating bullets," Bond said, his hologram flickering blue. "Both have good things and drawbacks, so tell me what you want to do."

"Let me guess—you've got this narrowed down to an automatic rifle and a semi-automatic shotgun," I said.

"How did you know?" he said with mock surprise. "We had to go big for the monsters *we're* hunting. The first option's a rifle with twenty-round magazines of big 400 grain .500 rounds that can penetrate solid steel. Its advantages over the shotgun are that it's more accurate and has less recoil. Its disadvantage is that it has less stopping power."

"Wow!" I said. "In that case, you must have a pretty nice shotgun there."

He grinned. "As a matter of fact, I do. In fact, they call it the Dracula Hunter after the infamous worms. The "Drac" for short is built with a 23 millimeter barrel that's usually produced for an anti-aircraft gun. The barrel's so big, you can fit your thumb inside it. But it only holds nine total cartridges. Now, keep in mind, each of those rounds is a 1,000 grain 4-gauge slug. What you lose in range and accuracy, you make up for in sheer stopping power."

"Nice!" I said. "I think the Dracula Hunters sound like the best option for both the giant, three-eyed hyenas and Owari. No, scratch that. The more I think about it, the razgit's third eye is off-center, you know? I'm guessing that means they hunt in packs and group themselves so that the ones with two eyes on one side of their head are facing the outside of their formation. That's the only thing that would make sense of it, if that wasn't a random mutation in the one I encountered. So, if we have to encounter a whole pack of those things, at least one of us is going to need something that's higher capacity. Why don't you pick up two automatic rifles and two Drac shotguns, as well?"

"Roger that," he said.

"One other thing," I said. "Remember that spherical

drone with omnidirectional laser turrets that Oxhorn gave us?"

"I like where your mind is at," Bond said with a chuckle.

"Yeah, but we can't use it on this op with lasers for the same reason we can't use blasters—the water."

"Hmm, good point," he said. "In that case, we'd get electrocuted, whereas in the case of lasers, we'd just get cooked."

I laughed. Laser cooking was quite a big deal in the future. It's how food printers made dinner so fast.

"Exactly," I said. "Do you think you and Steinbreaker could see if you could retrofit the drone with little machine guns instead? I mean, you're our weapons officer, and he's our ship's engineer."

"Hmm," Bond said thoughtfully. "We probably could, but in this case might run into two potential issues—time and bullet caliber—because the rounds that would be small enough for it to accommodate probably wouldn't have the stopping power we need."

"Yeah, I was afraid of that. Just didn't want that drone to go to waste, though, because it's such a cool weapon."

"Well, the drone's got a high rate of fire—it's just lasers, rather than slugs. So, what if we used *that* for your razgit hyenas? Then we could *all* get shotguns instead!"

"Perfect," I said. "See, I knew there was a reason I sent you to pick up our loadouts."

He laughed. "Okay, I'll be back soon."

As I hung up with him, acid still churned down deep in my gut. While these weapons would be a good start, if these vampire worms could get as big and fast as what we were learning about, we'd need much more to survive the night, but since we still hadn't been paid yet, we were getting painfully close to broke.

We were already over budget. Remaining funds were too low to even *think about* an armored boat.

Maybe that's why Mavgardon Rexlin hadn't felt the need to call us off of this job completely. He knew that without their lines of government support, we'd simply run out of creds and arrive at that conclusion all by ourselves.

Unfortunately, Braddock didn't know that.

All he knew is that I made him a promise and had been a royal stink on his planet before today. I had to somehow find a way to deliver, or none of us might even make it off this rock.

CHAPTER TWENTY-NINE

THE NEXT MORNING AT DAWN, my pad woke me up with the chime of a text. It came from Mercedes.

Top talked to me. You're back on the job.

I pumped my fist in the air. *Does this mean I'm a Centurion?* I typed back in a rush of thumbs.

You're a Contractor. Don't push your luck.

They probably hadn't reviewed my application after less than twenty-four hours. Plus, that wasn't Mercedes' job. Still, somehow, that message stung.

Please report to Barjinder Chadwick outside your window, she texted next.

Outside my window?

Without even stopping to get dressed, I ran out on the front porch. The bungalow that Tess had rented for our crew was on the side of a mountain overlooking the major commercial pier a six-hour boat ride from the caves where Braddock's brothers had disappeared.

I could already see people working and milling around. Fishermen, dock workers, restaurants opening up.

The busy pier seemed a far enough distance from the

volcanoes that nobody here worried about the Owari or even scavenging predators like razgits. They'd been driven away by land development to more remote locations to hunt without fear and we knew that the worms swam near the volcanoes.

Mercedes had said to look out my window. I blinked.

Because the moorings had a new addition—an armored patrol boat. A thrill shot through my chest, and I turned. "We're back on the job," I shouted, running into our bungalow, still shirtless and waving my arms.

The rest of my team was not so enthused.

Well, maybe they were and just lacked the get-up-and-go spirit at this hour after waking up from a dead sleep.

Or whatever.

"Everybody, up! Get dressed. Get your breakfast! There's a decommissioned cutter out there to pick us up, so let's show 'em that we're all professionals." I ducked into each of the bedrooms.

Tess squinted at me, cocking her head. "Is that a piece of lint hanging from your belly button or a gigantic spider?"

I glared at her. "Stop it. You have cybernetic vision."

"My eyes are fuzzy when I first wake up," she whined, turning over, pulling the blankets over her head.

With a smirk, I yanked off her covers and threw them into the corner.

"Pink pajamas with little piggies," I said with a chuckle. "Man, how classy is that?"

Without moving, she finally said, "Do you want me to hurt you? I *can*."

"Welcome aboard the *Magellan*, Mr. Stryker," Captain Barjinder Chadwick said, a sturdy Jagulen packed with muscle inside his bloodstained battle suit. It had seen action, some of it melee.

My sense was they'd just dropped anchor, since he started changing out of his armor, already focused on the next task.

"The honor is ours," I said, climbing onto his boat from the oceanfront dock, as the rest of my team stepped aboard behind me, Rubi with Steinbreaker in her backpack, Bodega, Zihan and Dr. Portinga, the volcanologist.

"Adams, give these people a tour and show them where they can stow their luggage," said Captain Chadwick, his catlike snout pulling back to reveal the long, yellowed teeth of a jaguar. He licked his lips, no less intimidating than any other Jagulen I'd met. I'd have to get used to it.

He was the boss.

"Right this way," said the fresh-faced twenty-something, Adams. He swept back his dusty blonde hair.

Since they were all working undercover as contractors for Task Force Cyberblade, none of Chadwick's men were in uniform. They looked the part as grubby pirates or smugglers who'd happened upon a fortunate score with this old Navy cutter they were serving on.

"The *Magellan* was decommissioned for its age and outdated enough at the time that the CMC didn't mind selling it to the highest bidder on the open market," Adams explained, addressing my question as we followed him across the top deck that swayed a little under our feet, open as it was to the chilling wind and saltwater air of the post-dawn.

He started at the stern. "This is our ramp for small boat or special forces insertions. We've got one major system in the aft, the combat craft retrieval system. It launches and recovers our seven-meter rigid inflatable boat, RIB, designed by the Navy for maritime counter terrorism, policing, anti-piracy or search and rescue. In our case, it's also great for man-overboard situations," he joked, making the universal sign for tossing back alcohol. "It only takes one person to operate and can launch the RIB in less than three minutes."

I frowned. This boat was impressive. Even in the age of space travel, the littoral or shallow regions of oceans had to be guarded and patrolled by someone, and that's exactly what this capable craft was designed to do.

"There you see our landing pad which can accommodate an Ectocraft or VTOL if needed," he said before leading us down metal stairs into the lower deck.

He pointed out the commanding officer's and officers' state rooms. Because of advancements in automation over the centuries as well as the specialized role of this vessel, the chain of command wasn't what I'd seen in civilian craft or Navy vessels of the twenty-first century.

Instead, they had a captain, his XO who also worked as the helmsman and navigator with the help of the ship's computers, a comms and sensors operator, a guy manning radar and sonar, and a ship's engineer.

"The rest of us are Gunner's Mates," Adams explained. "Our duties include the operation and maintenance of torpedo systems, gun mounts and other ordnance. But it's such a small crew that we all do a little bit of everything. Void, we're even deck hands and chore boys when needed —or as directed by Captain Chadwick."

After showing us the mess deck and briefing compartment, he led us into the forward berthing. "You can stow your bags in these cubbies," he said. "They lock, so here are your keys."

"Looks like we'll be sleeping in straightjackets," Bodega quipped.

"Those canvas straps?" Steinbreaker replied. "You've never slept on a small boat like this, have you?"

"Can't say that I have," Bodega replied.

That made Adams chuckle. "The seas can get pretty choppy, so these straps are to keep you from falling out of your rack when we go over six-meter swells."

"Oh," said Bodega. "A handy feature."

I don't know where Adams thought we were going, but let him give Bond a hard time. He could take it.

He took us through the engine room and back up to the top deck toward the bow. "Here's the pilothouse where the officers sit," he said.

"Tell us about these chain guns," I said, patting the single long barrel with a grin. It was longer than I was tall. "Looks like the bigger, meaner brother of the Bushmaster M242."

"We've got four Ethos Corporation T52's," he replied. "Two mounted forward, two aft. They're chain-driven auto-cannons. Metallic link belt with dual-feed capacity. The standard rate of fire's two hundred 50 mm rounds per minute. This can take down a light starfighter on a strafing run if you can hit its reactor inside a three-thousand-meter range."

"That'd make short order of an Owari worm," I said with a smirk.

"How do you like your sushi—*chopped?*" he agreed.

"Or would you rather scrape it off the bottom of the Kkoradian Abyss?" I said.

"I wouldn't go that far," Adams said, his brows rising with a shake of his head. "Have you ever seen one of the big ones?"

"No," I admitted.

"Stryker, we ship out this evening," Chadwick announced. He sauntered over to us, furry thumbs hitched in his belt over an open tactical shirt and green scarf the Jagulen wore around his thick neck.

"Going to brave the cave in the dark?" I asked him.

"That's why we've got this," he said with a jab at the tower aft of the pilothouse. "EOS, for surveillance and fire control with a whole sensor suite for intelligence, surveillance, reconnaissance and targeting. And don't forget about sonar and radar."

"You can see Owari those ways?" I challenged, knowing sonar and radar weren't very reliable for tracking sea life, especially when it was traveling fast.

"The Owari are hard to see in broad daylight, until they get within *sucking* distance," he countered. "Going out there at night is much preferred since that's when I'm told they're not typically active—which hopefully means less likely to notice and interfere with our underwater equipment."

"Except my scientist says they're underfed, so what if they're in the mood for a midnight snack?"

Chadwick just glared and said, "Duly noted."

I closed my mouth, this time determined to start things off on the right foot.

"We made contact with Emin Braddock last night and understand he wants a thorough search of the minor islands and volcanic coastlines, but Top instructed me to ask you for any relevant intel you've already gathered before we arrived to take over this mission," Chadwick said.

"Absolutely, I'm glad to share what we've got. According to his cousin, the last person to see Braddock's brothers may have been Absolom Stewart, the fisherman who took them out on the water the day they vanished. Here's the footage from his fishing boat's dashcam," I said, handing Chadwick the memory card. "The vid's last shot shows their boat entering a large cavern formed by old lava. Dr. Portinga here knows where it is. But that's all we've got."

"That's a great start," said the captain. "I'll watch this holo vid right away. So you know the coordinates of this lava cave?"

Dr. Portinga nodded. "I show you," he said. He projected a topographical hologram of the area in the three-dimensional space between the three of us from his quantum pad and pointed out the location.

"Hmm," said Chadwick, rubbing his long-whiskered snout pensively. "It should take my aerial drone about two hours to get there, an hour to scan it, and two hours to get back. That means we have time to kill, so Stryker, I need you and Dr. Portinga here to do a risk assessment on all the volcanoes in the region. Not Caldera Island—since it's already active. I mean the other ones on the minor islands that could pose a risk once we set out. I don't want any surprises tonight."

"Yes, sir," I said. "We can leave right away."

"Call me Chadwick," he said. "Could you get me a full report by this evening on any eruptions that might occur before our mission's completed?"

"Good question," I said. "Dr. Portinga?"

"Well, there are over a hundred in the region," the man explained. "So there won't be time to check all of them today. That means we're taking a small risk. But I've been monitoring the ones that *have* been active in the past five cycles with my seismic instruments, and there's really only one I think we should worry about. That's Mount Barabari. My readings have indicated it could be close to a massive-scale eruption. But I really won't know how big or how soon until I check the readings again today."

"Understood," said Chadwick. "Find out what you can, and let me know. Stryker, go with him to provide security and any assistance he needs."

I nodded, because we were dismissed.

Stopping at my cubby in the berthing compartment to pack some water and food rations, I noticed a package sitting there on my rack. My name was written on its brown wrapping paper, so I opened it.

A book of Oshwellian poetry. *I bet I know who this is from.*

Cracking open the leather-bound volume, I let out a cough from the layers of dust, then turned to the page demarcated by its bookmark and read the words—a simple poem with only one line.

Gazelles give up their path to a hungry lion when they're downrange.

It was a poem about knowing your place. I chuckled. The insinuation was clear.

Mercedes had let me back on the job since Mav Rexlin had made that request, but she wanted to make sure I'd respect the orders of the commanding Centurion. That wasn't me.

It was Captain Chadwick. And if I wanted to become one like him, I'd do well to heed her advice.

CHAPTER THIRTY

Dr. Portinga and I started our hike in the clouds that covered the base of Mount Barabari. I was wearing my armor and had the humongous Dracula Hunter shotgun slung over my shoulder, because this planet was insane in too many ways.

And one never knew. The fog was so thick that it shrouded the mountain in a white haze, within which the volcanologist would vanish if I let him get twelve paces ahead.

Branches cracked off to my left. Too many branches under too many feet. I braced my shotgun in the meat of my shoulder and squinted into the mist.

A trio of eyes shined through it, then another. And another.

All of them in trios with one off center, converging in a devilish arrangement that reminded me of tactical formations of enemy fighters if I'd seen it on my holo display.

My gun was cocked, my trigger finger ready. But its semi-auto magazine only held nine cartridges. How would this pack respond if I picked a few off? Would that scare the others away from us, or would it enrage them and make them go mad?

These were the wilds of a planet forsaken by common sense and decency for the greed and avarice that controlled populations, whose neglect had left the wilderness regions vulnerable to predators that roamed unchecked to prey on whoever they wanted.

My heart beat faster. "There's a pack of razgits following us," I whispered to the scientist.

"What? Oh!" he said with alarm.

"Just keep moving, and I'll keep an eye out. Bodega, you copy?"

"This is Bodega. Go ahead."

"We've got company. Large pack, probably bigger than we can appreciate in all of this voiding fog. Can you pick out any good targets?"

"Not yet," he breathed, sounding apologetic. "Visibility all around you is complete scrat, and that much condensation pretty much rules out lasers, anyway."

He was sitting back in our bungalow, guiding the orb drone above us remotely. I hadn't appreciated just how bad the cloud part of the cloud forest would be, but Bodega was right.

It rendered laser weapons worthless.

Not good news for the doctor and me.

"I've been around wolf packs before," I whispered. "This is like that, but a lot bigger. I think they're still trying to decide whether we're safe, so uncertainty's a good thing. Let's just pray that it holds out. Come on," I said to Dr. Portinga. "Let's get to the summit and get this over with. I don't like this. Beautiful but deadly—that's kind of a theme on your planet, isn't it?"

The scientist didn't answer, but I could hear him breathing hard.

The eerie biome of the cloud forest had been created by the combination of climate with the high elevation and proximity to the sea.

The watching eyes faded into the mist, but I sensed this wouldn't be the last time they ventured this close. And what I'd do then, I just didn't know.

After we'd reached one thousand meters in elevation, the condensation persisted to near white-out levels because of the cooling of moist air currents deflected up by the rocky terrain. For several hours, we climbed through a mind-numbing layer of clouds, straining for any signs of danger.

The high humidity fostered all manner of mosses, ferns, and climbing lichens which weighed down the trunks and branches of trees like heavy coats of green bedazzled with water droplets that sparkled in the morning light.

"You know," I said to Dr. Portinga as we climbed, "I get the natural beauty of living so close to all these volcanoes, and how they draw visitors from all over—and Oathel Beach has certainly built an incredibly lucrative tourist industry around all this that supports the local economy. I get all that. But I'm still surprised at how many millions of people buy homes and live so close to geological formations that technically could bury them and all they own in deadly lava any day of the week. You know what I mean?"

"I've lived here all my life," said Portinga. "The volcanoes provide both risks and benefits. Construction companies use volcanic ash as a cheap and renewable substitute for sand or gravel in making cement. And volcanic ash stimulates plant growth with essential nutrients—nitrogen, phosphorus, potassium—and its minerals create fertile soil where some crops can flourish. Some of the most productive agricultural areas in the galaxy are near active volcanoes."

"Wait a minute," I said. "In my ship on our way here, my AI Frederick told me that volcanic ash *damages* crops, but now you're saying it's good for the soil?"

"Precisely," said Frederick, "it's both. Do you see those transparent domes on your left?"

"I didn't know you were listening, buddy," I said with smirk. "Are you jealous of Dr. Portinga?"

"That's impossible. I'm a very limited AI."

"Sure, keep telling yourself that, Charles Dickens."

"That's impossible. I'm a very limited AI. That's impossible. I'm a very limited AI—"

"Yeah, that's enough. I didn't mean literally."

"Mr. Stryker, are you feeling disoriented?" Dr. Portinga asked. "Maybe we should sit down and rest. Take a breather. Sometimes the elevation can cause people issues."

"No, I'm fine. I was just talking to my AI. Forgot you couldn't hear him since he's inside my head. See, Frederick, now you just made me look like a dork. Go on, Portinga. You were telling me about volcanoes when my AI started talking about domes."

"Ah, yes, the volcanic ash can indeed damage crops and plant life, but it also makes for superior soil. To solve this dilemma, we've built enclosed agricultural habitats. Animals and crops live inside them without being harmed by the falling ash, while farmers carry that same ash into the domes to use for the soil they develop in there. The volcanoes also supply a source of geothermal energy."

"I get it. What you're saying is... it's all fun and games until someone's sublimated by molten rock," I pointed out.

"What are we looking for other than to check your instruments when we get to the top of the mountain?"

"Seismic activity," he said. "It's the greatest way to tell what a volcano is planning to do, when the next eruption may be and what damage it might inflict. That'll tell us if we're going to be clear to complete our mission in the next couple of days, or whether we need to wait or even possibly evacuate to avoid getting caught in a major eruption."

I groaned. "Seismic activity. So, earthquakes are an early warning sign."

"They are *the* early warning sign," he clarified.

"I haven't noticed any on Oathel Beach, but this is my first time on the minor islands," I said. "And we haven't been here very long."

"The past couple weeks on this mountain, they've been hitting six to seven times a day," he said soberly.

"Six or seven times a day?" I asked, shaking my head. "Come on, let's get this over with."

"Yes," he continued. "And this recent spate of earthquakes has yielded a fascinating look at some very unusual waveforms. Low-frequency, long-period waveforms we call VLP pulses."

"Oh yeah?" I said. "Why are they so unusual?"

"They've never been detected on Mount Barabari before and only have been at a select few other volcanoes, because we have to wait until it is safe from both eruptions and the risk of cave-ins to place special broadband equipment near the crater."

"Where the lava spurts out?" I said. "I can see why that could be a problem. So what are these tests revealing?"

"The epicenter of the quakes is happening right in ground zero of the most explosive eruption activity," he explained. "These seismic signals could have been caused by the buildup of rising gases inside the plugged chamber from rising magma. The pressure starts to build slowly, at first only in a shallow pocket below. But when that pressure exceeds the structural integrity of the formation, it can exert force against the rock walls and cause an earthquake."

"So what's different than usual about it?" I asked.

"It's both the frequency and severity," he answered. "Because this can indicate an unsteady upward movement of magma in the volcano's conduit. Earthquakes can intensify when crystalline, highly viscous magma coming up the conduit rubs against rocks in the conduit wall. These multiphase earthquakes could be the vibrations caused by this magma movement."

Suddenly, the ground started rumbling beneath us, and everything started to shake. I grabbed hold of a soggy tree branch to steady myself.

The ground began to splinter beside him, opening a fissure in the rock from the pressure cooker of gases building under us inside the volcano where we were standing. Gravel, then larger rocks tumbled from the higher elevations, pelting us.

A shard sliced open flesh on the doctor's arm. He whimpered and tried to staunch the bleeding with a handkerchief from his pocket. "Unfortunately, increases in seismic activity around volcanoes has been directly linked to activity *within* them!" he said.

"Are you saying this bad boy's about to blow its top?" I shouted over the roar of the earthquake.

"I'm saying it could very soon!" he shouted back.

The ground shifted. Dr. Portinga lost his footing. Slipping forward, he face planted, and his glasses cracked. He managed to clamp one hand around them, before flailing into a slide. My heart shot into my throat, and I fired the tow line from my right vambrace. Its monofilament shot out with pneumatic speed. The doctor, gripping a moss-covered stone shard embedded in clay, reached out with bloodied fingers.

Finally, he grabbed my line. I coaxed it through his hand very slowly so it didn't tear away at his skin and advised him to release it until he could get a better grip.

I drew him back up to safer ground and spread my armored body over him. Large rocks above us broke off, ricocheted and impacted my back as they tumbled down the mountainside. It felt like the entire mountain might split in two at any second. Squeezing my eyes shut, I covered the scientist and just waited for it to end.

Finally, the earthquake subsided, and I released a haggard breath, rolling over in exhaustion.

Dr. Portinga was wide-eyed with fear. "That was the worst one I've ever experienced," he said. "We've got to check my instruments."

Now making double time, we climbed the rest of the way to the summit. As we ascended above the cloud forest, the vegetation became sparse until on the mountain's apex, nothing remained but barren rock.

"See those gray electronic boxes marked with red flags around the rim of the crater? Help me. Hurry! We've got to check the readings to see if we need an evacuation."

An evacuation? This was going from bad to worse. I sprinted across the stony surface and picked up each of his seismographs then deposited them at the scientist's feet. I braced myself, as an aftershock rumbled through the mountaintop.

Portinga sped through the instruments' readings, then rocked back on his haunches and cursed.

"It's even worse than I expected," he said. "The tremors

have intensified so much since I last checked them that we're looking at a major event. I have a direct line to this planet's emergency response team, and I will call them right now."

"What does that mean for the people who live here?" I asked, remembering that Barabari and the other minor islands were home to ninety-one thousand residents.

"They have to evacuate if they want to survive," he said.

"The whole population of the minor islands?" I said.

"No," he said. "The minor islands could all be affected just by the *lava*. But clouds of ash will poison the air over this entire region—so all of Caldera Island must be evacuated. Every soul. Effective immediately."

A deep-throated yelp made the hair on the back of my neck stand on end. Raising my shotgun, I spun toward the source of the sound. The pack of wild razgits had crested the mountain's summit. They slinked around us in a perimeter, their lips curled back from salivating mouths.

Looking down the length of my barrel, I sighted the first one and pulled the trigger. The force from my shot ejected the spent cartridge and the next round automatically loaded.

The slug drove right through its brain stem, and the animal fell. The next three-eyed hyena charged me in a rabid gallop. I fired twice, and it squirted out blood, shambling forward into a skid. I had to dive on top of the scientist to keep him from being rolled over.

"Bodega, how is visibility?" I grimaced under the thing. "We're surrounded."

"I'm hunting targets of opportunity," he said.

The spherical drone rose from behind the mountaintop and flipped open. Its omnidirectional turrets opened up on the pack of ravenous creatures, blasting them with high-powered lasers. They cowered and bayed, worked up into a frenzy.

Others growled and their eyes roved us, unnatural in alignment and beast-like with lust. I wrenched my body out from under the hide of the one that was heaving its last and took aim at another razgit, pulling the trigger and making it drop.

Bodega's orb laid into their numbers with laser beams that singed and burned the hump-backed monstrosities until they started galloping down the mountain, howling and yelping as they fled.

Soon, the silhouette of my Ectocraft crested the milky horizon.

Bodega piloted it to our location and picked us up. We rocketed back to the *Magellan* patrol boat, where Captain Chadwick waited for an update, and Bodega touched down with our angling thrusters on the decommissioned cutter's wide pad.

As soon as we were cleared to disembark, the scientist and I headed for the pilothouse where the skipper was seated.

"Captain, Mount Barabari, a hundred kilometers from here, is getting ready to erupt," said Portinga. "I don't know how long we have for sure, but I estimate it'd be sometime in the next two days, and when it does, it will be catastrophic."

CHAPTER THIRTY-ONE

"ALL HANDS, TO BRIEFING, *NOW!*" roared the Jagulen. "This is an emergency meeting!"

The boat's small company of officers and crew, along with my people, snapped into action, racing down the metal steps one-by-one to the designated deck.

Chadwick paced the front like a predator, his feline ears twitching and his jaws working as everyone scrambled into the seats around the table. The compartment was cramped and devoid of much light. Limited ventilation made the air stale, and the tension was palpable.

"Everyone, if you haven't met him already, this is Dr. Portinga, our resident volcanologist who I just met today and who's been gracious enough to consult with us for this mission. He's just informed me that Mount Barabari is preparing for a massive-scale eruption in the next forty-eight hours. Evacuation-level event. First of all, doctor, how can we help?" Chadwick said.

"Well, for anyone who doesn't live here, which I assume is most of you, your personal preparations are minimal," said the scientist. "You could help with the planetary evacuation, but that won't start for another ten hours."

"Ten hours?" I said. "Why not sooner if it's such an emergency?"

"Because that's how the bureaucracy works on Vedana," said Portinga, grimacing. "The rich will leave quietly because they can leave from landing pads on their own property. But for the average citizens whose ships are docked in public spaceports, the government response team says they need that long to organize the evacuation without everything descending into madness."

Captain Chadwick rubbed his fur-covered brow. "Well, there is some truth to that approach. If all the ships docked at crowded spaceports took off at the same time, especially if people are panicked, just think. We'd be looking at all kinds of collisions and gridlock. You can't just transport billions of people off a planet in the blink of an eye. There are major logistics to making a plan like that happen on that magnitude."

"That being the case, I recommend calling off your mission or postponing it until a future date when the atmosphere has been cleared of particulates long after this eruption is over," said the scientist.

"No!" I said. "We can't do that. Look, Captain, I know you're in charge. I'm not going to question your leadership as the commanding Centurion, here, and if you can't follow through on this job, I can respect that. But I am going into that cave to find the remains of Braddock's brothers for reasons that are very precious to me—even if I have to go in there alone. I'll swim to the bottom and dredge up their skeletons, if that's what it takes."

"Haven't you read up on the Owari?" said Captain Chadwick in a skeptical squint. "You'd get eaten alive."

I blew out a breath of resignation. "I'd rather die knowing I did all I could than live the rest of my life in regret. What I stand to lose is not acceptable loss if there's one more breath in my lungs. At least, let me borrow that rigid inflatable boat stowed here in the stern of your craft. I'll pay good money for it, and then your people can be on their way."

Captain Chadwick's heavy brows furrowed and he pursed his lips, considering the situation. "When did you say the evacuation starts? Ten hours from now?"

Portinga nodded. "That is correct. But I need to get going. I've got lots of family here."

"You're free to go, and we wish you success," said the Jagulen captain.

Since the boat was still docked, Portinga got up from his seat and slipped out, then charged up the stairs to the top deck.

The captain leaned on the conference table that we were gathered around, casting his jaguar-like features in harrowing beams of white that vanished into the grimy shadows of the compartment.

"Stryker, I can see that this mission has personal significance for you, and I don't doubt that is for good reason. Mav Rexlin recommended you personally to me. But to everyone else on my team, we are Task Force Cyberblade. We have a mission to complete. Failure is not an option, people, because getting access to the Protectorate is a matter of galactic security. Now, that doctor said the evacuation efforts won't begin for another ten hours—and I can tell you from experience, they'll last much longer than that. We can be at that cave system in two hours at the *Magellan's* top speed, then we take four hours to gather what data we can and hope that it will be enough. After that, whatever the outcome, we return and join evac efforts with everyone else on this island. Eight hours round trip."

I nodded in acknowledgement but was elated.

"Now, here's our plan," Chadwick continued. "I'll include some additional details for the benefit of Stryker's team."

A three-dimensional holographic map showing the cave system's contours sprang to life on the table.

Chadwick manipulated it with his furry, clawed hands. "With its combination of laser, sonar, infrared and radar technologies, our drone has put together a pretty good picture of this cave system," he said. "Here you can see the outer cavern where Absolom Stewart's vessel entered with his clients, the Braddocks. As you can see here, its back wall extends all the way to the sea floor, but our scans have revealed that *behind* this wall is another chamber that's even bigger."

"So they teleported through a rock wall?" groused Steinbreaker, sitting on the table next to me.

I elbowed him. "Show some respect," I mumbled.

"What? It's a valid question," he replied, not because teleportation was possible, but because he didn't understand the point.

"This is much simpler than that," Chadwick answered. "When lava comes out of the ground, it naturally follows gravity, but as soon as it contacts air or water, it starts to harden into a crust. But the lava *inside* the outer crust's still molten, so it keeps draining downhill, leaving empty tunnels behind called lava tubes."

"So, you're wondering if the Braddock brothers might have gotten trapped behind a new flow of the stuff," Tess said, rubbing her chin.

The captain nodded. "Exactly."

"Who would enter a cave if you saw liquid lava dripping down from the ceiling?" Tess said with a scoff.

"It wouldn't have to be draining at that time," I pointed out. "They could've explored a deeper chamber of the cave system and then gotten killed by Owari worms, a cave-in, or some other means. Then, days later, a new flow of lava could've formed that back wall, subsequently cooling and trapping their corpses behind it forever, keeping everyone in the dark."

"That's our theory," said the Jagulen captain. "But not days afterwards. Later *that night*. My team's pulled the geological records for those very coordinates. We can't *prove* the Braddocks got trapped back there until we get inside, but we do know there was a new flow of lava in that location that evening after their guide returned home with his fishing boat—and no clients. Iverson, Kennedy, bring in our star witness."

The two men I recognized as Gunner's Mates dragged in a haggard fellow with hawklike features who looked gaunt and washed-out.

"Say 'hello' to Absolom Stewart," said Chadwick.

I shook my head. "You've been busy while Portinga and I were climbing that mountain."

Chadwick drilled me with a hard stare. "We are Task-force Cyberblade," he said.

I cleared my throat. "Of course," I said quietly.

"Tell everyone why you've been hiding, Absolom," the captain prompted him.

"I—I, well, yes, as you know by now, the Braddocks did charter a fishing trip with me that day, and they really wanted to explore the lava caves, and I tried to warn them about the Owari. They tried to offer me more money, but I refused. When you've been fishing for as long as I have, there's certain areas you know to avoid, no matter how much someone is willing to pay. But they were insistent. I think they were hoping to find something deep in that cave system. I can't imagine what they'd be looking for, but it got to the point that one of them shoved a gun in my back and started telling me details about each of my children that no one should know. It scared me. And I—in the panic of fear for my life—made a split decision. I told them we'd go but had to turn around after fifteen minutes whether they were back in the boat or not."

"At that time, was the back of the cavern blocked off like a dead end, or did they have access to a deeper cave system above the water?" I asked.

"It wasn't blocked off," he said with a frown. "Those caves go very deep, although your captain here has since told me there were new lava flows later that night."

"So what happened?" asked Tess.

"I don't know," said Absolom Stewart. "They hiked into the caves and didn't come back. It was very dark, and I was afraid to shine any kind of light in there for fear of drawing any attention from predators, but I did shout for them. After fifteen minutes, I got out of there, just like I warned 'em."

"Unfortunately, this is where things get complicated," said the Jagulen, hitching meaty thumbs in his belt. "The most recent lava flows have created natural dams so the passages we need to search can only be accessed now if we're able to cut a hole through that cave wall underwater."

"The water where the bloodsuckers live?!" snapped Bond. "Ah, man. Void, no!"

"How do we get through a wall like that safely—much less underwater?" I said. "I've heard volcanic rock can be really unstable. Couldn't we risk the whole thing coming down with traditional explosives?"

The Centurion nodded. "It's true—basaltic rock's fragile and prone to cave-ins, especially if we're sitting under the base of an entire mountain comprised of it. That's why we're deploying our remote drone to *cut* it. The *Dolphin* submersible is equipped with sonar, radar, and an inline diamond wire saw made for cutting underwater," he said. "We just need to make sure that drone makes it through the hole that it cuts and sends back images from the other side without interference by vampire fish."

"What could possibly go wrong?" I breathed.

"Iverson, Kennedy, Adams will man the autocannons in case any worms try to board our boat, but that really shouldn't be a problem because they can't climb and need water or some kind of wet slimy environment to move around. We've got a two hour trip, though, so I want each of you to orient Bodega, Rubi and Stryker to serve as backups as much as you can in that time frame on those guns, while Thorne will handle the fourth autocannon and keep the Rigid Inflatable Boat ready to go from the stern if needed. Now, Thorne, I only want you to deploy that thing if there's a realistic chance for survival for the one who falls overboard. We don't like to leave people behind. But we *also* don't want to risk the lives of everyone else on board out of misguided emotional reasons that only result in the loss of more life. Common sense is your friend on this mission. I, however, am not. Because of the time rush and our need to work together on this operation, I'm putting all of us on the same open comm channel. Don't make me regret that. Keep the small talk among yourselves unless you have something mission-critical."

The men voiced their agreement.

"We've got Drac Hunter 4-gauge shotguns if any targets present themselves at too steep an angle for your autocannons," I said. "Supercavitating rounds."

"Oh yeah," said Chadwick. "That goes without saying. But I'll say it anyway for those of you still fighting off last night's hangover. Supercavitating rounds *only* today. Don't let me catch you with anything else."

It was amazing how these bullets could fly through water, and I was looking forward to trying them out. But if all went well, hopefully I wouldn't have to and we'd be in and out of that cave with the proof Braddock needed of his brothers' fate.

"Now," said Chadwick, leaning over the table in a snarl, as the ambient white glow from the holo bank lit up his imposing frame. "We've got eight hours round trip for this mission. Then, we get the void off this planet. I know you don't have the security clearances I do, but let me assure you that this *is* a matter of galactic security. Braddock isn't our only way into the Protectorate on Samudra, but he might be our best. Yesterday was your day to get squared away. Today is your day to act."

CHAPTER THIRTY-TWO

THE *MAGELLAN* SPED through the coastal waters near max velocity until we slowed and drifted into the mouth of the chamber where the missing persons had vanished. The cavern engulfed us, blocking out daylight, in an otherworldly mystique formed by the accumulation of eruptions over eons of time, hardened into layers of volcanic rock with serpentine networks of shafts and tunnels beyond these confines that wove through the base of the volcano, some of them waterlogged, harboring worms.

Deposits hung from the ceiling like stalactites.

Ripples laced the walls where the lava had marbled into black basalt with impurities streaking it orange, red, and purple.

Light glowed from the pilothouse, casting Captain Chadwick and his officers in silhouette, including Underwood, who seemed like the odd man out as the engineer.

He was responsible for the operation, maintenance, and repair of engines and machinery, including propulsion, electrical power, fuel and water systems, but most of his duties could be performed electronically unless there was a problem.

"Deploying submersible," the sonar and radar operator, O'Malley, announced in a sober tone.

Iverson and Kennedy lowered it into the water from the bow of the craft as close as possible to the exact spot in the cavern's back wall that their instruments had identified ahead of time as the best place for it to cut.

"We have video," O'Malley announced.

A bit of the pressure we'd been shouldering released, and we all breathed. The inline diamond wire saw on the *Dolphin* submersible had started cutting into the layers of rock.

I set my jaw. My grip tightened around the action of my Drac Hunter. We held our collective breath and waited.

The Gunner's Mates manned their posts behind chain guns, fidgeting and nervous, as Bond, Rubi and I paced the top deck, ever-vigilant, with our loaded shotguns ready for any movement that wasn't right.

I heard something splash. Many things, actually.

"Okay, we're through," said O'Malley. "Wow, the cavern inside here is vast. I'm bringing her to the surface and raising the periscopic camera."

I adjusted the collar of the wetsuit I'd been issued by Chadwick, feeling a bit exposed without my armor, a bit like a big juicy bag of blood just waiting to be consumed for its nourishment by an organism that cared nothing for me, that cared nothing for any of us.

The armor would've protected me against bloodletting, but the skipper had forbidden it because in the black depths, it would do nothing but ensure drowning.

I wondered how deep the water went here.

Chadwick had gone over that in the briefing, but the

darkness and reflections on the water were playing tricks with my mind. Or was the soot deposits from the basaltic rock that had discolored it?

I couldn't tell.

Something moved underneath us. Or was that the shifting of light, casting a shadow from the pilothouse?

"I think I see it," said O'Malley. "The rock shelf that Chadwick was talking about. Yes—there it is. Okay, I'm approaching it."

My gaze roved the cave's deceptive contours. I couldn't make out the seabed below us. That might've been from the cloud of particulates, the cloud of something murky and dark. But our craft was bobbing on the still water, and I wanted to see the ocean floor, because it felt like we could be floating over depths that went down for leagues.

There was something about not being able to see how deep the water was below you. Something unknown and wrong about it. This was irrational.

Chadwick had showed us the hologram of it, but this seemed bigger in person, somehow.

My cybernetic hearing that had been a benefit was starting to feel like a curse as well, draining my concentration to distinguish the innocent lapping of water from splashing that might be a concern.

I thought I caught a *sloosh* of something heavy.

But I couldn't be sure.

"I see it!" said O'Malley. "I found the shelf. Guys, you wouldn't believe this. There's one—no, two—skeletons here. It's got to be them. They've got soft tissue. Not all decomposed, but their flesh is shrunken across their ribs, strips of it stretched too far over bones."

"Okay, can you identify the medallions that Braddock said they were wearing?" Chadwick asked excitedly.

"Wait—yes!" said O'Malley. "I see the medallions! Okay, bringing the *Dolphin* drone back to our boat."

"Captain, something's approaching our bow at eight knots. Closing quickly."

"Arm the torpedoes," Chadwick said.

"Sir, it's too late for torpedoes," said another man.

"Give me more information!" said Chadwick.

"Where did it come from?" O'Malley, the sonar and radar operator was incredulous. "Sir, it's a sea mine! There's some kind of mass around it. The mass is—is biological, amorphous."

I heard Chadwick curse quietly, and I knew why. The mine approaching us had us pinned inside the cavern with no way of escape.

"Brace for impact!" someone called.

A wake cut through the water, closing to the surface just before detonation. Our boat bucked from the explosion that tore a hole in the forward hull, pitching the crew astern the top deck as the craft listed.

Kennedy, one of the Gunner's Mates, fell into the water.

"Man overboard!" yelled Adams, and Thorne rushed to the Rigid Inflatable Boat. He started to free it.

But the chaos had distracted us from the fact that we were still moving, since the mine had pushed the *Magellan* toward the cave wall.

We impacted it.

Thorne, who hadn't properly braced himself since he'd been rushing to deploy the RIB, was thrown into a metal pole by the shift in momentum. The hull hung up, grinding against a shelf of basalt, then—pulled by gravity—slid back into the water, flipping Thorne over the side.

He hung on by the railing.

I grabbed his wrists, but a form dark and shiny emerged

from the depths, and before I could register what was happening, it had swallowed his lower half. The terror in his eyes pleaded with me for assistance, and I pulled with all of my strength on his forearms without tearing them out of their sockets.

But his skin, wet and slippery, slid from my grasp. He disappeared in the water.

Squinting into the foamy ocean, I fired at a slinking flash of something fast, brown and sleek. I fired twice more, uncertain of whether my rounds hit their target, but feeling better for it either way.

"One of the Owari has destroyed the submersible," O'Malley announced.

That wasn't good, because we needed that footage on the drone's camera. Without it, how were we going to prove to Braddock that we'd finished the job?

"Captain, these readings are haywire," said Underwood from inside the pilothouse. "I've got to get into the engine room to perform a manual override of the electrical systems, or these systems are going to melt down."

"Stryker, Rubi, Bodega, accompany Underwood to the engine room!"

"Roger that," Bodega and I said in unison.

"On our way," Rubi agreed.

I led the way. When we got to the lower deck, the corridor we needed to cross was submerged in meter-deep water from the breach in the hull. "Scrat," I said, gritting my teeth, as I left the safety of the metal steps for the waist-deep immersion in uncertainty.

My crew knew what to do, and I had total faith in them. We kept Underwood in between us.

A form slithered through the sloshing waves then suddenly breached the surface.

Its dorsal and lateral body was mud-brown, speckled black. But its mouth was what I wouldn't soon scrub from my memory, the jawless stacks of hook-teeth in row upon row of concentric circles. This one's circumference exceeded that of my own head.

Looking down the barrel, I placed my target just above the sight and pulled the trigger. My 1,000 grain bullet didn't slow down when it passed through the fat of the creature. The recoil pad took the edge off the kick, as the force from my shot ejected the casing, and the next one loaded automatically. I fired, blowing another hole, and again twice more.

A worm hurled itself up from the shallows. I plugged it with two rounds. Normally, bullets don't go far through water.

But these were supercavitating—designed with a tungsten-tipped, torpedo shape that created a bubble of gas around the bullet through Bernoulli's principle when fired through water, reducing the drag to next to nothing.

They could be fired from a submerged position to another underwater target, from above into the water or vice versa to lethal effect. A cloud of blood told me my aim had been true.

They were smart. Clearly they'd planned this out, including lying in wait with a leftover sea mine just out of range of our sonar sweeps, then pulling it here by its chain to breach our hull and level the playing field by forcing us into the one environment where they had the clear advantage.

The deep.

I turned my gun upside down and thumbed nine shells into the feeding mechanism from the bag on my belt then racked the bolt back and laid into the Owari that hunted us.

Blood spurted up from the shallows where my rounds devastated their bodies. The things were trying to crowd onto the boat and overwhelm us by sheer numbers.

This was ground zero, and Rubi and Bodega opened up on the living targets, careful to not hit each other in the relatively close quarters, which slowed down our rate of response considerably and made sure a certain number of them slid through our defenses and made their way up the metal staircase, which apparently must've been wet and slathered enough by now that they could traverse it.

Their bodies flexed in sickening heaves to inch their way up the steps, putting them in vulnerable positions to get shot, but we couldn't focus on those alone since we were trying to plug the hole through which they were boarding with enough bullets to make them draw back.

They didn't.

Somehow, we pushed through the tide of blood to get Underwood to the engine room while we stood guard outside it and shot bloodsuckers in the foaming waves that thrashed around in the corridor.

When we reached the top deck, word came from Centurion intelligence officers that Mount Barabari had erupted. The skies outside started to darken with blowing clouds of drifting ash.

Viscous lava from previous eruptions had plugged up the volcano's vents, keeping the vapors from boiling off, as the pressure of gases built up to a violent eruption unlike any in the planet's history. Fragments of rock and clouds of ash polluted the sky in the distance.

For hours, we fought against the Owari.

Our losses were heavy and numerous. We raked across

their flesh with shotgun rounds and high-caliber cartridges from autocannons, and they slid across our deck, sucking the blood from their hapless victims.

But in the end, it wasn't the volume of our bullets or the strength of our tactics or grit. It was the beckoning of those new sources of lava, the acidic waters their flows produced that drew the Owari away from us to this natural phenomenon.

When they left us, I dove off the side of the *Magellan* into the water.

Light beckoned me from the opening cut by the diamond saw of our submersible and led me into a chamber with the hidden cleft of rock. On it, I found the two dried up skeletons with thin wisps of dehydrated flesh that the *Dolphin* had started to capture on camera before it was destroyed.

And around their necks, I found the medallions like the one that Braddock had shown me.

I grabbed the medallions and dove back under. But when I returned to the surface, the skies were polluted with ash and Chadwick was screaming that we had to leave.

The survivors clambered onto the rigid inflatable boat the *Magellan* kept in her stern. Chadwick gunned its outboard motor and we shot across choppy coastal waters, watching Owari worms dive and resurface, mesmerized by the summit of their new destination.

My crew returned to our starship and lifted into the blackening skies, never to return to the wastes of the doomed planet, because I had Braddock's medallions in my cold fist.

I'd fulfilled his objective. Now, he'd have to give me access into the Protectorate.

I just needed to track him down.

CHAPTER THIRTY-THREE

For days, we'd been scouring reaches of space in our search for the Caudanum Mathum, Emin Braddock. The stars glared over our vessel in my viewport as if posing more questions.

I sat in my captain's chair, strapped in at the fore of the *Lizard King* with the Reckoning powered down in my lap, examining its blade. The plasma sword stood for something that Hidalgo hadn't been able to live up to but admired.

And now, it had passed down to me.

As we prepared to join forces with Braddock, I wondered if I deserved this weapon forged by Mavgardon Rexlin. Could I link up with the mogul from the League of Desai after everything I'd seen him do on Vedana?

After I knew those who'd struggled under his regime like Zihan and T'Amira?

I traced my thumb over the engraving on the sword's pommel. Three rings, interlocking.

Like the fates of my crew.

Three paths that Mav Rexlin had taught me about. Dedication, Solidarity, Defiance. The second was what he seemed to think that I needed to work on most to improve if I wanted to become a Centurion.

Just then, my quantum pad chimed with a text. I pumped my fist in relief, because it was him. "Braddock just sent me coordinates for a space station where we can meet," I announced to our team on our comm channel.

"About voiding time," Tess said from her workstation aft of my own.

"Finally, we're about to get paid!" said Bond.

"You can say that again," I muttered, punching in the coordinates on my console. "Celin-Ohmi, set a course for this heading."

"Captain, a vessel's hailing us," said Tess, sounding more curious than anything else. "It's a small transport shuttle. Civilian."

"Is it armed?" I grunted, sliding the Reckoning back into its scabbard.

"No weapon systems that I can detect," said Bond.

"Their captain's requesting visual contact," she added.

I frowned. "If they're unarmed, let's see what they want. Celin-Ohmi, belay that order to set a new course. Tess, put the skipper on the main viewscreen."

When the screen came to life, it wasn't with the face of the shuttle's captain. It was the broadcast of pre-recorded video. The footage brought me up short.

Yakuza gangsters lifted the critically injured body of Devon Fenstermacher-Dole to a stretcher. I knew it was him, because half of the telltale family crest he'd used to domineer Tess was still visible on his broken armor.

His face was badly disfigured.

The scene switched to footage played in fast forward inside an operating room. Robotic arms descended from a surgical base, performing procedures on Devon's riddled body, replacing areas with cybernetic parts.

Growing nauseous, I clenched my jaw. Devon survived, and now they were turning him into a monster as a form of psychological warfare, because they knew what it would do to Tess.

I could already hear her starting to break down from her workstation.

The next image on the screen was a happy family portrait, something we'd get on Earth from Olan Mills, a warm-looking couple in their mid-fifties, three teenage sons, a younger version of Tess.

Next was a photo of her as a child, riding a tricycle. Her eyes were the same. Blue. Full of wonder.

Then came a grainy clip of Tess' mother playing Christmas carols on a piano that was out of tune. Marekk-Thuul had found the flash drive in Devon's body and in his brilliant strategic mind, had started to put the pieces together. He knew what this would do to the woman, how it might almost break her.

It was his next shot across the bow.

Her screams were inevitable. I squeezed my eyes shut, because they were still hard for me to take.

"I'll kill that son of a bjorek!" she raged so loud over our comm that her voice distorted like a death metal song. "I'll kill him! I'll kill him!"

"Bodega, take command," I said quietly, unfastening my harness. I proceeded back to her station.

Tess was pacing and pounding the bulkheads.

Gently, I approached her, wrapping my arms around her waist. She pounded on my chest a few times. Her dark eyes ran wild with hate.

"Hey, it's okay," I said. "I'm here."

Her demeanor slackened. Tess collapsed into my arms, clutching my flight suit in her trembling fists, and cried. I held her there until the sobs subsided and promised her only one thing.

"You can forget he ever existed. Because when we're finished, neither Devon nor that alien captain will ever bother you again."

I felt arms pressing into my back and looked up to my surprise to see Bond and Steinbreaker and Zihan and T'Amira surrounding us. They'd pressed in together like the huddles before games outside the dugout in the twilight of summer when I was a kid. Like a team that couldn't be broken.

Maybe that was the point. None of us were worthy of the sword, but we were in the fight together.

Solidarity. This was my crew.

"Permission to engage that shuttle?" asked Bond.

"Come on, everyone, back to your stations," I ordered. "Terminate it with extreme prejudice."

By the time I was strapping back into my chair, Bond had fired enough laser power into the thing to create a critical failure in its reactor, and the shuttle exploded.

"I'm detecting no other ships in weapons range," he confirmed afterward.

"Of course not," I said. "Marekk-Thuul's just playing with us. We've managed to outwit him so far, so he's just trying to get into our heads. Celin-Ohmi, get us out of this system and to those coordinates that Braddock sent us on a course to shake off any other surveillance."

"Roger that, Captain," the mollusk replied.

Whatever it took to get into the Protectorate where they were keeping Oliver, and whoever I needed to be, I was here for it.

Activating my biomask, I resumed my identity as Henry Stryker. I withdrew the medallions that I'd fished out of that volcanic cave from their pouch on my belt, the proof that I'd done the mob leader's bidding.

My ticket to his undivided attention so that we could strike up a deal.

Dear Reader,

Right now, you're probably wondering how everything that's happened so far is related. Well, don't worry. Nothing in this series is random! I bring all the story threads together in Book 3. It's all connected. Trust me. In fact, here's the synopsis for Book 3:

Hope dawns. Gage discovers the truth.

.   .   .

Looking into how Pell, Devon, and Oliver might be connected leads to three opportunities. First, to become a ranking Centurion. Second, to face Tess' nemesis.

Third, to infiltrate the planet where his child's being held captive.

But his kid's caught up in a galactic plot between warring syndicates vying for control. Sarmonicus Pell waits behind a wall of secrets, human shields and orbital defenses. He won't be protected for long because the Centurion fleet is inbound.

And no expanse is too great a chasm for a Marine to cross for his son.

Thank you so much for your interest in the series! Here's the link to the next book:

https://www.amazon.com/dp/B0C2MZXMXH

I personally front thousands of dollars in production costs like artwork and marketing to make this happen before I get paid for my work.

Would you consider **preordering your copies of Book 3 and 4 today?**

Because that will ensure that I can continue to deliver

this series. Thank you! I couldn't do this without my amazing readers.

- Honored to be on this journey with you -
- Miles Rozak

Check out Book 3 at this link:

My Book

Printed in Great Britain
by Amazon

25699815R00178

STAR CENTURION

The greatest risk is the unknown...

Tyson Gage's four-year-old was kidnapped from Earth by the most notorious criminal syndicate in the galaxy when they traveled eight hundred years back in time.

To mount a rescue, Gage must fly behind enemy lines.

Outgunned and outclassed, he's being hunted by Yakuza's fleet, and details emerging from Tess' past could break up their crew.

His last hope? Become a Centurion to uncover the secret the League is keeping from the civilized worlds. A secret so explosive it could put the whole federation in danger.

A secret that has everything to do with why they've abducted his son.

THE BELOVED CHARACTERS, IMMERSIVE WORLD BUILDING, AND BREATHTAKING ACTION ARE BACK IN BOOK TWO OF THE # 1 AMAZON SERIES:

1 Bestseller in Space Exploration
1 Bestseller in First Contact Science Fiction
1 New Release - Bestseller in Space Opera
1 Bestseller in Galactic Empire Books
1 Bestseller in Space Marines

MP
MEGAULCITE
PRESS